Praise for Marilyn Ida Horowitz and *The B...*

"This provocative novel weaves ... ex, wrenching emotion, Jewis... at the hea..."

—Kenneth John Atchity, ... and author of *The ... Matrix*

"A galvanizing work combining espionage, paranormal phenomena, religion, intrigue, and the realization that everything is political. Horowitz synthesizes these ideas within a psychological tapestry that showcases the decision-making prowess of a woman juggling survival and cultural identity."

—Charles Coleman, Film Program Director, Facets Cinémathèque, Chicago

"A fast-paced political thriller that never loses sight of its heart: a skeptical woman searching for love and a faith she can live with, all while saving the world. A truly original heroine."

—Chap Taylor, screenwriter, *Changing Lanes*

"Funny, fast-paced, and highly enjoyable."

—D.P. Lyle, award-winning author of the Samantha Cody and Dub Walker thriller series

"A devilishly delicious feast and deeply imagined comedic thriller blending Kabbalah, the Bible, contemporary times, geopolitics, and life's absurdities in Portnoyesque fashion."

—Mark Rubinstein, award-winning author of *Mad Dog House* and *Love Gone Mad*

"A fun book, original and full of surprises."

—Abby Westlake, writer and widow of author Donald Westlake

"Horowitz's storytelling—twisty, sexy, smart—is so skillful, it's hard to believe this is her debut novel."

—Michael Zam, former Associate Director of Programs in Humanities, NYU

"Well-drawn complex characters, tight suspense, action, and a healthy sprinkle of sexuality make this book a satisfying read."

—Kristen Houghton, award-winning author of *For I Have Sinned: A Cate Harlow Private Investigation*

The Book of Zev
by Marilyn Ida Horowitz

ISBN 978-1-940192-78-9

Published by
 köehlerbooks ™

210 60th Street
Virginia Beach, VA 23451
212-574-7939
www.koehlerbooks.com

The BOOK of ZEV

A NOVEL BY

Marilyn Ida Horowitz

VIRGINIA BEACH
CAPE CHARLES

"The only thing necessary for the triumph of evil is for good men to do nothing."

—Edmund Burke

PROLOGUE

Dawn in Cornwall

HE ROSE-TINTED MIST cast an otherworldly glow over a small English seaside town in Cornwall. Its ancient stone cottages stood dark and still as day snuck in. At the far edge of town, in a tiny thatched-roof house overlooking the ocean, Gwydion Myerscough unlatched the padlock on a five-hundred-year-old battered oaken door as he balanced a tray with a mug of black coffee and banana muffins. He clicked on the overhead light and walked into his study—a dusty, wood-paneled room stocked floor to ceiling with books—and set his tray on his desk. He bit into a muffin as he pondered the ocean view outside his lace-curtained window.

Gwydion was considered one of the preeminent psychics in the world, although he hadn't left his cozy bungalow for many years and had never advertised his services. People found their way to him only by referral. The bank of clocks that filled one entire wall of the study, and which were set to the various time zones of his clients, were the only obvious clues to their identities or their whereabouts, or, for that matter, to Gwydion's unique calling. He worked with many kinds of people, anyone from cab-drivers to world leaders who needed his help, and had changed the course of history more than once. Others might have been thrilled to have a direct link to "the other side," as he called it, and to be able to predict and change the course of history, but Gwydion, at best, was a reluctant volunteer. "It's a blessing and a curse," he often said. "The blessing is being able to do some good. The curse is knowing what is going to happen in my own personal life and having to watch difficult things unfold in their own time." He had recently endured the death of a grandchild, and it had nearly killed him.

But what was done was done, and on this particular morning Gwydion was worrying about a recent talk he'd had with an autocratic Asian leader who had asked him point-blank whether he should form an alliance with a group of Muslim extremists who were interested in purchasing nuclear weapons, of which the Asian leader happened to own a few. The call had put Gwydion in a dark mood. These fanatics were in the news of late, and their conviction that a world war was necessary to summon the Messiah and bring about Judgment Day terrified him.

At fifty, Gwydion was strikingly handsome in an aging-rock-star sort of way. He wore his long, dark, gray-streaked hair loose, so that it flowed down to the middle of his back. His piercing blue eyes were set in a long face framed by a square chin and softened by the John Lennon-style round, wire-rimmed glasses that he kept perched on his nose. He was the runt of his large Cockney family. He had been terribly close to his dad, a car mechanic who had his own garage, which was still run by a few of Gwydion's older brothers. The baby as well as the runt, he had seen his first dead person at six, and afterward, he'd attempted suicide several times.

Finally, Gwydion had been sent an angel, who explained that he had been chosen for this service by—surprise—a version of himself in another time and space. Gwydion fought this destiny for a few years until one day when a lorry ran him over and he was able simply to get up and walk away, unharmed, to the astonishment of onlookers. Realizing that he was trapped, or gifted, or both, he resigned himself to his fate. His father was a religious man, but somehow he understood Gwydion's struggle and stood by him. His dad was the first thing he thought about when he awoke, and the last thing he thought about before he went to sleep. It wasn't that he couldn't communicate with what was his father's "soul" but that a soul with a corporeal presence is completely different from a disembodied essence. His "Da" had truly disappeared after the death of his body.

The threadbare, oversized red cardigan sweater that Gwydion wore when he worked had belonged to his father, who had been massive at six feet five inches tall. Gwydion was a wiry five feet eight inches—but, in his view, the sweater fit him just fine. If you asked him what he would want in terms of an earthly reward for his service—and he had counseled as many as ten thousand people in the last thirty-five years—his eyes would fill with tears, and he would say without hesitation, "Just give me another hour with me dad." He spoke in a heavy East London accent, and of all the things of which he could have been proud, the circumstance that most pleased him was that he'd grown up in the same East End London neighborhood as Ozzy Osbourne.

He finished his muffin, clicked on the telly, and sat down at the sixteenth-century partner desk, which reputedly had once belonged to Casanova. How he came to own this particular desk could be the subject of a book, if he ever got around to writing it. Gwydion pushed back the sleeves of his sweater, revealing deep and jagged scars on his wrists from his final suicide attempt, at age twelve.

He sipped his coffee as he watched. On the television, Mahmoud Zarafshan, the president of Iran, was speaking about how Israel must be destroyed. "He thinks he's the bloody Second Coming," Gwydion said aloud then giggled, because the truth was Zarafshan did. *How do you get to be him?* Gwydion wondered. *How do you go from being a simple traffic engineer to the puppet for a gang of religious zealots running the country—and possibly one of the most dangerous men in the world? Strange.* It had occurred to Gwydion that America's duly-elected-by-the-people president Bush had also been a puppet for his own group of local fundamentalist crazies. Cowboy hat or turban, what was done in the name of God remained shocking.

Gwydion had a theory about all this—that the ability to reason is the enemy of goodness, because it separates the mind from the heart. After talking to so many people about intimate things, he had heard the entire spectrum of criminal, murderous behavior, and it never ceased to amaze him how these people could defend any action, however monstrous, under the banner of "reason" if they tried hard enough—killing the Jews, or the blacks, or the illegals—and that the reason was always that such action would serve the greater good of those who happened to be the "same" as the murderer. Yet concepts like "greater good" didn't hold up if one stayed in the realm of faith. If you were a believer in your heart, your sense of personal liability would keep you from spiritual ruin, but the application of reason offered a million opportunities to create loopholes. Gwydion did not excuse bad behavior regardless of the seeming logic behind it. "Actions speak louder than words" was what his dad had always said, and he agreed.

Gwydion recognized Cindal's gentle knock, and she smiled nervously as she peeked her head in, looking around the room as if expecting to find someone there with Gwydion. She was a plump, pretty blonde, and she wore a short, sexy pink robe with terrycloth mules. "Is it safe to come in?"

It was a fair question. There had been occasions when odd and unexplained things happened in the study. After the World Trade Center had been blown up, a tall, gray-haired woman in scorched and tattered clothing had appeared at the front door of the cottage, giving her name as Lorraine Smith and saying she had come urgently to meet with Gwydion. Cindal had politely escorted the distressed woman to the back of the study and lingered as Lorraine explained to Gwydion that she was there to find her husband. She had seemed confused when Gwydion explained that she was three thousand miles away from the tragedy.

Gwydion immediately realized what had happened, and he gently asked Cindal to get them some coffee as he did not want her to hear the distressing truth: Lorraine's husband had gone into the next world, and Lorraine herself was already dead! Nonetheless, Gwydion knew he had to tell her, and when he revealed the news, Lorraine did not understand and leapt up to argue her case. Cindal returned with coffee and muffins just in time to see the woman vanish into thin air, a crumpled tissue on the floor where she once stood.

Understandably, Cindal was shaken, and it took several days for her to calm down. The last straw had been when a client, an abused woman, showed up unannounced on Gwydion's doorstep. Rather than giving her a reading, Gwydion put her in his car and drove her directly to a shelter. A day or so later, the enraged husband, a large man with huge hands, stormed past Cindal into the study with a shotgun and told Gwydion that unless he revealed his wife's whereabouts, he was going to shoot him! Gwydion laughed and said, "Do you know who I am?"

The husband replied, "Yeah, you're one of those weird ones. You see the future."

Gwydion laughed harder and said bitterly, "Yes, and I know there is life after this one, so go ahead and blow me head off, mate. You'll be doing me a favor."

At that point, the man began to cry. Gwydion was able to take him to a specialist in anger management, and a successful resolution was reached. But after that, Cindal put her foot down, and, as a result, Gwydion stopped seeing people in their home. Yet the fear and anxiety that Cindal associated with the study lingered on.

Gwydion patted his lap, inviting her to sit. After nineteen years of marriage, he still fancied his wife like crazy. She padded across the room and nestled against him. They watched a BBC newscast. She fed him a bite of muffin. "Wonderful," he said, feeling a smug sense of victory. These days he was forced to use his wiles to get her to make the muffins in the first place, as she professed to be a kind of New Millennium feminist and often refused to cater to his whims, just because she could.

On the television, Iranian president Zarafshan addressed

the General Assembly of the United Nations. The English sub-titles revealed he was denying the Holocaust and, furthermore, was calling for the destruction of Israel. The speech concluded, and the BBC newscaster, a pale man in a drab suit, came on-screen: "The president addressed the General Assembly of the UN in New York City earlier today, causing shock and outrage when he demanded that Israel be cast out of the UN."

Gwydion thought to himself, *Yeah, we heard that—shouldn't you be pointing out what a sick fuck he is?*

Cindal asked, "What is that crazy man chuntering on about?"

"Oh, these extremist dickheads believe that there will be a resurrection, the world will end, everyone will be judged, and the good will be sent to heaven and the bad to hell. Most dooms-day prophecies foretell that there will be a terrible war that will precipitate the end of the world and the coming of the Messiah. Zarafshan and his mentor, the real power behind the throne, figure that they can speed up the Second Coming by getting the war started sooner. Ridiculous, of course. But I'm afraid they are serious. And they need to be stopped."

Cindal shook her head and snuggled deeper into her hus-band's lap as he put his arms around her. He loved the way she smelled in the morning, a combination of a sweet, floral per-fume and fresh milk. "Gwydion, is there any good news on this morning?"

He flicked the remote past several satellite channels, finally settling on some American all-night news show broadcast out of Washington, D.C. The presenters, one a disheveled and seem-ingly drunk Irishman with curly, gray hair and a fake smile, the other, a too young, overly sexy redheaded sidekick, sat in matching chairs on a raised dais. They watched a video playing on a flatscreen located above and between the two of them. In the video, a tall, slightly stooped but handsome man in his thir-ties, wearing a peaked cap, walked along a street where a large building was under construction. As he walked beneath some scaffolding, a sixteen-foot steel I-beam came crashing down out of nowhere.

Cindal gasped. "Oh, my God!"

Gwydion felt a cold but unseen hand on his shoulder—the spooky sensation that always indicated it was time to go to work. He clicked off the telly, grasped Cindal gently around her marvelously slim waist, and lifted her off his lap.

"What did you do that for? We'll never know what happened to the poor bloke."

"Time for work. It will be as God planned it."

"Oh, c'mon with the mystical stuff!"

"There are no coincidences, only the appearance of coincidences."

"Okay, Merlin—if you're so good, what are we having for dinner tonight?"

"I don't know, but I know what we're having for dessert." He reached out an arm and patted her bum, his hand electric on the soft, smooth skin underneath her short robe.

She giggled and tried to slap it away, but he pulled his hand back too quickly. "Some psychic you are," she laughed, then said sternly but with a smirk, "Self-fulfilling prophecy does not a psychic make!" She giggled again, amused at her own clever remark. "We're having steak, Mister Wizard." She slipped out of the study, closing the door behind her.

Immediately the air shifted and the room grew cold. Gwydion could hear the murmuring of far-off voices, a faint chiming of bells, and what sounded like the nervous fluttering of a flock of birds. The temperature dropped precipitously, and his glasses fogged in the sudden frost. His study filled with shadows and a strange hammering. He blinked and found himself rushing down an endless corridor filled with thick, purplish smoke. He came to a heavy wooden door, opened it and entered. Gwydion now stood in a duplicate version of his own study, but the furniture was transparent, as if it were made of glass, while, ironically, there was no view through the windows, just opaque darkness. There was a crackling fire in the hearth, yet Gwydion could see his own breath. A life-sized stone sculpture of an angel, complete with huge, curving wings and a floor-length gown, sat with its back to the door, posed as if staring out at the black nothingness beyond.

"I am here," Gwydion said, and the short hairs on his arms stood on end as the angel's chiseled wings moved slightly. Gwydion had never gotten used to it; his guts twisted as the angel turned toward him, the angel's face a mirror image of Gwydion's own but possessing eyes colder than his. This was Gwydion's guide—an angel with no name. Neither of them spoke; they simply nodded to each other knowingly, and Gwydion sat in his chair, turned on his computer, and clicked on his e-mail. On the screen were the latest of the dozens of requests he got for consultations every day, and more of them popped into view as the computer sprang into action. At the top of the list, there appeared an e-mail from Zephaniah Bronfman, whom Gwydion had just seen on TV. He raised a quizzical eyebrow. *So he survived—but how? It is a miracle.* The next one down was from nycprivatechef@hotmail.com.

The angel said in a voice colder than the grave, "No miracles, only the appearance of miracles. Give that Zephaniah fellow your next appointment, and the one below it, the cook, that one too. They both will have a role to play on a larger stage. Make sure that you tape your conversations, and send the tapes off directly after each one. We will tell you what to do just before you speak with them."

"Okeydokey." Gwydion paused, then asked, "And what about my consultation with the Korean president's aide? Is nuclear war a real threat?"

"Yes, it is, and more than that, Zarafshan believes he is the Twelfth Imam, and thus the one who must facilitate the resurrection. He is very dangerous, and the outcome is by no means clear."

"Why doesn't God stop him?"

"What makes you think He won't?"

"God didn't stop the Holocaust."

"Zarafshan doesn't even admit there was a Holocaust. That doesn't make it true."

"Doesn't make it false, either. And God did allow six million plus to die."

The angel sighed. "Arguing with God accomplishes nothing."

"I am not arguing. I am asking."

"Yes, that's a discussion for another time. Free will factors in here. Every human has a choice, you know that."

"Did I really have a choice?"

"We have discussed this many times. Your soul is a volunteer in the Army of Light. This one, this . . . Bronfman is too."

Gwydion smiled wryly. "He just doesn't know it yet."

The angel nodded. "For now, it's time for you to take your nap so I can dictate the conversations you will have."

"Zarafshan must be stopped."

Gwydion waited, but the angel did not respond, so Gwydion dutifully went over to the sofa, lay down, and closed his eyes. The angel leaned over and whispered in his ear. He felt himself falling into a paradox of sunlit darkness.

When Gwydion awoke, he was back in his worldly study. The sun had set outside the open window, and as night fell, the sky was tinted a dark-navy blue streaked with pink and purple. The noise that woke him was Cindal knocking—the signal that dinner was ready. "Be right there," he called, then walked over to the computer and responded in the affirmative to both Zephaniah Bronfman's and nycprivatechef@hotmail.com's e-mails. *How will this drama play out?* he wondered. From experience, he knew that, whatever happened, free will didn't prevent tears. He headed for the door, but before he left the room, he turned and looked back at the computer and mused, "I hope poor Bronfman had a drink when he got home. He's going to need it."

Gwydion took off his dad's sweater and went in to dinner.

CHAPTER 1

Love Is a Bullet

 INSE THE LAMB CHOPS in cold water, pat them dry. Sharpen the small knife and cut off all the fat. Take a nail scissor to get any strings. Take the tulip pan, put in a little oil, and turn the stove on high. Quickly chop garlic and fresh rosemary and press mixture into the soft meat. Salt the face of the chop and pour out any extra oil in the pan. Put the chops in the pan. Add a splash of red wine. Pour a glass.

The satisfying sound of meat searing. *Rinse bunch of arugula to make sure there's no sand. Spin-dry and taste. Still sandy, shit. Rinse it again, turn the chop over. With water running, open microwave and turn sweet potato. Heat for three minutes. Turn over chops, first salting them and pouring off grease from pan.*

A few minutes later, the entrée was ready. *Voilà!*

Santiago, Sarah's Ecuadorian helper, came into the large, stainless-steel-and-chrome Upper East Side kitchen carrying four empty salad plates. He was compactly buff, a baby-faced blond with watery blue eyes and a goatee. No taller than she, with a gentle smile, he could have been twenty or forty—it was hard to know. He was dressed in a black shirt and pants. "They loved your kosher *lardons*," he said in heavily accented English.

"They wanted to know how you did it." Sarah smiled. Translating haute cuisine into kosher fare was something for which she was known.

"I bet they do." Santiago picked up two of the lamb plates and left, then returned for the other two. Sarah meanwhile took out a pan of roasted winter vegetables, plated them onto a maroon platter, and drizzled them with truffle-infused oil. She had found a French chef in Avignon who sold kosher-certified products. It always amused her because truffles were dug out of the ground by pigs, which were definitely *not* kosher. Santiago returned for the vegetables.

"Do they seem happy?"

"Go look for yourself."

"You know I never do. It's bad luck. If I so much as set foot in there, something terrible will happen."

Santiago smiled and left carrying the vegetable platter.

Now that the entrée was served, Sarah poured herself a small glass of wine, drank it back, and refilled her glass. Sadness settled on her like the raven over Poe's chamber door. She felt so alone. The hard part was never the cooking of these gourmet meals for clients. What was hard was how to know what to do with herself when she got home. There was no longer anyone there with whom to share the leftovers. She started coffee and put the strawberry-rhubarb pie in the oven.

When the gig was over, Sarah took the bottle home and finished it while she did some yoga. The irony of mixing the two was not lost on her, and when she attempted to move into the "downward dog" pose, she fell and lay on her mat, laughing.

The trouble was that her drinking was getting heavier—and sometimes she became a blackout drunk. And when she got really loaded, she hid things in strange places, or moved some of her treasures from one hiding place to another. The most important one was a necklace from a lover she tried not to think about. *Where was it now? Where was he? Where was . . .*

She fell asleep in the middle of her thought on the yoga mat. She awoke, hours later, abruptly, cold and stiff. She began the

yoga exercise known as "the breath of fire," pumping her stomach in and out, but was too hung over and had to stop. Sarah
sobbed, got ahold of herself, and thought about how much she
hated God. Why had He arranged matters so that, in her world,
she could never be considered the equal of a man, just by dint
of her sex? The anger took her out of her lethargy, and she got
up off the mat. How long was this going to go on? Ever since
her divorce, mornings were difficult. Sleeping was hard enough,
but no matter how late she awoke, Sarah's memories chased her
like some lingering nightmare. When she tried to see what was
actually making her feel so blue, it was always the same thing:
an image of the pale ocean in winter, in black and white. With
it would come the disembodied face of her ex saying something
cruel, or a time when they had fought. Then her mind would
skitter away like a bug, and she would try to distract herself with
the details of the upcoming day.

Early mornings, especially Sundays, had been their special
time. But as her marriage had disintegrated over its last five
years, she and Michael no longer woke up and made love. Instead, he worked into the early-morning hours as a bartender
and often slept in until noon. Sarah would get up and take an extra yoga class, then walk by the East River. No matter how much
the esoteric discipline improved her mood and the beauty of the
river lifted her spirit, underneath she was sick with disappointment—and hated herself for it. She knew better. She believed
that life was inherently meaningless and that the attempt to give
it meaning was doomed, because it was always false. Even her
work was futile. *Cook for ten hours, eat for ten minutes, rinse,
repeat.*

What a fool she had been to fall in love with a man, any man.
For a brief time the way Michael had made her feel thwarted her
chronic nihilism. He had filled her with that most evil thing—
hope. Michael resembled Clark Kent from *Superman.* He was
tall and muscular. Dark, curly hair fell forward on his high forehead, framing an intelligent face with a cleft chin. Horn-rimmed
glasses topped off his profile. Sarah had hoped the marriage

vows would be kept, and furthermore that the two of them would always inhabit that euphoric state known as "being in love."

It had lasted for a year or two, and then somehow, the connection had slipped away. Sarah found herself living with a man who would do anything for her except the one thing she needed. In short, he had stopped making love to her for over a year before the end. Once she saw that the magic was gone forever, she ended the marriage although her married friends all seemed to have accepted that it was natural for the romance to end, and that a descent into a comfortable sort of brother-sister arrangement was fine. They didn't understand why she would give up such a good and decent man and risk being alone. Was it "good and decent" not to try to meet the other half of a relationship halfway? She wanted a life filled with romance—and she had never felt as alone as she did on those sexless mornings. The worst was knowing that he hadn't wanted to try. He kept saying that he couldn't, but a book she read to try to understand his behavior stated bluntly that "couldn't" meant "wouldn't." She keenly remembered the dreadful recognition when she'd read those words.

Today was the worst so far. Well, it was a Sunday. She felt like the Little Match Girl in the fairytale, who is not allowed to come in out of the snowstorm until all of her matches are sold. The child dies, unloved and unnoticed. Sarah felt the Little Match Girl's pain and could not comfort herself. She just had to wait it out, and usually this agony would pass into her unconscious because she was too busy prepping a new cooking job.

Thanksgiving was the beginning of one of her busy seasons. Perhaps it was the nearness of the holiday; the whole idea of celebrating the rape of the original Americans depressed her—Jews and Native Americans had a history of persecution in common. Or perhaps it was because she and Michael had become engaged over a Thanksgiving dinner she had cooked for him and his parents. He was not Jewish. She had made a turkey basted with beer and a pound of the fattiest bacon she could find. It was a trick she'd learned from Carlos, her neighbor and fellow chef.

The meal was a success, and Michael had buried the ring in the stuffing. Sometimes, now, she wished he had choked on it.

Later, when she proudly showed her ring to her mother, the response was: "Oh, it's so small. Mine was three carats." Sarah had thought but not said aloud, *Yeah, but Dad was paying you off for Grandpa's connections. He admitted that he never loved you—at least this guy loves me for myself.*

Sarah walked into her bedroom and collapsed onto the bed. She looked around and had to admit that it would not be inviting to any man. Some time ago she had painted it a pale blue, which had since morphed into a color she imagined the skin of World War II concentration-camp victims had when liberated, and the sheets and bedspread were tired and worn. Two not-hung but expensively framed Brassaï photographs of people in bars stood in a corner. Her brass bed faced a simple oak dresser with a mirror. She looked at herself warily. Reflecting back at her was a thin, sad woman in her thirties with long, curly red hair and discontented gray eyes.

Her nightstand featured a cheap ceramic lamp, a battery-operated alarm clock, and a large statue of the Hindu elephant deity, Ganesh, known as the "remover of obstacles." A beat-up brass incense holder was nearby, and, as was her habit, Sarah lit the half-used stick of incense and performed her morning wakeup routine, which involved stretching, breathing, and massaging the various parts of her body associated with each of the seven energy centers, or chakras. It never made her feel appreciably better, but the chanting of ancient words somehow gave her a moment's respite. She had loved Hebrew as a child, and the Gurmukhi words warmed her in the same way. Because there were so many celebrity gods in the Hindu pantheon, she didn't mind singing prayers to them. Conversely, though, she bitterly resented the Hebrew invocations because of their mono-theistic focus.

On the nightstand next to Ganesh she kept her most prized possession: a zippered coin purse that Sylvie Anne Jones, her grandparents' cook, had given her. The image of the Statue of

Liberty was embroidered on the worn cloth, and it had two pockets. Inside one was the paper message from a fortune cookie that read: BEWARE OF WHAT YOU WISH FOR. Inside the other was a token for the subway and a MetroCard. Sarah had kept the metal token as a souvenir, even though New York City had done away with coin tokens years ago. When Sylvie had left Sarah's grandparents' employ, she had given the purse to Sarah with the admonition, "Only ask the Lord for what you need, and always keep enough money so you can take a ride." Ever since then, Sarah made sure there was also a current MetroCard in the pocket so that she could take a trip on the subway. She opened the purse, read the fortune, and smiled sadly. There was nothing she wished for, nowhere to go, so she was probably safe, at least for now.

She pulled on a once-white terrycloth bathrobe, padded over to her yoga mat, and again attempted the breath of fire. After a few rounds, she gave up and walked across the hall.

She found herself in the kitchen. It was equipped with professional-quality appliances and utensils. A French-farm-house-style table, with a warm yellow-and-gray paisley runner and wooden chairs with matching cushions, gave the room charm. A big poster of a red Ganesh hung on one wall, over a pine bookcase overflowing with cooking and yoga books. Next to the bookcase stood a matching filing cabinet. Sarah opened it. The files were neatly kept and color-coded. She filed them chronologically based on the date of the event.

Cooking had been good to her, and she loved it, but not like a religion. She was annoyed by the attempts to exalt cooking into some other realm. Wasn't cooking its own reward?

On a recent date, a fellow chef bragged about things like having an egg poacher that heated water to the perfect temperature every time. "Oh, so you are reducing art to science," she had said caustically, expecting a laugh.

Instead, he leaned forward and said earnestly and proudly, "Yes, that's exactly right," and gave her that look that said, *See, I am so great—you should sleep with me*. She had passed on the offer, as she had on so many others.

She reviewed the file for one of her upcoming jobs, a five-course banquet for four. She intended to prepare veal tenderloin using an ancient recipe she had found in a book on biblical foods, but would add a few modern touches such as balsamic vinegar in the marinade. She smiled for a moment at her own foolishness. Better to stay detached and keep her distance from anything that smacked of relevance.

As she made a shopping list, Sarah felt despair settle upon her like a saddle on a horse. She bucked, hard. No way did she want to go there, another fruitless journey into the land of woulda-coulda-shoulda—and why hadn't Michael been willing to try? She'd felt so hurt when he just refused to explore any of the usual options to resolve marital stress: He scoffed at therapy, ridiculed counseling. She'd chalked it up to his blue-collar upbringing, hoping that "wouldn't try" meant "couldn't try" so she could avoid blaming him directly. She hated blame, because even when it seemed appropriate, it worked like a seesaw: He was to blame, but she was equally so. Perhaps if she knew what her transgressions were, what she had done, that knowledge would ease her suffering. Sarah believed that there was never any randomness in the universe; rather, she accepted that, on some level, she must prefer suffering or she wouldn't be doing it—practicing it, as if *suffering* were her religion. She found herself stifling tears and knew she'd better get moving.

She poured herself into a cold shower—a yoga trick. Ice-cold water always improved her mood. As the water hit her white skin and dampened her waist-length, curly red hair, she shouted, "*Waheguru*," a Gurmukhi expression that was equivalent to "Thank God." She enjoyed speaking in Gurmukhi, which was a language older than Sanskrit, like Aramaic was to Hebrew. She had studied Hebrew until she was bat mitzvahed, but had since lost the ability to read or speak it.

Ironically, she, a fallen Jew, specialized in elegant, upscale kosher cuisine—"Safe *treif*," as she privately referred to her style of cooking. She made dishes that would not ordinarily be allowed under the kosher dietary laws by creating acceptable versions of such off-limit items as bacon. Her clients marveled at her skills, but she felt like a fraud because she herself was a bit of an anti-Semite. She blamed the Jews for always attracting their own suffering, and she fumed when she saw the ridiculous appearance of the Chasidim with their archaic clothes and hairstyles. Standing out was a sure way to get into trouble. Was it necessary to highlight the differences and shove them down other people's throats? She had never read in the Bible where it said, "When observing my laws, be sure to alienate every other culture in a thousand-mile radius." Absurd. It was part of the reason she hated God. He wasn't explicit enough, and when humans misinterpreted His lack of clear instructions, He blamed them! Talk about passive-aggressive behavior. She'd been married to a passive-aggressive man and well knew that you could never win. And to be stuck for all eternity with a passive-aggressive deity—that was a good definition of what hell would be, and she was stuck in it, forever, whatever "forever" meant.

Sarah felt the same way about the Sikhs. So many Kundalini yoga practitioners also adopted their religious doctrines and lifestyle. The Sikhs wore turbans as part of their religious practice—and this outlandish costume, plus strident dietary restrictions, also made them a target. At least they were not obsessed with being victims—perhaps that was why this style of yoga appealed to her.

The Jewish obsession with the Holocaust also maddened her, because on a certain level she felt the Jews were writing the instruction booklet for the next Hitler and confirming their candidacy for victimhood. How should the need to preserve their heritage be approached? At least reframe the perspective so that history could admire the strength the Jews had shown in surviving. Make it into a David and Goliath story, and flaunt the fact that, in spite of near obliteration, they were the only . . . well, what were they, really? Was being Jewish a religion, a nationality, or a culture? Maybe all three—but, regardless, theirs was the only ancient culture that was still extant. They needed to present themselves as victors, not victims. She understood that you preserved culture by reenacting it, so if people were interested in maintaining the past by adhering to a specific dietary code, which did not give detailed instructions on how to orchestrate genocide, she was glad to participate.

Sarah felt that being Jewish was a curse, and the idea that she was part of a race that had been "chosen" infuriated her. *Yeah, we were chosen all right—chosen to be tied to God's whipping post, like Job. To be exterminated. Thank You for making us part of the Final Solution. Thanks for nothing, God. Thanks for making this hell—for that is surely what life must be—and sticking me in it, and trying to sell it to me as something good.*

However, kosher cooking had been good to her. The Shively building where she lived near the East River was pricey. The complex consisted of six separate five-story buildings surrounding a central courtyard, and each building had a lobby with stairs at each level that went down to the yard. There were two wrought-iron-gate entrances, one on 77th and the other on 78th. There was even a driveway so that she could pull the van she used for work very close to the stairwell nearest her duplex. She'd been able to buy two apartments on the fourth and fifth floors and to break through. A spiral staircase ran between the two floors. The best part was that she had two kitchens and was able to do much of the preparation for each job at home, ferrying the food with Santiago's help anywhere in the city or the outlying boroughs, where she often worked. One kitchen she kept strictly kosher, for that was much of her business, though Sarah herself did not observe.

Each floor of the Shively had two apartments, and Carlos lived right across the hall, so it was cozy and convenient all around. Carlos was Sri Lankan and impossibly handsome, with dark, shoulder-length hair, creamy beige skin, large doe eyes, and a perfect pink mouth. He moved like a dancer but liked to brag about his stint in the Sri Lankan Army, where he had been the equivalent of a Marine and had jumped out of airplanes. He was now a private chef to some fancy woman downtown who entertained diplomats and celebrities. Sarah and Carlos were close friends, and he would often drop in after work with a half-bottle of some remarkable wine left over from dinner, a tin of unfinished caviar, or lobster tails. In fact, that was how they first met. She had recently moved in and was prepping a job. He had knocked on her door and said without preamble, "I'm Carlos. Do you eat lobster tails?"

"As long as they're kosher."

He thought about it, then laughed at her joke.

They'd been fast friends ever since. Carlos was a true Casanova, and more than once she had hidden one of his lovers in her apartment while another was coming or going. This particular episode of depression had been launched in part by the words Carlos had said to her during his most recent unannounced visit.

He'd shown up a couple of days earlier with a bottle of fabulous Bordeaux and announced, "I think I am truly in love with Laura."

"But you work for her."

"So? It could be dangerous?"

"Yes, honey. Love is always risky. Especially with your boss. And besides, Carlos, she's a woman, and I thought you're . . ."

Carlos laughed. "How can you get to be so old and still be so innocent?"

"I got married at an early age."

Carlos nodded. "Um-hmm, and that was all over, like, two years ago. We need to find you some loving."

"It takes time to get over things. You know the rule: half the time to get over a relationship, based on the time you put in. In six months, I'll be ready."

"Yeah, whatever. I saw this movie once, and one guy said to the other, 'How do I get over this woman?' and his friend says, 'Best way to get over one woman is to get on top of a few others.' "

"Not funny. I am no slut."

Carlos sighed. "And you'll be sorry when you're old."

"I know, but it's that fucking 'chosen people' bullshit—I can't!"

Carlos looked confused. "But you don't keep kosher or go to

church."

"Synagogue."

"Whatever. You work on the holidays. You love bacon. You tell Jewish jokes." He looked her up and down. "You, my dear, are a hypocrite, hiding behind some Jewish ideal to justify avoiding love."

"You assume you get to love through sex."

"How else?"

"Oh, you are such a *man!*"

"And you assume that if you mope around long enough, some prince will stumble across you and save you. You are such a *woman!*"

"I date."

"Yes, that's true, but as far as I can tell, you never take any of them out for a test drive. Don't you get whatever the female equivalent of blue balls is?"

"No, Kundalini yoga reshapes your libido. You channel all that energy back through your chakras."

Carlos nodded. "Okay. But if you don't need something, you don't really go after it. I know you're lonely."

"Really? How do you know?"

He picked up an empty wine bottle. "You never used to drink alone."

Sarah knew he was right. "I know," she mumbled, her voice shaky with unshed tears. Carlos handed her a box of tissues.

"But don't worry. You can't hide. Love is a bullet with your name on it."

"Oh, well, that makes me eager—*not!* But it sounds about right. Love's always going to wound you, and it's often fatal."

"Everything is ultimately fatal. We are all going to die. At least the physical-body part. So I say use it before you lose it."

"You sound like an ad for sneakers! 'Just do it.' I never thought of you as a walking platitude."

"Well then, let me pile on another one: It's better to have loved and lost than never to have loved at all. By the way, I have a referral for you. Are you booked for Thanksgiving yet?"

"I haven't committed."

"Good! He's a live one, ready to be caught," Carlos said with a wink. "Play your cards right—get those pigs in the blanket just right . . ." He made a rude gesture with the thumb and forefinger of his left hand, then pushed the forefinger of the other hand through the hole he'd formed. "Why do they call it that? Pigs aren't kosher. Anyway, hook up with this guy, you could retire. He's a doctor—plastic surgeon to the stars—and recently divorced, like you. The ex-wife and kids are in Boca with a new stepfather."

✿

Sarah met Dr. Hirsch at his office on Fifth Avenue. His building occupied the entire southeast corner of 72nd Street. Two pretty receptionists managing a full waiting room greeted her. Sarah was quickly ushered past the patients into his lavish office. He sat behind an expensive desk with nothing on it. There were photos of the family and of Dr. Hirsch with well-known movie stars and politicians. *Trust Carlos to find a celebrity doctor.* Dr. Hirsch stood up and offered his hand. "Call me Ed." He spoke with a slight Long Island accent but had a startling baritone voice. *Very sexy.* In fact, he was perfect: handsome, in a Semitic way, tall, with a patrician nose and curly, graying hair, and attractively dressed in Gucci loafers and a crisp, white doctor's coat—the kind of guy her parents wished she had married.

But Sarah was wary because she had seen her mother always having to put up with her father. He held the purse strings, even though he had gotten that purse from his father-in-law. She had witnessed her mother become terribly unhappy in all of her choices and stuck because she didn't have financial freedom. Sarah had sworn that she would never be financially dependent on any man.

She could tell he liked her. He came and sat on the edge of his desk, less than a foot away from the chair in which she sat.

"I hear you are a great chef."

She smiled. "You're too kind. How many guests will there be?"
"Eleven, plus me."

So she would be cooking for twelve Jews. There were the phrases for groups of animals such as a "murder of ravens" and a "gaggle of geese," so what did you call it when a bunch of Jews hung together? She remembered—it was a *minyan*, which required that there be ten or more men gathered in order to hold a Jewish service. Of course, women didn't count.

He seemed to read her thoughts. "Yes, we'll have a *minyan*." He said something in Hebrew, and she pretended to nod appreciatively, not wanting to be found out.

"I brought a couple of different menus," she said, handing him a folder. He scanned them, three menus with variations of a four-course Thanksgiving-dinner theme, each listing a soup, salad, entrée, and dessert: turkey soup with *kreplach,* a salad with cranberries and walnuts, classic roast turkey and trimmings, and an array of baked goods that she would create using the kosher guidelines; or turkey-giblet soup and honey-glazed turkey with pesto stuffing, plus wilted-spinach-and-mushroom salad. The third menu was the one that made him smile: *kreplach* soup, roasted turkey stuffed with *challah, fines herbes* and mushrooms, sweet-potato *kugel* and creamy *parve* peas. He nodded, pleased. She handed him another document with her price list on it. He scanned it and frowned.

"Okay, I know you get what you pay for, but how about a ten percent discount?"

She concealed her annoyance by crossing her legs in a sexy way. Men always tried to nickel and dime women when they would never argue with a man over money that way.

She said calmly, "Do you want me to cook ten percent less than excellent? Shall I only cook everything ninety percent done?" She crossed her legs the other direction, showing a tad more thigh. She examined her cuticles. And waited. A long minute passed. Then finally, he spoke.

"I've had two other bids, and they were both lower." He seemed stunned that she wouldn't negotiate.

"You get what you pay for, Dr. Hirsch." She stood up to go. "I gave you three references, and I am sure you understand what I offer." She glanced at the door.

"Wait, I know you have a stellar reputation."

"Would you like me to do the dinner or not?"

He surveyed her ringless left hand.

"Will you have a drink with me?"

She'd forced herself to smile, though she felt like slapping his smooth, complacent face. "Is that part of the deal?"

He smirked. "No, but . . ."

Sarah moved in close. "Perhaps we can discuss that after the party." She gave him a flirtatious smile. He grinned. He had long teeth, and they were perfectly white. She wondered if he ate his own home cooking. *Is any part of him real?*

"Fair enough."

"Great. So, if you would like to engage me, I need half up-front."

"Do you make your own *kreplach*?"

"From scratch."

"My mother used to make them. I miss them." He pulled out his book, wrote out the check, and signed it. "How will you serve them?"

"Your choice, boiled in soup or fried as a canapé. Whatever you prefer."

"Will there be soup?"

She was bewildered—they had both looked at the menu and seen soup featured clearly. "Your wish is my command—there will be soup."

They shared a smile. As she took the check, she enjoyed a private joke with herself: She'd been taught to cook not by her *bubbie*—her fat, white-haired cultural-stereotype grandmother—but by Sylvie, the cook. Sylvie was descended from slaves who had escaped on the Underground Railroad, and she was a deacon in her church. She was black, truly: the color of cooking chocolate. Sylvie's voice was warm and resonant. There was always a smile, a hug (as long as no one was looking), and a cookie.

She taught Sarah little tricks: how to carve a radish into a flower, how to use powdered sugar to make smiley faces on pancakes, as well as classic techniques such as how to render chicken fat. As a child, Sarah was desperate for warmth and mothering, and Sylvie had provided both. Sylvie would tell Sarah Bible stories while she cooked the family dinner. Perhaps Sylvie's vivid retelling of what Sarah thought of as myths explained Sarah's lack of interest in Hindu mythology, which she found violent and unsettling in its moral message. Arjuna's dilemma in the *Bhagavad Gita* actually annoyed her. *What sort of literature affirmed the necessity to go to war against one's relatives, however hateful?* Sarah's favorite myth was the story of Purim and how Queen Esther had tricked the evil Haman into showing his true colors, thus saving the Jews.

Sylvie had told her the story many times, making the point that Jews and black people were a lot alike. Later, when she was older, Sarah realized that, while there were similarities, Jews had never sold their own into slavery. Sarah wished that Sylvie could have been her mother.

Sarah's own mother was beautiful and accomplished but detached from Sarah because her focus was completely on her husband. She liked to shop and read while Sarah wanted to garden and cook. Her maternal grandmother was the original model of emotional remoteness, a redhead who spent a great deal of time doing volunteer work. She had been a force in the Jewish charity Hadassah and was rarely home.

Sarah's father worked with his father-in-law and was almost never around. Her grandfather was a multimillionaire real estate developer, and Sarah's mother had grown up with nannies and a butler. Sarah's mother spoke of herself as lonely: a poor little rich girl forced to shop by herself at Saks Fifth Avenue— but she still neglected Sarah. Even so, Sarah often found herself wishing her mother could have been happier.

Nowadays she often thought of her mother, her recollections tinged with guilt because of her love for Sylvie. Until Sarah's grandfather died, there were formal

Friday-night dinners, which were served at a long, antique table that sat sixteen, with four courses and two servers. There was a lot of shop talked at the table, and Sarah found the long dinners excruciating. She would escape into the kitchen and "help" the heartbreakingly beautiful Sylvie cook.

Sylvie was more attractive than Lena Horne, yet she spent her life raising two bastard kids, taking care of her sick mother, and cooking for a Jewish family. She had a rich contralto voice and sang hymns, which she taught to Sarah as she was cooking brisket or making chicken soup. She explained to Sarah that some of the hymns were actually encoded messages that helped her relatives trying to escape slavery make the connection to the Underground Railroad. Sarah's favorite was "Swing Low, Sweet Chariot," because the song referenced a stop on that secret path to freedom: a town in Ohio where fugitive slaves could hide and rest up. This locale was atop a mountain and accessible only by crossing a river, and only the villagers could lead the runaway slaves to safety. So the lyrics in the chorus went:

I looked over Jordan, and what did I see?
Coming for to carry me home
A band of angels coming after me

This was code, so that the escaping slaves would know to wait for the "angels" to come and get them. Sylvie was the great-great-grandchild of one of the slaves that had hidden in that very town.

But one Friday when Sarah snuck into the kitchen, Sylvie was no longer there. Sarah was bereft and threw a tantrum when told that Sylvie was gone and was never coming back. Sarah wept and pleaded. She refused to go into the dining room and sit during dinner. Sarah's mother slapped her for being fresh. A tiny scar would remain next to her lower lip on the right side where the edge of her mother's diamond ring had cut her face.

Sarah bled copiously, so her mother left her in the maid's room with an ice pack and sent the new cook, a portly, light-skinned black woman named Mary, in to her with soup. Sarah lay in a fetal position, the ice pack pressed to her lip. She was beyond grief, beyond tears. Mary, who smelled of vanilla, sat down on the edge of the bed. Her voice was musical, from some foreign island. "C'mon, my little one, you must eat—and keep up your strength."

"I wish I was dead."

Mary chuckled.

"There was a very famous actress with your name."

"I know. Sarah Bernhardt. And don't tell me I'm being dramatic."

"Tosh, tosh!"

"How could she just leave without saying goodbye?"

Mary examined the wound. "The bleeding has stopped. What about a Band-Aid and a little soup?"

"No. I'm never eating again."

Mary left and returned with a Band-Aid and a small package wrapped in pretty blue paper tied with a shiny silver ribbon.

"Sylvie didn't have time to say goodbye, but she left you this."

Sarah eagerly opened the package. Inside was the coin purse with the embroidered Statue of Liberty.

The message was on another piece of the blue wrapping paper and written in clear curving script.

Dear Sarah,

It was time for me to go. I am leaving you this purse so that you remember me. Freedom comes from two things: having resources and having wisdom. There's a little token here for the subway train so that when you are a little older you can take a ride and get away from things. The fortune is the best advice anyone ever gave me. I will always love you and hold you in my heart.

Your friend,

Sylvie

Instead of feeling comforted, Sarah felt abandoned. The scar near her lip was tiny, but it seemed to her no one ever told her how pretty she was after that. She slept with the change purse and often dreamed of her friend.

Sarah always longed to see Sylvie again, and whenever she saw a woman of color who looked remotely like her, Sarah would startle like a horse.

She snapped back to the present. Ed Hirsch thrust into her view, looking pensively at her. "Was there anything else?"

"No," she said, flustered, and stood up. "I look forward to working with you." She shook hands and ducked out quickly.

Sarah took the bus across town to the Farmland Market on Broadway. Upon boarding, she carefully opened the change purse, which she always brought to job interviews as a good luck charm. She paid the fare with the MetroCard she kept inside, then picked up the vintage token and rubbed the smooth, worn surface between her fingers, thinking fondly of Sylvie before putting it safely back. The purse would go back on her night table as soon as she got home.

Farmland was packed solid. It was a New York institution filled with fresh fruits and vegetables and every gourmet treat imaginable. The market took up half a city block and had open bins along the sidewalk filled with colorful produce and flowers. Inside, the space was divided into narrow aisles that were crammed full of Thanksgiving shoppers, jostling for space with the workers who continuously replenished the fruits and vegetables. In the back of the store was a fish counter, a butcher, a huge cheese section, and an entire refrigerator case filled with kosher food. Sarah wore sunglasses and avoided meeting anyone's gaze. Usually, the bustle cheered her up, but today she felt trapped and panicky. She broke into a sweat. Her heart was pounding heavily, and although she felt like thick cotton was encasing her brain, she knew that she was in the midst of a panic attack. *Waheguru, Waheguru, Waheguru*, she chanted mentally and began the breath of fire. She went outside to get some air.

Across the street from the market stood a health club that

boasted an outdoor climbing wall. Sarah stared as three female gym rats attempted to scale to the top. They were all working hard. Normally, Sarah would have enjoyed watching this absurdity, but today she had a thought that made her gasp: *I am equally absurd! I too have been climbing the wrong mountain—my whole life!* A pain shot through her heart—*not only wrong but a false mountain as well.* No wonder she felt such existential despair—it was true; her life *was* meaningless! A desperate giggle escaped her lips. It was grimly amusing to have meaninglessness confirmed, as opposed to the usual vague cloud of doubt that seemed to block out any sun from getting close enough to warm her heart. She admitted finally that she had always known on some subconscious level that she had spent her life "climbing the wrong mountain," so, of course, nothing in her life had ever felt real.

What about the cooking? Was that also false? Chuang Tzu, the Zen philosopher, wrote, "Last night I dreamed that I was a blue butterfly. How do I know that today I am not a blue butterfly dreaming that I am a man?" Was she asleep having a nightmare from which she couldn't rouse herself or was she just awake in Sodom?

Sarah needed a sign—something that would pull her out of this accelerating downward spiral. She decided to abort her shopping mission and do the only thing she could think of, which was to take a yoga class. She realized that she had been able to keep up a steady breath of fire and that she was once again calm. *Waheguru.*

CHAPTER 2

IN THE BLINK OF AN I-BEAM

PART OF WHAT SET Zephaniah on his journey was a story he'd heard from his *zayde*, or grandfather, at a wedding. In Zephaniah's upbringing, men had little social interaction with women, and he was still nervous in their presence. But the men and women were not segregated at this less-religious-than-usual event. He sat with Hal, a former dentist now in his eighties, who had recently been widowed. Hal, although white-haired, was still a tall, handsome man with a hooked nose and playful blue eyes. He'd been on the dance floor since the reception began. When he came back to the table, he dismissed the frisky seventyish woman, who was clearly interested in him, with a cheek kiss and an empty promise to call her. Hal poured two glasses of wine to the brim and handed one to his thirty-two-year-old grandson. Zephaniah was also tall, broad-shouldered, and handsome. Hal frowned. "Zev, why aren't you dancing?"

Zev shook his head helplessly and shrugged. *Zayde* Hal patted his arm. "Okay, my friend. Drink this. I understand. The idea of sleeping with one woman for your entire life is just too much to bear. But here, today, one dance is just one dance."

Zev, surprised at this blasphemy, nodded.

"What's wrong with you? Are you shy?" *Zayde* looked around

the ballroom, and with a sparkle in his eyes noted that there were many single women present and that over the course of the evening many of them had paraded in front of Zev, smiling and signaling interest. "Aside from the fact that you're thirty-two and unmarried, live at home, have probably never had a woman, and aren't willing to play the game in our little sect, nothing is wrong! Listen, I never told you this—your father would *plotz* if he knew I was revealing it to you now—but my mother, your great-grandmother, was the bookkeeper for a synagogue. As you know, my stepfather wasn't Jewish. So every Sunday my mother would bring me and leave me at the Hebrew school—and then she would go off to church with my stepfather! One day I was so early that only the rabbi was there. I told him my plans to join up, and he explained the difference between the army and the navy: The navy was cleaner, and in the army you could get trench foot—the trenches were so full of water that the soldiers' feet would rot in their boots! This could be fatal, so, when it was time, I joined the navy. Got in the day before they closed to volunteers."

Zev offered a weak, obligatory smile, then lifted his glass. "To the navy!"

The two men drank their way to the bottom of the bottle without talking. Zev watched as the women and girls danced. One girl had round, flaxen curls. She caught his eye and smiled. He looked away, full of desire. In a fantasy, he saw himself dressed in an SS uniform and jackboots, approaching her and grabbing her from behind. With one arm, he swept the china dishes and glassware onto the floor while the other hand flipped her dress over her head and tore off her panties. As he bent her over the table, the tablecloth ran red with spilled wine. At the last moment, he pulled out of her and came all over her perfect behind and her satiny blue dress.

Hal followed Zev's gaze. "Yes!" the older man said appreciatively. Zev snapped back to reality. "You know what else? That same rabbi told me that one's first job is to survive, whatever that means: not to lose oneself. Staying alive is more important than any rule."

Zev shrugged. "This is news?"

Hal smiled. "Wait. So, when I was in the navy, I tried to keep the Jewish dietary laws, but one day, when I hadn't eaten for three days in France, God help me, I ate a pork chop. I waited and waited, but God didn't strike me down. I knew then that the rabbi had been right, and that it was a mighty force, this God who could create a Holocaust yet save a poor Jewish sailor. That was the day I truly began to believe. So never doubt Him, my young Zev. Always do what you have to do to keep yourself alive, and God will support you."

The irresistible strains of the *hora* began, and Hal stood up. "This is my cue. Come, help me lift the chair of this poor *meshugana* who's already got his balls cut off."

Zev was confused. "But you just said I was wrong not to be married."

"I didn't say you were wrong; I said you didn't fit into our little group. I've had some drinks, so don't quote me, but don't let them get a rope around your neck! Once you marry, your life is no longer your own. Find out who you are and what you want first. Don't get buried under tradition."

As they lifted the groom in the chair and carried him around the room, something snapped inside Zev like an electrical short in one of the machines he inspected at work.

Then the women danced, and his mother came over to the table and said, in Yiddish, "Zev, you could have your pick. It doesn't have to be Rivka." He shook his head. He could feel an imaginary noose tightening around his neck.

The blonde wandered by one last time, but Zev did nothing and went home drunk. He lay down in the bed he'd slept in all his life, and, as he had so many times before, he pleasured himself until he fell asleep fully dressed, his fly open.

In his dream, he was a child and stood by a railing watching Jews herded by German soldiers into the ovens, still alive, and heard them scream. Thick smoke, redolent with the smell of burning flesh, filled his nostrils, choking him. He tried but couldn't wake up.

Then the dream shifted, and night had fallen. In the moon-light, through an iron gate set in a twisted, barbed-wire fence, these same German soldiers pushed wheelbarrows full of cre-mated corpses over to an open pit and dumped their ghastly cargo into a smoldering heap.

He awoke bathed in sweat, gasping for breath.

This was a recurrent dream. He'd read books on Hitler's Fi-nal Solution and was no longer sure if what he'd read influenced what was in his dreams—or if, in fact, they were somehow vague, disturbing memories. In the books, the doomed Jews were sent into the rooms alive, gassed, and their bodies burned, but in his nightmares they were always stuffed directly into the cremato-rium while still alive. It made Zev shudder every time he remem-bered his dream. He feared that he'd been a prison guard in a previous life and was now reincarnated as a Jew. God certainly knew how to mete out punishment.

Maybe that was why Zev had never felt secure in his world. He couldn't understand how this had been allowed to happen, and could never get satisfactory answers to his questions through his studies. He therefore emotionally turned away from spirituality after his bar mitzvah. In fact, as far as he could tell, there was no God. The good thing about Judaism was that he wasn't required to believe; he merely had to follow the many rules laid down in the Torah and the Talmud. So he refused to say the many blessings drilled into his head since childhood by his father, but sometimes they slipped out. His inner rebellion was expressed as a boycott against the basic moment-by-moment experience Orthodox Judaism offered: the endless litany of prayer. Not only three times a day—Jewish law prescribed blessings be said with such frequency that there were ones for almost every waking moment. His father, Chaim, was very observant and a stickler for the details of every ritual and prayer. His entire relation-ship with him as a boy had been a relentless cross-examination and tutorial as to what prayer or blessing should be said in any given moment or situation. There was even a prayer for success-ful bathroom functions.

His mother never questioned or protected him from his father's endless barrage.

Bitterly, Zev remembered as a child having been given a baseball card of a famous player. His father had made him tear it up, because one of Judaism's many rules was that practitioners were not to worship any form of idol, and Chaim had felt the baseball card was a form of idolatry, albeit a secular one. Zev had kept the torn pieces in a drawer for many years. He didn't want any part of a punishing god.

In the morning, once dressed in his uniform of a black suit and white shirt, Zev knew he should now "lay *tefillin*"—don the leather straps used in the morning prayer—and recite the customary blessings, but he also knew he wouldn't. He'd once looked up the origin of the word "prayer." The Hebrew word was *tefillah*, and the root of the word, *pillel*, meant the act of self-examination. There was no point in that.

To disappear was what Zev wanted more than anything else at this moment—to be able to leave the house unseen and just escape. He began to pray, uttering, "*Baruch atah Adonai, Eloheinu . . . ,*" which are the opening words of many blessings. He caught himself, put on his cap and his *tzitzit* (the fringed garment that all of the men wore), and went downstairs.

☗

Chaim sat nursing a hangover, an untouched bagel and lox before him. The constriction from wrapping the heavy leather straps of the *tefillin* had left red welts on his left forearm and wrist. Zev smiled inwardly, as he knew his father was repenting for having gotten so drunk the evening before. Like Zev, Chaim wore a rumpled black suit, an open-necked, white button-down shirt, and black leather slippers. The tails of his *tzitzit* peeked out, and his *yarmulke* sat crooked on his head. He ignored his son's entrance. Nothing new here.

Ruth, Zev's mother, sat across from her husband as usual. They looked up at each other without speaking, but Zev could recite the unspoken conversation by heart: "When will it be our turn to dance at *your* wedding? All of your friends are married with kids . . ." Ruth, a once pretty woman with strikingly dark eyes and eyebrows, carried an extra twenty pounds underneath her faded, flowered housecoat with a zipper down the front. Her wavy black hair, streaked with gray, was kept back with a plain clip. She opened her mouth to comment, but Zev looked at her pleadingly. "Okay," she uttered, as if he had spoken, "do you want me to toast your bagel?"

Chaim nodded and said, "He's thirty-two years old—it should be his wife who's asking him that!" Hebrew was the language spoken in the house.

"Don't start, Chaim. We all drank too much last night."

Ruth put the bagel in the toaster oven and pushed the TOAST button loudly. Chaim rustled his newspaper in silent protest. Ruth poured him more coffee. He gave an obligatory little smile of thanks, but it was accompanied by a glare. She returned it, rolling her eyes in Zev's direction. How often had Zev watched this dance between them? They would make up in a few minutes, then turn their ire onto their only son. It was a rare circumstance to have only one child in this community, where the command to be "fruitful and multiply" was taken literally. Zev had required a Cesarean section. The operation was botched and resulted in his mother's inability to have more children. The silent blame lurked at the edge of any argument directed toward him.

At least it was Monday, so escape from this day was possible, if only to go to work. But the thing that gnawed at Zev was the growing realization that work was the *only* escape at his disposal. There was never anyone he wanted to call or see, nothing else he wanted to do. The strictly defined responsibilities of his religion dictated everything in his life outside work, though he never did more than he had to, mostly going through the motions.

As he sat at the breakfast table, what *Zayde* Hal had said the prior evening resonated in his thoughts. *God wants you to survive.* Did that mean just the body—or was the soul allowed to eat a metaphorical "pork chop" to maintain its life? One of the blessings that he didn't say had to do with thanking God for putting the soul into a body. How could you be grateful if you really weren't? His head hurt, and he rubbed his temples.

Chaim was a tall man with an unkempt gray beard. Zev looked so much like him that there could be no mistake of parentage. Chaim had the piercing eyes of a prophet, and the community revered him as a scholar and teacher. Zev knew that he was a great disappointment. His father had wanted him to become a rabbi, and it was only after Zev had nearly died of measles that he backed down and allowed Zev to follow the path of math and science, the boy's true passion. Zev realized that he could not remember a time when he and his father had talked outside the realm of study or discussed day-to-day things. Not one! Maybe it was for the best, because Chaim lacked any sense of humor unless he was the one making the joke.

Zev sat down at the table. Could they tell he hadn't prayed? Ruth looked at him as she poured him coffee.

"So, did you have fun?"

"Yes."

"Why didn't you dance?"

If he wanted the argument to start, all he had to do was answer her, because any answer would light up the fireworks.

"Good coffee," he said, swallowing the whole hot cup at once. She smiled.

"Chaim, why don't you ever tell me my coffee is good?"

Chaim picked up his cup and exaggerated drinking, smacking his lips, and rolling his eyes—"*Oy*, Ruthie, your coffee is like nectar!"—but his smile was genuine.

Ruth laughed, shedding twenty years. "Your father—he's always such a comedian!" For a moment, Zev basked in the brief wave of happiness his parents shared, but he knew the next Psalm in the *siddur* would be the two of them ganging up on him.

Zev stood up abruptly. "Time to go," he said.

Chaim frowned without looking at him. "What about tonight? Will I see you in *shul*?"

"I may have to work late."

His mother cleared his plate, her lips pursed disapprovingly. "The Torah is more important than any job." It was okay if his father criticized him, but he could predict the response when his mother nagged.

Chaim immediately derailed her. "Look at our boy, Ruthie. What a provider he'll make! How hardworking is our son! Did he tell you he's up for a promotion?"

Ruth looked surprised. Zev stepped back as she swooped in for a hug. He hated to admit it, but any physical contact with his mother made his skin crawl. She enveloped him in warm vanilla-scented plumpness. He gently released himself and traded his *yarmulke* for the peaked cap he wore in the outside world.

"I didn't want to get your hopes up, Mom. I didn't want to tell you until it was done."

Ruth nodded and began to clear the breakfast things.

☼

Zev drove the blue Toyota the forty-five minutes to work. The United States Patent Office was located in Alexandria, Virginia. It was a picturesque summer day, and Zev was so moved by the beauty that a blessing formed in his mind unbidden, but he dismissed it and instead tuned the car radio to a classic rock station—a guilty pleasure. The heavy metal band Metallica belted out "The Unforgiven," a cut from their *Black Album*.

New blood joins this earth
And, quickly, he's subdued
Through constant pained disgrace
The young boy learns their rules
With time the child draws in
This whipping boy done wrong
Deprived of all his thoughts
The young man struggles on and on, he's known
A vow unto his own
That never from this day
His will they'll take away

Zev sang along, his good humor restored.

When he had first gotten his job, the imposing brick façade of the Patent Office building, with its central tower and curved walls, had impressed him. How proud he had been in earlier days to work for this office, the place that validated and approved great inventions, which when they reached fruition would benefit all humankind. But these days, the process had become corrupted by greed. Zev had acquaintances but not many friends because he had been taught to keep his distance from the *goyim*.

Still, Zev was hardworking, dependable, and kind. He was considered a brilliant troubleshooter, even a reluctant genius, and was always ready to help a colleague with a tricky problem. There was one guy—Mitch Wallis—a hot-blooded, rusty-haired Southerner with a heavy accent, who, at the very least, Zev had an understanding with, though their interaction was largely limited to going on coffee breaks together from time to time. Mitch was always urging Zev to come out to the airport bars with him and pick up women. He would recount his amorous adventures with stewardesses and lonely, traveling businesswomen. Zev longed to take him up on his offer but never dared to. There was one bar at Dulles that Mitch said was especially good: Pig and Whistle. Imagine him going somewhere with "pig" in the name. He realized that it was past nine A.M. and stepped on the gas.

Zev parked the car, reached over, and fished his ID lanyard out of the glove compartment. He hurried to the employee entrance in the rear of the building, still accessible beneath a maze of scaffolding and steel, part of a massive new wing that was being built. He was squinting through the bright sunlight toward the cool, dark tunnel that led to the entrance when he suddenly heard a man yell, followed immediately by a deafening *snap*, like the cracking of a whip. A massive steel I-beam whooshed by Zev's face, missing him by an angstrom unit—it was so close that it clipped the edge of his hat and sent it flying. The beam crashed into the pavement with a thunderous bang that hurt his ears as shards of shattered concrete flew in every direction, followed by a dense cloud of dust. Zev felt the rush of cold air created by the falling steel flatten his clothing against his body. The ground shuddered at the impact, and tears rushed into Zev's eyes. *This is what 9/11 must have been like*, he thought in an instant that seemed like an hour. *Baruch atah Adonai*, he silently prayed. *Thank You for sparing my life.*

He instinctively clapped his hands to his ears and fell back, reeling. Then he folded down into a squat, collapsed to his knees, felt the blood rush in his bowels, and out of him came a sound—something between the scream of an infant and the howl of one of the victims in his nightmares. He smelled his own sweat, hoped it wasn't urine, and realized he was dripping wet and suddenly cold. *Where is my hat?* Some workers rushed over to see if he was okay, but in his panic Zev jumped to his feet and bolted before the workers could get to him. He saw his cap nearby, scooped it up, and slapped it on his head just before he ran.

Zev would later recall something bizarre about the incident, as if the falling beam wasn't peculiar enough. As he raced away from the building he was sure was collapsing like the World Trade Center, he had seen a TV camera crew that appeared to be filming the whole thing! He would later remember thinking, *Boy, these gonifs don't miss anything anymore!*

Zev sprinted for two blocks before he stopped, gasping for breath, and placed his hands on his knees to steady himself. After a few moments, he righted and walked the side streets to collect his wits. At one point he thought he saw a woman with a mike in her hand—*the TV camera crew again?* But he was in no mood to talk to anyone, so he lost her by slipping down an alley and circling back to his car in the Patent Office parking lot.

The building was still standing, Zev noted. He drew a deep breath as he surveyed the scene and police cars surrounded the site. Still shaking, Zev climbed into his car and prayed for strength. *Maybe I should find a shul.* He headed for home, but halfway there he began to shake so much that he feared getting into an accident, so he pulled into a rest-stop parking lot, turned off the engine, and fell asleep.

CHAPTER 3

Not Your Basic Yoga Class

HE KY YOGA STUDIO was housed in a well-kept brownstone on 59th Street and First Avenue. The second-floor space had floor-to-ceiling windows, and from her yoga mat, Sarah could see the Roosevelt Island Tramway, where they had filmed the climax of the movie *Nighthawks*.

Sarah changed in the dressing area, a small white room plastered floor to ceiling with posters of the nine gurus upon whom Kundalini yoga practitioners lavish their attention. Several of the women chatted while they dressed, and the exchange of banal life details depressed Sarah further. It wasn't that she was particularly suicidal, just that she saw no reason to soldier on. And yet, here she was. She envied the women who saw value in the minutiae of existence. Maybe some of it would rub off. The dress code was white, so she put on a white camisole top and knee-length leggings; her hair was pulled back in a ponytail. She could not bring herself to cover her head—too much like Judaism.

The teacher, Sat Siri Kaur, was a distinguished Australian Sikh in his fifties. He had a waist-length gray beard and wore a white turban and white robes. Sat Siri motioned the students to sit cross-legged on the purple mats, and he moved his hands into prayer pose. Sarah sat in the back row, one of the few not dressed in the same flowing white clothes and turbans. The invocation *"Ong namo, Guru Dev namo"* ("I call upon my true self, I bow to the teacher within") was sung three times, followed by three minutes of the breath of fire. The practice of Kundalini yoga involved doing five things at once: measured breathing, movement, hand positions, eye positions, and the recitation of sacred prayers or mantras.

The goal in Kundalini yoga is "to remember who you are," Sat Siri said, and Sarah pondered the implication that memory was somehow a metaphor for reconnecting with the self. Did memory, and indeed the self, survive the life and death of the physical body? Was the body merely a temporary dwelling for some fluid, timeless consciousness? Was *that* the self? And why did this cultish practice appeal to her, even though she resented the relentless and obsequious entreaties to the various gurus?

Sat Siri continued, "Today we are going to do a set to connect with our true selves, the great teacher within, the part that connects to God." Sarah felt herself smile a little and relax. Maybe it was the optimism that she enjoyed. They were all so sure that God was right there and that they were connected to Him. If she could connect to the God within—well, they were going to have a talk. Meanwhile, she committed herself to the class.

Sat Siri asked, "Where is the self? By that I mean, where is it located in your body? If you can find the self, you can have a glimpse of God, as the self is part of Him. Most people assume it's an idea, a concept—but before we begin, I will show you where it lives in the temple of your body. But always remember: If you are in a body, you are attracting trouble. Stand up and assume the tree pose!" Sarah and the other students arose.

Suddenly she felt exposed, powerless. The soul that was trapped in her corporeal form squirmed like a fish on a hook. She tried to focus on attaining the pose.

Sat Siri directed them to bend one leg and place it above the knee of the standing leg, and then to balance there, hands together. Sarah easily conquered the exercise, though she wobbled a bit.

"Where is the self?" he asked again. No one knew. Sarah wished he would get to it. He continued, "I know all of you think the goal of this *asana* is to be still. In fact, I see that each of you is swaying to various degrees in order to hold the posture. The self can be experienced in that attempt to regain balance—the 'self' is in fact a verb, not a noun."

Sat Siri then gestured for them to drop the pose and sit down. He took them through a series of simple poses and instructed them in chanting, breathing, alignment, and eye and hand movements. He spoke as he demonstrated. "Kundalini yoga often requires the student to hold eyes and hands in precise positions, to chant and move the body all at the same time. Because there is so much going on, the physical part of our yoga is often very simple. However, the many repetitions of a seemingly innocuous movement—such as almost clapping hands but stopping just short of actual contact, followed by a series of equally simple movements—become an aerobic challenge because of the sheer number of repetitions, often a hundred and eight. Each group of exercises is called a *kriya*, which also means an emotional break with reality, the intention of this performance. Each *kriya* addresses a specific emotional issue and offers a cure. These exercises are part of a secret oral tradition that is over five thousand years old and was brought to America by our beloved Yogi Bhajan."

Sarah followed along. Her arms were stinging from the almost-clap repeated one hundred and eight times; her legs were tired from one hundred and eight frog squats; her guts hurt from one hundred and eight sit-ups done with raised legs. As she lay exhausted on her mat, the teacher spoke again. "The purpose of movement in all yoga is to relax the body and mind so meditation can occur. Please lie down in corpse pose, or *shavasana*, and breathe normally. Mentally repeat the mantra, *Sat Nam*, which in English means roughly 'true name.' "

As she lay on her mat, arms and legs outstretched, repeating the mantra, she was startled to hear a voice say, "It is safe for you to remember your true name—your true name is Judith."

Sarah opened her eyes to see who was speaking, but there was no one beside her. She heard the voice again. "Sarah, it's safe for you to know who you were." Sarah was not sure what had just happened, but she'd heard the voice so clearly that it had to be taken seriously.

As much as she hated God, she said aloud, "Thank you." She had asked for a sign and received one. Reincarnation was one of those optimistic ideas that made Kundalini yoga so appealing to her. She didn't believe in it for a second, because if you couldn't remember something, how could you know if you had actually experienced it?

She'd already forgotten the yoga set she had done, and she waited impatiently until the class was instructed to sit up and sing the closing invocation three times. *"Sat Nam. Sat Nam. Sat Nam."*

CHAPTER 4

THE GENERAL AND THE COOK

AT HOME, SARAH GOOGLED the name Judith, half-intrigued, half-annoyed. She had been taught that when you die, you cease to exist. That was God's dubious promise to the Jews. She knew He was selling them more fucking lies. Sarah had technically "died" after a head-on car accident as a teenager, and while experiencing the passing of her body, she had remained conscious. Knowing that there was some kind of eternal life was not comforting—on the contrary, the idea that you kept participating in this chaotic, pointless hash was part of what made things unbearable. In how many more bad romances would she be trapped? How many more pointless jobs would she have to do?

Yet she hated to sleep. Slumber should have been her salvation. *I make no sense to myself.* That was the biggest truth of all. When she honestly looked at even the happiest moments in her marriage, she could see the edges of the experience as if she were watching a film. She was always aware that she was the audience and not the star. That this hell went on for eternity—and pompous fools insisted *this* was God's plan? If so, then why in the same breath did these same pontificators piously claim that no one could know God's plan? *Fools!* They didn't listen to themselves. They didn't want to know His plan, which was the real truth. *If God made us, or some of us, in His image, then what was His plan for Himself?* That was a better question. She'd once made the mistake of asking Carlos. He laughed and said, "We're here to have sex, eat, and fart. Our job is to produce methane." He felt no moral obligation to do anything further.

She poured a glass of wine and tried to ignore what had happened in the yoga class as she experimented with a new recipe for *challah* with rosemary. The dough had to rise for a couple of hours, so she settled down to do some serious Googling.

Still, the idea that she had held some mythic importance in some previous moment of consciousness was actually exciting. The feeling made her afraid—*hope kills*, she reminded herself sternly. She knew that Jews shouldn't believe in reincarnation, but if God didn't want her to, why had He shown her a different truth?

Sarah typed in "Judith." She took a gulp of wine and clicked ENTER.

What came up on her computer screen were a series of Web sites all referring to a biblical Jewish heroine who had saved her village from certain death.

No surprise that the Book of Judith was part of the Apocrypha, a group of writings mysteriously not included in the Hebrew Bible. *Fuckers.* Even the Catholics recognized the story. According to that fabulously accurate resource—the Web—the Judith story had been part of the Hanukkah celebration throughout the Middle Ages. She couldn't find out when it had been discredited, and truly, in all of the Hebrew School Sarah had attended, Judith had never been discussed. It would figure, Sarah thought, that in a past life she would have been an ignored heroine. When she examined the scholarly Jewish sites, they seemed busy trying to discredit the story as a work of fiction, unlike that utterly believable Hanukkah tale about the brave Maccabee tribe that first led a revolt in their mountain town, then consecrated the defiled temple in Jerusalem. (And as an aside, no one seemed to mind that a priest had killed one of his own congregants and then many Assyrian soldiers!) This bunch of bozos hadn't even thought to bring enough oil for the eight-day consecration, then covered up their poor planning as a miracle when the lamp burned for the entire period despite their incompetence.

Her hatred of God increased tenfold. *You are definitely male, and I curse You for all Your fucking lies! You just wanted a servant class so You made women and gave them breasts, but we women got uppity and forced You to backpedal. My grandfather was right to thank You for not making him a woman!* Sarah was so angry she threw her wineglass across the room.

But the story was interesting nonetheless, and Judith seemed to be one of the few women in the Bible who was a victor and not a victim. Now that was refreshing and intriguing in and of itself.

In the same period of history as the Hanukkah story, King Nebuchadnezzar, who was also responsible for the situation in Jerusalem that the Maccabees had to rectify, sent his general, Holofernes, to capture all of Judea. Holofernes laid siege to the city of Bethulia and cut off all of the water, so the townspeople were near death from thirst. Judith lived in Bethulia and was described thusly:

Judith . . . was the daughter of Merari, the son of Ox, the son of Joseph, the son of Ozel, the son of Elcia, the son of Ananias, the son of Gedeon, the son of Raphaim, the son of Acitho, the son of Eliu, the son of Eliab, the son of Nathanael, the son of Samael, the son of Salasadal, the son of Israel. And Manasses was Judith's husband, of her tribe and kindred, who died in the barley harvest.

For as he stood overseeing them that bound sheaves in the field, the heat came upon his head, and he fell on his bed, and died in the city of Bethulia, and they buried him with his fathers in the field between Dothaim and Balamo. So Judith was a widow in her house three years and four months. And she made her a tent upon the top of her house, and put sackcloth upon her loins and wore her widow's apparel. And she fasted all the days of her widowhood, save the eves of the sabbaths, and the sabbaths, and the eves of the new moons, and the new moons and the feasts and solemn days of the house of Israel.

She was also of a goodly countenance, and very beautiful to behold, and her husband Manasses had left her gold, and silver, and menservants and maidservants, and cattle, and lands. And she remained upon them.

Sarah thought that Judith did not handle her widowhood very well and could have used some of her wealth to ease the pain.

When the townspeople had run out of water, they had wanted to surrender. Uzziah, the leader, convinced the angry villagers to give God five more days to save them, and the followers agreed. When Judith, the beautiful and devout widow of a wealthy landowner, heard the news, she was offended that God was being given a time limit and that surrender would not save them from certain death, since angering God might result in the same or a worse fate. She called Uzziah and the elders to her and admonished them for giving God a time limit as if He were human. Instead, she offered a daring plan. Since she was respected, and since "there was none that gave her ill word because she feared God greatly"—and of course, since she was a wealthy widow with a pedigree—they agreed to let her go to face the fearsome Holofernes, accompanied by her maid.

Sarah liked this passage, where Judith spoke to the elders:

Listen to me, rulers of the people of Bethulia! What you have said to the people today is not right, you have even sworn and pronounced this oath between God and you, promising to surrender the city to our enemies unless the Lord turns and helps us within so many days. Who are you that have put God to the test this day, and are setting yourselves up in the place of God among the sons of men?

You are putting the Lord Almighty to the test—but you will never know anything!

You cannot plumb the depths of the human heart, nor find out what a man is thinking; how do you expect to search out God, who made all these things, and find out His mind or comprehend His thoughts? No, my brethren, do not provoke the Lord, our God, to anger.

For if He does not choose to help us within these five days, He has power to protect us within any time He pleases, or even to destroy us in the presence of our enemies.

Do not try to bind the purposes of the Lord, our God, for God is not like man, to be threatened, nor like a human being, to be won over by pleading.

Therefore, while we wait for His deliverance, let us call upon Him to help us, and He will hear our voice, if it pleases Him.

For never in our generation, nor in these present days, has there been any tribe or family or people or city of ours which worshiped gods made with hands, as was done in days gone by—and that was why our fathers were handed over to the sword, and to be plundered, and so they suffered a great catastrophe before our enemies. But we know no other God but Him, and therefore we hope that He will not disdain us or any of our nations.

For if we are captured, all Judea will be captured, and our sanctuary will be plundered, and He will exact of us the penalty for its desecration. And the slaughter of our brethren and the captivity of the land and the desolation of our inheritance—all this He will bring upon our heads among the Gentiles, wherever we serve as slaves, and we shall be an offense and a reproach in the eyes of those who acquire us. For our slavery will not bring us into favor, but the Lord, our God, will turn it to dishonor.

Now therefore, brethren, let us set an example to our brethren, for their lives depend upon us, and the sanctuary and the temple and the altar rest upon us. In spite of everything, let us give thanks to the Lord, our God, who is putting us to the test as He did our forefathers. Remember what He did with Abraham, and how He tested Isaac, and what happened to Jacob in Mesopotamia in Syria, while he was keeping the sheep of Laban, his mother's brother. For He has not tried us with fire, as He did them, to search their hearts, nor has He taken revenge upon us. But the Lord scourges those who draw near to Him in order to admonish them.

Amazing—one of the few times a woman commanded authority!

Then Uzziah said to her, "All that you have said has been spoken out of a true heart, and there is no one who can deny your words. Today is not the first time your wisdom has been shown, but from the beginning of your life, all the people have recognized your understanding, for your heart's disposition is right. But the people were very thirsty, and they compelled us to do for them what we have promised, and made us take an oath which we cannot break. So pray for us, since you are a devout woman, and the Lord will send us rain to fill our cisterns, and we will no longer be faint."

Now came the part Sarah liked the best.

Judith said to them, "Listen to me. I am about to do a thing which will go down through all generations of our descendants. Stand at the city gate tonight, and I will go out with my maid, and within the days after which you have promised to surrender the city to our enemies, the Lord will deliver Israel by my hand. Only, do not try to find out what I plan, for I will not tell you until I have finished what I am about to do."

Uzziah and the rulers said to her, "Go in peace, and may the Lord God go before you to take revenge upon our enemies."

So that night Judith got herself dressed in her best clothes. She passed through the gate with her maid and walked across the valley to the encampment of Holofernes. There, she explained to the guards that she wanted to provide the general with information about the best means of entering Bethulia.

When she was admitted to his presence, Judith explained that the siege had caused the Jews to turn away from their religion, and so they therefore merited destruction. She maintained that God Himself had sent her on this errand. She would show them the best way to make the conquest without a single Assyrian soldier being harmed. The process would take five days. All of this pleased General Holofernes very much, as did Judith's beauty. Out of his lust, Judith and Holofernes came to an agreement: he would not harm her, and she would be allowed to leave the camp at night for prayer. This, Judith claimed, would allow her to learn from God exactly when the city should be attacked. For three days, Judith stayed in the camp, eating only the food her maid prepared and carried with her in a cloth sack. Each night she was allowed to leave and make her prayers to God, unattended by Assyrian guards.

On the fourth night, sure of success, Holofernes held a banquet in order to seduce Judith. She arrived dressed in her finest clothes and bearing gifts. Judith was famous for her cheesemaking and had brought plenty for the general, as well as her own extra strong wine. She fed him chunks of cheese, and he washed them down with her wine, convinced that he was about to successfully seduce her. Judith got Holofernes drunker than he had ever been, and he ordered everyone to leave so they could be alone. He moved to kiss her, and promptly passed out. Now that she was alone with the sleeping general, Judith prayed for strength and, using his own sword, cut off the leader's head in two strokes.

Sarah admired her power—Judith had definitely cooked more than cheese. How else would she have known where to place the sword so that it would cut between the bones?

With the help of her faithful maid, Judith put Holofernes' head in the bag she had used to carry her special food, and the two women left the camp upon what seemed to be their nightly errand of prayer but didn't stop until they reached home. At the gate of Bethulia, she called for entry, showed her trophy, and told the men to mount an attack on the Assyrian camp the next morning.

Meanwhile, the Assyrians ran to Holofernes' tent to rouse him and saw what had happened. Spooked—terrified—the Assyrians abandoned the camp, and without bloodshed, the Israelites took possession. There was great wealth left behind, and supposedly all the best things of Holofernes were given to Judith, who then passed them to her late husband's heirs.

Sarah wondered if Judith had ever remarried. She was

pleased that Judith's culinary skill had provided the method of
tranquilizing the enemy, but beyond that connection she saw no
resemblance or purpose for her having been told this.

There were no accidents, of that Sarah was sure—only mys-
teries surrounding the events. But why did the inner voice tell
her she was the reincarnation of a heroine? What did it mean, if
anything? Aside from being Jewish, from cooking, and from not
handling . . . widowhood—for truly she admitted that's how she
saw the split with Michael—well, Judith and she had nothing in
common.

Maybe Judith should have taken off the sackcloth and ashes.
That should have been so obvious. Had it really been necessary
for this elaborate magic trick to shed light on the situation? For
all His protests, God did seem fond of the Jews: the eight-day
candle of Hanukkah, the plagues on their enemies, the parting of the Red Sea for Moses, the Burning Bush. Of course, the
Holocaust was still an anomaly, but maybe it had, ironically,
reunited the Jews. It seemed to Sarah that, on balance, the inner voice had connected her to a has-been biblical heroine who
had largely been dismissed in traditional literature and history,
though the purpose of this new information remained unclear.

The timer went off. She checked the dough, and it had risen
perfectly. She put it on a large cutting board and divided it into
four equal parts. She coated her hands with flour and rolled the
portions into long, round logs, braiding them together into a
single loaf. She covered the bread and set the timer for another
hour.

So, if her true name was Judith, was she a current incar-
nation of whatever that eternal essential self or soul was? She
noted that the Judith story was relegated to the books of the
Apocrypha, not the Bible. The Apocrypha was a selection of
books that were deleted from the Bible in 1885. They were removed for several reasons including the fact that they did not
toe the party line, but also to reduce the cost of printing the King
James Bible.

Fine, I am reincarnated from an actual person in a heroic

story denigrated to a fairytale, whereas God's keeping a candle burning with no oil for eight days is unquestionably the gospel truth!

She half-smiled. Sarah also reflected on the fact that Judith had made a statement upon her return to the Israelites that she did not have to sleep with Holofernes, which would have been considered evil back then despite the victorious outcome. It would be deemed evil now, despite modern "enlightenment." The double standard did seem to be firmly entrenched throughout history.

She'd read that the Hindu gods invented humans because they were bored. *If we are entertainment for them,* she thought, *then Judith's story is rich and unusual.* This paradigm seemed more honest to Sarah than the pablum of Western religion that always alleged some kind of character-building lessons humans were supposed to learn. To Sarah, this kind of rationale was tantamount to a scientist who conducted heinous lab experiments and told the rats he was torturing that it was for their own good. *Maybe God did have a plan that involved love and paradise and world peace, but if He made us in His image, shouldn't He have put Himself through His own gauntlet first? But then, shouldn't world leaders have to win wars by dueling each other before sending thousands to their deaths? If we were made in God's image, then our human history was a mirror of His— hardly a good résumé for the man in charge! If He had been forced to give birth, things would have been different.*

History—and she meant *His story*—was a tragic tale in which virtually all worldly events were and continued to be caused by insatiable greed. Was God greedy? How could humans be if He wasn't?

When she'd gone to see the film *The Matrix*, she found a perfect allegory for her worldview, and had smirked in agreement during a scene in which the evil robot Agent Smith is torturing the virtuous, self-sacrificing human Morpheus, who would rather die than reveal the secret that would, if released, destroy the human race. Agent Smith gives a monologue that defined

Sarah's feelings:

Every mammal on this planet instinctively develops a natural equilibrium with the surrounding environment, but you humans do not. You move to an area, and you multiply and multiply until every natural resource is consumed, and the only way you can survive is to spread to another area. There is another organism on this planet that follows the same pattern. Do you know what it is? A virus. Human beings are a disease, a cancer of this planet. You're a plague . . .

Sarah had no children and felt pity for those who did. *Breeders*—that's what Carlos called mothers. It was all so complicated, but in the end, she thought, *Why would you want a virus to spread?* The question that confused and troubled her was: *What is the damn point of this endless narrative?* Sarah's mother had been a true existentialist—able to understand the meaninglessness of living yet still able to have a hopeful sense that somehow there was value in it, even if it was not the salvation offered to us by so many religious leaders. Sarah had not gotten the hang of that. In Sarah's version of the Lord's Prayer, the lyrics went like this: "Forgive us our trespasses, and we will forgive Yours—and oh, yes, those who trespass against us too." Maybe God and the Devil were one, and our pathetic human attempts to convince ourselves that hell was indeed heaven endlessly amused them.

Where does this overwhelming tsunami of bitterness come from? Sarah wondered. *Here I am, a human being who has had mystical experiences that included surviving death. Why fight so hard for this bitter enlightenment that keeps me bobbing on the sea of the collective unconscious?*

The one thing she felt sure of on a gut level was that faith was not the cure for despair, as the religious-marketing geniuses had suggested. The real problem was that His existence in no way mitigated her existential despair. None of the known solutions were helping, including immersing herself in the work of cooking. And this state of mind had existed long before her wedding and never really gone away. Her joke about her marriage was that it had worked for so long because Michael had "pre-rejected her," just as her father had done, so she knew the parameters.

This was another of the reasons she hated God. You were judged if you couldn't get it right, and no one could. Having to cook this kosher Thanksgiving dinner reminded her of how the many kosher laws were intended in part to provide endless opportunities for Jews to follow God's rules. The exception was that you could eat *treif*, or unclean food, if your physical survival depended on it. *Phooey! So when do you feast?* There was no moment when the possibility of not doing wrong existed, just as there was no moment when you were not in a relationship with a punitive male force. It was like being a child again, and certainly her earthly father had been critical and judgmental—was that redundant?

She looked around her cozy kitchen—the nonkosher one—with its restaurant-style stove and gray, granite countertops. The floor consisted of tiny black and white tiles. The cabinets were made of light shellacked pine. It felt like a French country kitchen with its yellow and gray dishtowels and curtains that she had bought on a visit to Provence. She worked at a square wooden table, where she usually ate her dinner, alone, and that she also used as a loading area when she was catering. She preferred to prepare food at home whenever possible.

She always said a Jewish prayer before she cooked, admitting to herself that she was quite sure God would strike her dead if she didn't. As much as He pissed her off, she did not doubt His ability to affect the physical world. She said the only one she remembered, one that sounded like: *"Baruch atah Adonai, Eloheinu, melech ha'olam, borei p'ri hagafen."* It was one of the blessings said over the wine at the Friday night *Shabbos* meal. She wished she remembered more but had lost her ability to read or speak Hebrew when her mother attempted suicide by trying to jump out of a twenty-third-floor window during the reception of Sarah's bat mitzvah. Her father was having an affair with a secretary, and her mother had been despondent and threatening to kill herself for several weeks. The preparations for her party had been slapdash—no photographer was hired, so, mercifully, there were no photos of the event. But, in spite of everything, her memories were happy—the food had been great because Sylvie had cooked it.

The timer sounded again. Sarah glazed the bread with egg, put the loaf into a four-hundred-degree oven, and set the timer for thirty minutes. She was exhausted and dozed off in her chair.

When the timer went off once again, she awoke just long enough to take the bread out, set it on the counter, and turn off the oven. *Shit!* She'd forgotten the rosemary.

CHAPTER 5

A Narrow Escape

ZEV AWOKE TO THE buttery sun streaming through the windshield, a terrible cold stiffness radiating from his bones. He got out of the car and stretched. His mind led him to the words of the Afternoon Prayer, but instead the lyrics of the Metallica song came back in so loudly that he couldn't remember the blessings. Shaken, Zev got back behind the wheel and drove straight home, the radio off. He decided to skip *shul* and focus on getting warm.

The Bronfmans lived in a modest Cape Cod-style house with a nice lawn and a picket fence on a street of similar houses. From the driveway he could see the *shul*, the tallest building in the neighborhood and the center of the religious community, of which he was supposed to be a part. Chaim was away teaching at the *shul*, and Ruth was shopping. *Good.* He needed a moment's peace.

In his room, Zev stripped off his clothes and got into the shower. He soaped his long, muscular white body. His chest was thickly planted with hair, and his gut was punctuated with the six-pack abs he'd gotten by doing one hundred push-ups and one hundred sit-ups the way *Zayde* Hal had taught him when he was bar mitzvahed. "It's all downhill from here, *boychick*," he had said. "Remember, you are going to die. The question is: How do you want to die? No need to be sick. Stay fit. Don't get fat like your father."

Zev had been shocked to hear Hal talk about his own son that way. Hal had pulled up his shirt to show off his taut gut. He smacked himself lightly with his hand and said, "This is a symbol for your mind. Your father is soft, and his mind is so busy being on God he has become simple. Don't be like him, you hear? Keep your mind sound and your body hard." His grandfather then got down on the floor and showed him the right way.

Zev had been too hungover to do exercises in the morning, so he did them now, thinking he should go talk to Hal; but he suddenly felt so tired that, although daylight streamed in through the curtains, he pulled on pajama bottoms, got into bed, and slept. He dreamed again of the ovens. This time giant beams fell, landing on the flames and putting them out.

When he awoke, Ruth and Chaim were standing over him, and Dr. Heimowitz held his wrist, taking a pulse. It was dark outside. "Oh, finally, he's awake," Ruth exclaimed. "We were so worried!"

Chaim nodded. "You gave us a scare, my son."

"Oh, hey, Zev—how are you feeling?" Dr. Heimowitz was a portly man with the same kind of unkempt beard and hair that all the men in this community sported—except for Zev and a few of the other younger men. Stains from his dinner besmirched his white shirt. He let go of Zev's wrist and put his stethoscope against Zev's chest. He listened, nodded, and stood up, satisfied. "So?"

"Okay," replied Zev.

"Your mother tells me they couldn't wake you. They called me."

"I don't understand. I took a nap, that's all. What time is it?"

Dr. Heimowitz stroked his beard, frowning. "You don't remember?"

Zev shook his head.

"*Did* something happen to you?" he asked, putting emphasis

on the first word.

Zev decided not to reveal what had happened. "I've just been working too hard."

He tried to get up, but Dr. Heimowitz put a firm hand on Zev's shoulder and gently pushed him back down in the bed. "It's Wednesday, Zev. You've been asleep for almost thirty-six hours. That's why your parents called me. We saw it on the news. It's a miracle."

Zev shrugged. "I was lucky. No big deal. Enough already. I gotta sleep, but now I can't miss any more work." He felt so tired. "Where's *Zayde*?"

"He's been here, off and on," Ruth said. "We'll call him after the doctor leaves."

Zev lay back, too tired to argue.

"He's suffering from exhaustion," the doctor pronounced. "He needs rest. Let him stay home the rest of the week. The rabbi will want to see him when he's stronger."

"I want to talk to *Zayde*," Zev said, and fell asleep.

He awoke the next morning hearing his mother calling his office, telling his boss that he was sick again—incredibly, it was Thursday already. *He could have been killed!* The thought made him oddly numb. He got out of bed and looked around the tiny room in which he had lived since childhood. It was a boy's room painted light blue, with a pine bedroom set—twin beds, dresser, desk, and nightstand. Several plaques and trophies attested to his academic achievements, but the room did not have a personal feel. Would he die in here a bitter old man? He got down on the floor and managed only a few push-ups and sit-ups before he lay back in bed, exhausted.

It was almost nine A.M.—he'd be late, but he had to get dressed and go. Then he remembered that his mother had already called him in sick. He was compelled to get out of bed, out of his parents' house, but work was the only place he could think of to go. Chaim was already at *shul*, but he'd have to get past Ruth.

"Where do you think you're going?"

"Work."

"But you're exhausted. Dr. Heimowitz said—"

"If I want that promotion, I should go. I'll take it easy."

"Wait, I'll get your thermos and lunch. I made extra for Dad."

She quickly poured the leftover coffee into the thermos, wrapped a sandwich in tinfoil, and put everything in his lunch cooler. She came for a hug, but he backed away. She looked hurt. "Mom, I could have a bug or something. I don't want to make you sick."

A minute later, Zev jumped into his car and drove off. *My mother is still making my lunch*, he thought. *I must call Zayde.*

As he walked to his office, coworkers and colleagues, some of whom had hardly ever spoken to him before, greeted him heartily. At first he was perplexed—surprised to observe, so he thought, that he was apparently more well liked than he had given himself credit for, at least on the surface. Then he remembered the TV crew. *They know*, he suddenly realized.

Zev's job was to review patent applications, which included rigorous testing of the obligatory prototypes submitted for approval. His office was a small one but had the luxury of a window. Still, it looked more like a storage room. Mechanical devices of every description filled the shelves and the lone bookcase. There were boxes of applications stacked on the floor. There was a small *mezuzah* inside the door, and, as was his custom, Zev kissed his finger and touched it as he entered.

He sat down in his worn leatherette desk chair and looked out the window at the parking lot, where he had nearly been killed. He checked his phone messages. There was one asking him to come to his boss's office and a trio of them from HR as well. He was cold in the air-conditioned space, so chilled he stamped his feet to get the numbness out and rubbed his hands as if he were in a blizzard. He kept a sweater in his bottom drawer. He retrieved it and put it on. Mitch stuck his head in. "How's the miracle man?"

"What are you talking about?" feigned Zev, a little annoyed.

"Why, it was all over the local news," Mitch drawled. "All

over!"

"I almost got killed."

"Yep. You know what I'm going to say, right? Come out drinking with me. Every woman will be at your feet when she finds out you're *that* guy."

Zev smiled wanly. "When I feel a bit stronger." He tried to keep his teeth from chattering.

"Yeah, I get it. FYI, you should sue them. You'll be able to retire. Rest up and we'll go next week." He waved and disappeared from the doorway.

Zev went to meet with his boss. He decided he would clean his office once and for all, later.

♔

Fred Kalop was a tall ex-Marine in his early sixties with a steel-gray brush cut, bright-blue eyes, and a perpetual tan. Training in engineering had been his sole reward for three brutal tours of duty in Vietnam. Fred was proud of his military service but bitter that he'd never gone on to get a law degree, because becoming an attorney would have guaranteed him a much higher place—and a fatter salary—in the U.S. Patent Office.

Fred's office was larger than Zev's, with two windows. There were family pictures on the wall. He was a neat freak and the office was tidy, the shiny desktop being empty except for his computer. The door was open, and before Zev could knock, Fred motioned him in and to a chair. Zev parked himself, trying not to shake with cold.

"You all right?"

Zev nodded, an unspoken apology in his eyes.

"I want you to see this." Fred turned his computer screen toward Zev and hit a button. A grainy security tape of the I-beam falling replayed itself. Fred stopped the image with the beam in mid-fall, where it seemed to balance on Zev's nose, his cap a blur above his head.

"You are one lucky son of a gun! Of course, if you'd been to work on time . . ."

Zev nodded, queasy but surprised by this degree of joviality from a boss who was known for his anti-Semitic attitude. Zev waited for the punch line. Just *what* was the point of this meeting?

Fred leaned forward and said, "You gonna live?"

Zev was taken completely by surprise. "I wasn't hurt," he said. "A little shaken up, I guess."

"Exactly. You know it wasn't our fault."

"No one said it was."

"If you sue, it won't be us. You'll have to sue the contractor."

So that was it. That's what they feared.

"I wasn't hurt. I'm not going to sue anybody."

Fred leaned back with a sigh of relief. "Now, that's mighty sensible of you!"

Zev stood up. "Is there anything else? HR called three times."

"No, don't worry. I'll take care of that." Fred also stood up. "I'd like you to take two weeks of paid sick leave. You've had a nasty shock." He offered his hand, and Zev took it.

Zev left the office lightheaded. He reached for his cell phone to call his folks—but he didn't. He had cheated death, and so he was going to try to do what he wanted for a change. Instead of driving home, he stopped at an ATM and took out a thousand dollars. He had never done this before. Mostly his salary went to help pay his parents' household expenses, but he also had a good chunk of money in savings owing to frugality—and the fact that there wasn't much for him to spend it on.

Zev drove to the nearest mall. He bought himself a pair of tight black jeans, a black T-shirt, and a new leather jacket. He also acquired black bikini underwear, socks, and a pair of black Converse Chuck Taylor high-top sneakers. He stopped at a drugstore, where he procured a pack of Trojan Magnums and a disposable travel set with a razor and a toothbrush. He called *Zayde* Hal, but there was no answer.

His phone rang. It was Ruth. "How is it going? How do you feel?"

Revulsion washed over him. "I feel fine, Mom, but I'm going to have to work late tonight, maybe very late."

"Your first day back? It's not right. You want I should talk to them?"

Honestly, how old was he?

"No, Mom, don't worry."

"When you're feeling better, Zevelah, Rivka's mother called and asked if we could move forward."

"Okay, when I am stronger."

"Zev, you're not getting any younger. With that promotion, you could afford—"

He cut her off. "I have to go into a meeting, Mom. I'll see you when I see you." His eyes filled with liquid, and he blinked it back hard. He felt distanced from everything he knew. Somehow, death's constant immanence had moved him to a new place of perspective. *What am I doing in this shabby suit, in this shabby world, in this shabby life?* He walked to his car and got in. The holy books instructed Jews to appreciate God's creations—good food, good weather, love. Perhaps he had been disobeying God up until now. He'd heard somewhere the catchphrase "Living well is the best revenge," and laughed inwardly. Perhaps not well, but at least he was living. He turned on his rock 'n' roll station and blasted the music out the windows.

He drove to the airport and checked into the Marriot, room 111. As Mitch had told him, Pig and Whistle was the hotel bar, and the intended mecca of Zev's new life.

Zev's nondescript hotel room had a king-size bed and a window that overlooked the airport. He threw the safety bolt on the door, and for the first time ever he was truly alone. He took off his shoes and walked around the room in his socks. He stood and looked through the window, watching a plane land and another depart. He clicked on the TV. An entertainment menu appeared, complete with adult films. He opened the door to the minibar. There was every kind of liquor in there. None of it was kosher.

Zev went into the bathroom and shaved. He combed his hair straight back instead of parting it on the side. He replaced the black suit and white button-down shirt with the black jeans, the black T-shirt, and his new leather jacket. A stranger stared at him in the mirror. He smiled back at him, then sighed and looked away.

Mitch insisted that women would flock to him, but how could he make the most of the situation without letting them know who he was? Mitch stressed that consenting parties often used pseudonyms. Was he really going to do this?

Zev called Hal, but again there was no answer. He was tempted to leave the hotel, to drive away and check on his *zayde*, but knew that if he left he would never have the courage to return. He needed a different, more secular name. He took his ID out of his wallet and hid it amongst his folded clothes. "Hi, my name is . . . James." That was it—James . . . *James what? James Hetfield?* That was the name of the lead singer for Metallica. Unsure, Zev posed in the mirror and rehearsed, saying it aloud until he felt confident. He took the elevator down to the lobby level. As he walked to the bar, he readjusted his leather jacket so that the collar was up, a more casual and "hip" look, much more befitting a "Jim."

It was five twenty, and the Pig and Whistle was more than half-full. It had a pleasantly cozy feel, with a square, central bar manned by a pair of sexy female bartenders. Tables covered by red-and-white-checkered cloths and topped with candles lined the pub. The cute barmaids in short skirts who zipped around carrying trays of exotic-looking drinks mesmerized Zev. He had never been in a bar before, but "Jim" had a lifetime of experience in taverns of every description, and so Zev pulled his shoulders back and sauntered confidently up to the long mahogany bar. He wanted to see what others were drinking. A pretty blonde with curls that cascaded to her shoulders sat a few seats down. She looked up as Zev approached, flashed a smile, then looked away. She wore a frilly pink top that showed modest but inviting cleavage. Zev was smitten, but before he could claim the empty seat next to her, a well-groomed but heavyset man in an expensive suit blocked him. "Let me buy you a drink?"

Zev was suddenly depressed. Just his luck—his one romance was over before it ever began.

"No, thanks. I'm doing fine," the blonde said softly but in a way that made it clear that her answer was final. But the man did not heed her cue. He leaned in close to her on the pretext of waving his hand to summon the bartender. A tan line on his left fourth finger gave his married state away.

"Oh, c'mon, my money's not good enough?" He signaled again to the bartender and said loudly, "Bring her a refill." But before the man could sit, Zev found himself sliding into the empty seat. "Hi, honey," he said, with the kind of smile Chaim would give to Ruth that always melted her. "Got caught in traffic. Sorry." The suit backed away, mumbling an apology. Zev was six feet two inches and looked tough and intimidating in his new outfit.

Once the suit was out of earshot, the blonde said ironically, "You're my hero." Zev colored and looked away.

The bartender, a black woman showing major cleavage, approached them, giving Zev a smile of approval. "Thanks, pal, you saved me having to throw that guy out." Zev cleared his throat. The bartender leaned on the bar in such a way that Zev saw another inch of creamy black skin. *Wow.* "Next one's on me," she said.

Zev pointed at the blonde's nearly empty, oversized martini glass. "I'm almost afraid to ask."

"Ask away." His blonde *shiksa* goddess bestowed a smile.

Zev smiled nervously. "Can I buy you a . . . ah . . . one?"

She glanced at him—a sideways appraising look—sternly with no smile. A long moment passed while she pretended to consider her options. Zev could feel sweat suddenly roll down his back.

At last, the blonde nodded and tapped her glass. "Cosmo again, Ruby. And thanks, mister." She had a lovely, breathy voice, and each sentence ended up sounding like a question. He warmed to her and felt himself relax. Ruby looked at Zev until he broke out of his trance.

"Oh!" Zev said. "I'll have a beer." Ruby rocked back on her heels and waved a hand at the selection of bottles lined up behind the bar. "Corona," he said. That's what Mitch said he drank. "With lime." He breathed a sigh of relief. The drinks came.

"He was a creep." The blonde drained what was left in the martini glass. She waited for Zev to make a move, then saved him the trouble. She leaned forward and said, "Hi, I'm Rachel."

He put out his hand. "Jim." The lie had rolled off his tongue. He waited for lightning to strike him down. But it did not come. "Cheers!" he said. She smiled and held up her glass to clink.

"What shall we drink to?"

Zev looked unsure. She looked thoughtful, then said with a laugh, "What about . . . narrow escapes?"

"Yes," he agreed. "Narrow escapes." He was sure she was not Jewish in spite of her traditionally Hebrew name—but how to ask her about such? And really . . . did it matter?

"So, Jim, what brings you to D.C.? Or do you live here?"

"No, I work for . . ."

He had to catch himself, as he hadn't prepared a response to this line of questioning. He cleared his throat and said, "I'm here from Chicago on business." It sounded important! Could it be this easy?

She smiled politely. "What kind of business?"

"I'm an engineer." That much was true. He reached up to adjust his hat, but he wasn't wearing it. "What about you?"

She shrugged. "I'm in education. I teach third graders."

"I wish I'd had a third grade teacher that looked like you. I'd probably still be in grade school."

"Thank you!" Pleased, she nodded, waiting for more.

Inwardly Zev was panicking, but he thought about how smooth his grandfather was with the ladies and hoped that maybe such skills were in his blood. "What do you like best about teaching?"

"Well, I love children, so mostly being around them, showing them things. I also teach Sunday school, and there I enjoy telling them all the Bible stories."

"You read the Bible? Old or New?"

"The New Testament, mostly."

So here was Rachel, his *blonde trophy*—how on earth was he going to get her into bed?

"What do you like best about your job?"

"That I get to travel and meet new people." Each new lie made the next one even easier.

She ate the cherry off the swizzle stick in her drink. She chewed delicately, showing neat white teeth. "My girlfriend was supposed to be joining me, but she couldn't get a babysitter."

Zev digested this and finished his beer. "Would you like another?"

She nodded. "What do you do for fun when you travel?" Rachel asked. He looked around the bar. There were several couples dancing. She followed his gaze. "Do you dance?" Here it was, here was his chance. Could he fake it?

"Not well."

"Me neither."

Ruby brought their drinks, and they toasted again. He watched Rachel take a sip. She was terribly pretty, and Zev felt paralyzed. She looked up over her glass at him with a shy smile. "Would you like to try?"

They danced to the latest pop songs. A slow number came on and she posed, right arm up, left arm extended. It was the decisive moment. He had no idea of what to do, but she had insinuated herself inches from him. He found himself dancing, taking tiny steps, as he was terrified of stepping on her feet. She smelled of alcohol and lovely perfume. She was so soft, so tiny. He put his arm more closely around her, and Rachel leaned her head against his shoulder. He could feel where her bra bit into her back and her pantyhose dug into her waist. It was as if he were floating somewhere outside this clunky body that was gently undulating with this soft, exotic creature.

Someone turned the lights down. In the dim room, he watched to see what the other men were doing and was able to imitate some of the basic steps. Zev felt both panic and desire.

Okay, this is enough. Besides, I should get home and check on Zayde. His parents were bound to be getting worried. One more song and he would ask for her number. She gazed into his eyes, smiled, then looked down. Zev realized with a shock that she had just let him know she would sleep with him.

Emboldened, he pulled her a little closer and slid his hand over her bottom. She didn't protest.

"What time do you have to go to work in the morning?" she murmured, pressing against his chest.

"My first appointment is not 'til noon." In an instant, Zev imagined a patent application for a machine that would tabulate all his lies. Or did God already hold that patent?

"Perfect. My place is nearby. Walking distance." She smiled up at him and pulled him away. "Let's go."

His heart leapt from his chest in triumph, then contracted in panic as he thought, *What if I blow it, come too soon? What if she likes oral sex? Will I be able to find her G-spot?* His mind raced through all the stuff he'd read online, some of it pretty kinky, but the only information he could remember came from an issue of a men's health magazine—and a tame publication at that—at the barbershop where he got his hair cut: "If you're afraid of coming too soon—have a quick one in the can before you get into bed."

"Come on," she urged, gently tugging his arm.

He followed her outside to the street. He realized he was dead drunk. He would later remember almost nothing of the euphoric walk to her place except some vague instructions to himself as to how to find his way back. As he put his arm around her, she pressed against his side. They swayed under the streetlights and down the sidewalk to her place. At a red light, he leaned down and kissed her. She pulled away and said, "C'mon, we have the light."

His inner tutor continued while they walked. It said, "Go slow, touch her gently, concern yourself with her pleasure, not yours," and other such bits of man-of-the-world wisdom. He would move gently then, resolving to go slowly, long enough for her to take her pleasure, but the main thing was that, unbelievably, she wanted him.

At last they arrived at Rachel's apartment. She turned the key in the lock and looked at him seductively as she slowly pushed the door open for him to enter first. Once inside, she led him down a hallway to a pretty bedroom with pink ruffled curtains and a matching bedspread. She lit a candle, sat on the edge of her bed, and turned the radio on, low, to some dreamy music Zev did not recognize. "*Shhh*," she whispered. "Let's be quiet."

She took off her shoes and lay back on the bed, her arms cradling her head. She smiled at him expectantly, then closed her eyes. He sat next to her and leaned down to kiss her. He reached behind to unhook her bra, struggling to pull off her tight skirt. She helped him take off the black T-shirt and fumbled with his belt as he kicked off his shoes. Both of them naked, he sat up in the bed and took her onto his lap. She straddled him, and they kissed. His brain went on automatic pilot as his hands touched her plump white breasts.

He thought he would go crazy but strained instead to heed the inner voice that commanded, "Slowly! They like it slowly! Make it last." He felt her softness—her wet, silken inner reaches. He was doing it at last—he was making love. She convulsed and cried out with what Zev hoped was pleasure. All of the alcohol he had drunk merged with his physical exhaustion, and he passed out.

Then, in his dream, he and Rachel floated together like the subjects of a Marc Chagall painting, lying on a red magic carpet drifting across scenes from the ancient world described in the Bible. But his dream transformed, and when he looked over at his beloved, he saw that she had the snout of a pig. Abruptly he awoke in a panic and pulled on his jeans. He went out into the hall to the bathroom, collecting himself as he washed his face.

When he came out, a sturdy little boy of about eight was standing by the bathroom door in airline-pilot pajamas and matching slippers. He held a model jet airplane in one hand.

"Hi, I'm Aaron," he whispered. "What's your name?"

"Zev."

"That's a funny name. Are you a giant?"

Zev smiled and knelt down.

"No, I'm a friend of your mom's," he whispered back.

"Is my mommy a whore?"

Zev was taken aback. In his community, children were not so precocious.

"No," he said. "She's a nice lady. She just gets lonely sometimes. Do you get lonely?"

Aaron looked at him, unsure. "I mean, aren't there times you wish you were with somebody . . . a friend?" Aaron looked down.

"I guess so. I miss my daddy. Are you sure you're not a giant?"

"Yes. Where is your dad?"

"Oh, he died in a plane crash and went to heaven. I wish he'd taken me with him."

"Why?"

"Because he's my daddy!" He looked at Zev as if he were an idiot. "Don't you have a daddy?"

Zev nodded.

"Well, don't you want to be with him?"

Zev thought about how little he'd ever wanted to be with his father, who he'd always perceived as a bossy, overbearing, humorless man who had slapped him for the simplest infraction.

"Of course I do," Zev lied.

Aaron smiled. "Want to play Legos? I'm building a big jet." Irresistible. This was why Zev had become an engineer. He loved to build things and to discover how they worked. He followed Aaron into his bedroom. It was the same blue as Zev's own room, with similar pine furniture. There was a definite airplane motif: The room had aircraft-themed sheets and bedding and a hanging airplane mobile that looked down upon a tall, antique wardrobe that stood next to the bed, separated from it only by a small night table. A large framed photograph of Aaron, Rachel, and a man in a pilot's uniform was propped up on Aaron's pillow.

Zev sat on the floor with Aaron and helped him build a big jet with swept-back wings. As it began to get light outside, Zev stood and shivered, realizing he'd been sitting shirtless and barefoot on the floor in a draft.

"I should go back to bed," Zev said.

Aaron's eyes filled with tears. "But you just got here! Why are you leaving? You don't like me. Just like Daddy. If I'd been good, he'd still be here!"

Aaron began to cry. Rachel rushed in, wearing a red silk kimono. When she saw her son, she gathered him in her arms and said accusingly, "What did you do to him?"

"Nothing. We built the rest of his airplane, and then I said I should go back to bed. He just started crying!"

Rachel looked at Aaron. "Is this true?"

"He doesn't like me. He'll leave just like Daddy."

Rachel shot Zev a helpless look.

"I don't have to leave right away, Aaron. I can stay for a while."

Aaron sobbed more loudly. "I don't believe you!"

Rachel rolled her eyes and said, "You'd better go."

"But—"

"Just go."

Zev felt like he'd been slapped in the face. He looked at the sobbing boy and his distraught mother and sneezed several times in a row as he headed for the door to retrieve his clothes. He dressed hurriedly. He wrote his cell number on a piece of paper, almost scribbling "Zev"—but he caught himself and simply scrawled, *Call me. Jim.* He left the paper on the nightstand, feeling cheap.

"Bye, Aaron. Bye, Rachel," he called from the door of the apartment, but, of course, there was no reply. He shut the door and left.

CHAPTER 6

Trapped in the Matrix

HE NEXT MORNING, SARAH performed her exercise routine but found herself having a bad case of what she called her "mystery sobs." Ever since Sylvie had disappeared, there had been days when Sarah woke up unable to stop crying for more than a few minutes. She would go about her business while allowing her body to just weep until it was done. She tried to be kind to it, and was aware that her mind immediately disconnected, like a parent disowning a child. Her body seemed like a separate being, with its own needs and wants, and somehow whoever it was that considered herself "Sarah" was trapped inside it, waiting for it to decay and rot around her. It was hard to be enthusiastic about the future.

But this sobbing thing had of late become a serious symptom that, in her past, was always followed by a terrible illness. It was invariably triggered by some event that could only be described as traumatic—Sylvie's disappearance, the end of her marriage, and so on—then illness would follow. Once, it was three months of pneumonia, another time a month of flu. Why now? Nothing had really happened to set her off, or had it? Sarah could not afford to get sick, and so she focused on trying to understand what she could do to avoid a seemingly inevitable outcome. What had happened lately? Work had been going well, the money was coming in . . . Then she realized that, somehow, it was learning about Judith that had precipitated this physical expression of total despair. She was truly being mocked, reminded that not only did she feel that life was meaningless but that she had no purpose and never would. Worthless was what she was and always had been—a pathetic little virus. How was she going to get through this day?

She hadn't even been able to remember to put the rosemary in the fucking bread. She had left the loaf out, uncovered, and now it was as hard as a rock. She threw it in the trash but then extracted it and wrapped it up. Even stale it would make good stuffing.

There was only one way to get through this day: distraction.

She poured a large glass of wine and climbed back into bed. She turned on the TV and watched *The Matrix* again. The storyline centered on Neo, an alienated, drug-dealing computer programmer given a chance to become the savior of the sci-fi world in which he lives by saving the human race from robots who have conquered the planet. His challenge is to discover what is real and what is part of the computer-generated dream that keeps the humans enslaved as "coppertops"—energy batteries that fuel the artificial-intelligence universe created after a nuclear war has destroyed the earth. This was why she loved the story. She often thought that if she could get out of the matrix of her existence, she too might do some larger good.

In her favorite part of the film, Neo escapes from his ordinary life and meets a mentor, the legendary Morpheus, who is one of the few humans who survived the war and is now the head of the resistance movement. Morpheus gives Neo the choice of two pills: a blue one that will lead him to the truth, and a red one that will lead him back to the world he *believes* is real, and remove his doubts about such. He chooses the blue pill and finds himself transported to the "farm"—acres of human beings asleep in pod-like cradles connected by wires to the giant central matrix that leeches out the energy of the human coppertops, who are being kept asleep in the waking dream of what Neo imagined was the real world. Horrified, Neo must literally unhook his body from a pod and disconnect the wires. In doing so, he discovers that his actual body has never been used and has no strength. He escapes through the sewage system and nearly drowns before his mentors rescue him.

Sarah sat watching, rapt. In her mind, she *was* Neo. The experience with the faux mountain climbers was the first step, and she felt that she was now on a path to the truth. She cried on and off.

On-screen, Neo is saved from the sewer and ferried onto the ship, the *Nebuchadnezzar*—ironically the name of the king of Babylon in the Judith story. Neo is saved but then has a nervous breakdown, or *kriya*, when he realizes everything he has accepted as real is false. Sarah acknowledged that she was having a mini-*kriya*, and once again she calmed down. Wistfully, she wished that she had some important destiny like Neo. He was "the One," a being prophesized to save the humans. What was she? A cook.

When the movie ended, Sarah had regained control and was ready to prepare Hirsch's Thanksgiving feast. She would tackle the *challah* with rosemary again, but her first step was always to create a picture of what the final presentation would be. For this purpose, she used Smith's modeling clay in harvest colors, which she arranged on the various dinner and serving plates so that she could refine the arrangements to her liking. The clay came in one- to five-pound bricks of brown, orange, yellow, and green. There was a kids' craft store down the block, and she'd discovered the moldable material one day when she was asked by a prospective client to demonstrate what a meal would look like but hadn't the money to buy the food speculatively. It was a strange request, but she landed the job and had used the clay to test out new ideas ever since.

After getting the layout correct, she added various decorative items to the shopping list, including doilies and purple kale.

She returned to Farmland and methodically bought every

item on her fifty-item list. She'd previously ordered the turkeys from Epstein's, a kosher butcher in the Bronx, and sent Santiago there to pick them up. She didn't trust the delivery service at Farmland and arranged for them to hold all ten bags until Santiago could retrieve them.

When she returned home, Sarah looked over the menu and to-do lists and began to assemble the equipment she always took with her when she had to cook on site. The menu was going to be lavish within the guidelines of the dietary laws, of which the most basic was "Thou shalt not cook the calf in its mother's milk." This excluded dairy from a meal with meat in it. Fowl had not originally been considered meat, but since it now was, the laws had to be observed. No butter in the stuffing, only margarine or olive oil.

Her kosher kitchen was similar to her other one except that she had decorated it in the blue and white colors of the Israeli flag. There were two complete sets of everything—one designated for meat-based meals and the other for milk-based or dairy meals. Although she knew the letter of the dietary laws, they meant nothing to her—they were yet another way of religion intruding into Jews' lives by making the practice of eating a further opportunity to disobey God's rules. Did it ever stop? Could you ever get any alone time in a world where God was always sticking His big nose in? She sighed and gathered her tools, an assortment of utensils including five very sharp knives in varying sizes, which she kept in a special canvas bag with a sleeve for each tool.

CHAPTER 7

A Knockout of a Thanksgiving

ANTIAGO RANG HER DOORBELL, and Sarah buzzed him up. A minute later, she opened the front door, where he stood with a big grocery box. They kissed on both cheeks, European-style. She looked disapprovingly at the box.

"They fit two in there?"

"No, the other one's in the truck. I knew you would want to look." He brought the box in and set it on the kitchen counter.

She peeked inside. The bird was perfect. "Thanks. Is the van downstairs?"

Santiago nodded.

"I also stopped at Farmland and picked up the order." She gave him a smile. "See you in fifteen."

He picked up the box with the turkey and exited. Sarah got into the shower and twisted her wet waist-length curls into a chignon. She briefly looked in the mirror at her naked form. Everything seemed to be holding up. She touched her breasts and scowled. They could have been a touch bigger—*enough!*

She practiced the breath of fire as she put on her cooking uniform of white T-shirt, black-and-white-checked chef's pants, and patent leather clogs. She added lipstick and considered perfume. She tended to be "all business" when she was on a job, especially with a first-time client. She decided to use a little of her favorite fragrance, *La Nuit Exotique*, just for herself.

Santiago drove the van across town. The afternoon before Thanksgiving was quiet on the East Side, and he and Sarah made the trip in a few minutes. Santiago drove well. "This will be a happy Thanksgiving for me too," he said in his heavily accented English. "I have been here for almost one year, and you and Mr. Carlos, you help me to stay here." He stopped for a red light, and Sarah was surprised to see tears in his eyes.

"You earned it," she said, handing him a tissue.

"Thanks to you, Miss Sarah. But I must tell you one thing: I will be leaving you after New Year's. I am homesick and want to return."

"Of course," she said. "I know just what you mean. Thanks for giving me so much notice. You know I rely on you."

"I know. I am sorry." She wished that some geographical location mattered to her like that.

Hirsch owned a brownstone off Fifth Avenue. He met her at the door wearing a navy T-shirt, gray sweatpants, and expensive sneakers. He was buff, she would give him that.

"Hello, Chef Sarah," he said, smiling, and walked her through the huge entranceway with a black-and-white-tiled floor, wood paneling, and terrifying African sculptures. "Let me give you the tour."

He walked her into a high-ceilinged living room done in bachelor beige with brown leather sofas, lime-green accent pillows, and the largest flatscreen TV she had ever seen. There were a number of Andy Warhol-style prints of movie stars on the wall clearly designed to coordinate with the room. "That's quite a TV" was all she could manage.

"My mother's an interior designer." That explained the statues—there to scare off any female he might want to bring home.

Then to the dining room, equally lavish with the same black-and-white and wood-paneled theme. "Lovely. Your mother is amazing."

He smiled and led her to the kitchen, a state-of-the-art room again with the black-and-white-tile motif. But this room was warm and had some life to it. "This is beautiful," she said. "Do you cook much?" She went to find the right set of pots and pans.

He shook his head. "Once in a while. My ex-wife used to try to cook. She was useless." Sarah was surprised at the rancor in his voice.

"Where are the meat pots and pans?" He looked at her blankly. She realized that the kitchen was not kosher. "I'm confused. Didn't we agree that this is to be a strictly kosher meal?"

"Yes, why?"

"This kitchen is not. Perhaps I should cook at home and return with the meal."

Hirsch shrugged. "But the food is, right?"

She nodded.

"And so is the chef, so that makes it all right. Please cook here."

Sarah pasted on a smile. "As you wish." Santiago came in with a box of supplies and left.

When they were alone, Hirsch moved in close to her and said, "You look great with your hair up, and you smell wonderful."

She laughed. "You're kidding, but thanks."

He lingered as she unwrapped her knives and began to unpack. "Can I watch?" he asked.

"No."

"Why not?"

"I prefer privacy."

"Is that why you don't work in a restaurant?"

She shrugged. "Not my style."

"I have friends who could get you on the Cooking Network."

"Thanks, but no thanks." She sharpened her knives and unpacked the box of supplies.

"How long have you been cooking?"

"Too long. All that info's on the Web site."

"What is your goal?"

"To make this meal excellent." He came and picked up one of her knives. She gently took it out of his hand. "Now, don't you need to go to the gym or something? I promise that you'll need to work this dinner off."

"Okay."

Santiago came in with another box. "Where should I put this?" Sarah gestured and turned her back on Hirsch. He waited, but when he realized she was ignoring him, he left. She sighed with relief. She was annoyed at his attitude. Things should either be kosher or not. It was disrespectful to dabble in this arena. She had been raised kosher when at home, and her parents had acted devout in front of their own parents but always cheated when they were out. After her bat mitzvah, she had rejected all of it because she was considered a second-class citizen. It occurred to her suddenly that maybe the reason she had selected Michael in the first place was that he pre-rejected her in the same way—she had never been Number One. His work and his mother had come first. It sounded like Hirsch had the same priorities.

She assembled her ingredients and put Santiago to work chopping onions and washing vegetables. When he was done, he left the kitchen and began setting the table.

She liked to work in complete silence, reciting a yogic mantra repeatedly until she stopped thinking and was consumed by the work. *Aad Guray Namay, Jugaad Guray Namay, Sat Guray Namay, Siri Guru Devay Namay.* Over and over. It translated loosely as "I call on the primal wisdom within. I call on the ancient wisdom. I call on the true wisdom beyond. I call on the God wisdom within."

She used margarine, which she did not enjoy, and oil. The turkeys were quickly washed and basted. She made Sylvie's favorite stuffing recipe, which called for *challah*, mushrooms, peas, onions, and chicken fat. Sylvie's secret had been to soak the bread in broth instead of water. Sarah used the stale *challah* from the "mystery sob" morning, and it reminded her of another Thanksgiving, when Sylvie was making the stuffing and Sarah was helping to shuck peas.

They sat at the kitchen table. Sylvie wore a white apron over her pink uniform, her veined, dark chocolate hands with their chipped red nails separating the broth-soaked bread.

"Can I do that?" Sarah asked. Sylvie took the peas away. She held Sarah's hands and placed the soaked bread in them, but held them so Sarah could not knead.

"Who gave us this bread?" Sylvie asked, smiling. She had prominent cheekbones, curved red lips, and her voice was breathy and deep.

Sarah felt warmed by the memory of that smile, as she had all those years ago.

"God did," she said

"How do we know that?"

Sarah thought for a moment.

"God makes everything."

"Good girl, now squeeze the broth out."

"Sylvie?"

"Yes?"

"Are your God and my God the same?"

Sylvie nodded solemnly and smiled. "Why?"

"Your God seems nicer. Mine doesn't like me because I am a girl. He never gives me what I want."

"I can't believe that—God likes boys and girls the same. And you are such a good little girl. What is it that you want?"

"No, He doesn't. When my grandpa puts on his tefillin, he thanks God for not making him a woman. If God loved me, He would have made me a boy. Your God loves you, and you're a woman. I prefer your God."

"Child, your grandpa was just thanking God he didn't have to suffer the agony of giving birth."

Sarah said, "So why didn't God make it so everybody has

to give birth?"

Sylvie had no answer, and Sarah knew then that God expected people not to ask questions, in spite of what her mother called "the Talmudic tradition." She was still asking and not getting an answer.

Sarah pulled herself back to earth and concentrated on her work. *Soak the challah in broth, caramelize the onions, continue to recite the Gurmukhi blessing. Aad Guray Namay.* Supposedly, the blessing offered protection, its vibration moving time "nine feet." The idea of shifting time spatially intrigued her and cheered her up.

Sarah hummed a snippet of a poem by Rumi that a singer named Mirabai had transformed into a song: *"If love taps on your window, let it in, but shut the door of your reason, even the smallest hint changes love again."*

Hirsch arrived, a little breathless and sweaty in his gym clothes.

"Smells great in here."

"It's the onions. Good workout?"

"Yes, just ran five miles."

"Wow." Sarah thought running was asinine because almost everyone she knew who ran eventually got injured.

"Will you help me select the wine?"

Sarah nodded, secretly annoyed at the interruption. She gave the pan of onions another quick shake and combined the stuffing ingredients in a bowl so they could sit. The turkey corpses sat expectantly in their pans. Why did things have to die to feed other things? She had always appreciated the practice in kosher cooking of draining all the blood out of the animal so that somehow it ceased to be a dead creature—but again, more of God's head games. Dead was dead.

"Okay." She wiped her hands and followed him across the kitchen. The door to the wine cellar was in the far corner near the back door.

Hirsch led her down the stairs to the wine cellar. The low-ceilinged room, with its stone walls lined with dusty wooden shelves filled with bottle after bottle, was unexpected in New York City. It looked like a set from one of Sarah's favorite movies, *Notorious*, a retelling of the Mata Hari story directed by Alfred Hitchcock. Ingrid Bergman played a loose woman who becomes Claude Rains's lover in order to secretly investigate his Nazi dealings. The wine cellar is pivotal in the story, as that's where the smuggling integral to the movie's plot occurs. Bergman's character redeems herself by being willing to die to expose her husband. Cary Grant played the love interest—a disapproving male spy who ends up falling in love with Bergman and saving her from certain death.

"I have been collecting wine since I was a young man," Hirsch said. "One of my many regrets was marrying a woman who didn't appreciate fine wine. Do you drink?"

"I've been known to." *And too much lately*, she thought. *Way too much.* He showed her two bottles, one a Chardonnay, the other red French Bordeaux. She nodded approvingly. "Are they kosher?"

"Yes, it has to be kosher," he said. "My mother is coming." Sarah wondered if the mother had designed the nonkosher kitchen. She moved toward the door, mulling why he'd brought her down there, then he caught hold of her and kissed her. And stuck his tongue in her mouth. An instant of shock, then cold anger coursed through her veins. It wasn't the first time, nor would it be the last, but it was always insulting.

She pulled away and headed for the door. "This is against my rule. I don't shit where I eat." She tried to keep her voice level. There was no reason to ruin the job.

"Bend a little," he smiled. "It won't hurt you." She hurried up the stairs.

Realization flooded her mind. *Bend a little.* Maybe that one thing was the whole reason for her misery.

With Michael, she'd kept bending her rules, making excuses for him, giving away little bits of herself in the hope of being loved. It was like the fake climbing wall or the false human world of *The Matrix*. She could feel the edges of her artificial reality crumbling. *Never again*, she thought. *I am not doing that again.* She crossed the kitchen to the stove. He came up the stairs, his arms full of bottles. He walked toward her, but she said, "If I don't get the turkeys in the oven, there will be no dinner. Maybe take the red out so Santiago can decant it."

"No problem, Chef Sarah."

She looked at the clock. It was a little tight. She quickly stuffed the birds and got them in the oven. She heard the doorbell ring. Hirsch appeared with a tiny, wizened woman with a cap of black hair wearing a red silk dress and a lot of jewelry. "This is my mother."

Sarah wiped a hand on her napkin and greeted the tiny wrinkled one. "A pleasure." Mrs. Hirsch looked her over coldly and left the kitchen without a word. Hirsch gave her an apologetic smile and followed his mother out of the room.

☗

Santiago served, and things were going well. Hirsch stayed out of the kitchen until the very end. But he came in when Santiago left to get the van.

Sarah had a glass or two of wine and was carefully putting her knives back into their special cases. "It was delicious. You are everything I was told about you. My mother is raving about you."

"Thanks."

"Can I take you to dinner tomorrow night?"

She wondered how bad this was going to get.

He came toward her. She put a hand up. "No, please. I told you, I have a rule about this."

He was drunk and fumbled for his checkbook. He leaned on the counter near the stove and struggled to guide his hand across the page.

"Once I pay you, that's over." She kept quiet, as she wanted to be paid. He signed the check with a flourish and held it out toward her. "C'mon, take it." She reached for it and he stepped back, giggling. She took another step and again he stepped away. "I want to give you a huge bonus," he said coyly.

I bet you do, she thought, and deftly snagged the check from his fingers. "Thank you so much." She realized that her knives were still on the counter and moved to collect them, but he was fast. He grabbed her wrists, lifted her arms over her head, backed her against the Sub-Zero fridge, and kissed her a second time. She moved her face so the slimy obscenity landed on her cheek. "Let me go," she said.

"You know you want me." He giggled again. There was a grope, a silent skirmish, then Santiago was there, between them, skillfully extricating Sarah. Hirsch made a grab for Sarah, and somehow she hauled off and punched him. He flew backward and landed flat on his back with a thud. He struggled to get up but was so drunk he couldn't. Santiago grabbed the knives and the last box. "Let's go," he said and dragged Sarah away.

They dashed to the van, which Santiago had left running. Santiago gunned the motor, and the van screeched away like a scene from a gangster movie. They drove south on Fifth Avenue and turned east on 58th Street. There were a few random snowflakes falling.

"I want to stop at the bank."

As Santiago pulled up to one, he gave her a shy smile. "Miss Sarah, you gave him a punch." She nodded. Normally she would have waited to go to the bank, but she had never knocked down one of her clients before. Should she call him? She hadn't seen blood, but they'd left so fast, she couldn't be sure.

Sarah deposited the check into the silent ATM. She had never hit a man before—or anyone else, for that matter. She was concerned—how much trouble could he make? She was lucky that Santiago had been there as a witness, so why was she worrying about Hirsch? She was the one who had been assaulted. She was ashamed that she had hoped that he might be "the one"— there was that damned thing again. *Fuck hope, and fuck you, while I am thinking about you . . .*

She thought of the old joke about the man who is drowning

and believes that God will rescue him. A sailboat comes and the man refuses. "I'm waiting for God to save me." Then a submarine comes, and the man waves it on. "No, I am waiting for God to save me." Then a motorboat comes along, followed by a yacht, and finally a cruise ship. Each time the man refuses help. "No, I am waiting for God to save me." Suddenly, a loud voice booms from the sky. "Schmuck! Who do you think sent the boats?"

Sarah laughed aloud as the cash machine swallowed Hirsch's check. "You sent Santiago. Thank you," she muttered and glanced upward. Then her sour mood returned. "But you also sent Hirsch! What are you trying to do to me?" What would have happened if Santiago hadn't been there? It was a chilling thought, but perhaps the point was that God had sent the boat. Or maybe the point was that He had caused the shipwreck in the first place—and why was she the person who always noticed such things? Someone had let the snake into the Garden of Eden too.

CHAPTER 8

THE MORNING AFTER

T WAS SEVEN A.M. Zev was not jubilant. He felt empty and aching. There had been no waking kiss, no billing and cooing, no second helpings. The damp morning grayness chilled his bones as he stood outside Rachel's townhouse apartment. She lived on a street of prefab townhouses, and it was a road that got a lot of airport traffic. He could see signs to the airport and planes taking off thunderously in the distance. He turned on his cell-phone GPS and typed in the address. He was less than a ten-minute walk from the hotel. *Does she do this often?* he wondered. His phone rang.

He looked at the number, hoping it was Rachel, but, no, it was his parents. He was in no mood. Zev knew that they were concerned, as he had never spent an unplanned night away from home before. He needed time to formulate an excuse. He suddenly wished the steel beam had done its work. He could not bear the idea of his life stretching endlessly before him in its present form. *Am I in what the gentiles believe is hell? Not some fiery pit but this everyday mundanity called "daily life"?*

As he walked back to the hotel, a truck passed him. On the side it said CHURCH OF GOD. He reframed it in his mind as "*Shul* of God." Instantly and irrationally, in a way that made sense only to him, Zev suddenly decided that's what he wanted to do: go and study the world, maybe looking for a god whom he could believe was worthy. The great rabbi Hillel had said, "If you don't stand for yourself, who will stand for you?"

He sighed heavily and began to walk back to the hotel.

He changed back into his old clothes and carefully bagged his new ones. He thought of leaving them, but the thrift in him prevented such.

It was close to nine A.M. When he drove up to his parents' home, his anxiety grew exponentially. The morning sun cast a bittersweet honey light, reminding him of a painting he had seen where it was both night and day at the same time.

He pulled into the driveway and parked in his own spot. Ruth would be shopping and Chaim would be at school. Rachel was a teacher, and she seemed like a good mother—but did she bring many men home from that bar? How long had she been widowed? He wondered if she would call. If not, if he went back to the bar, would she be there?

He entered the house quietly, carrying the plastic bag containing his new clothes. He took an apple from the fruit bowl on the kitchen table and headed up to his room. It seemed terribly small to him: tinier than ever before, with its twin-size bed that was too short for his long legs. He could never marry Rivka. She was a sincere person and deserved someone who accepted this way of life. He'd endured endless *yenta*-ing and being hawked as an eligible bachelor since he turned eighteen. He sat on his bed, unsure whether to unpack or pack up and leave. He must have fallen asleep sitting up, and Ruth's entering his room with his laundry jolted him awake.

"So you decided to come home," she said. He yawned loudly to avoid answering. He was emotionally many miles away from the fury of his mother. She berated Zev for making her worry. "Where have you been?" She put down the laundry and wrung her hands. "We were up all night calling the hospitals! You never came home from work. We were afraid you had collapsed somewhere. It's not like you to worry us so." She looked at him suspiciously. "Where were you? Why didn't you call?"

"I fell asleep at my desk. I had so much catch-up to do, I stayed working and I fell asleep."

"We called you and called you."

"My phone ran out of power. Sorry I worried you. Should we call Dad?"

Ruth nodded and looked him over critically. "You look tired. I was right—you went back to work too soon."

"You're always right. The boss sent me home. He told me to take two weeks off with pay."

"I always said he was a good man. You must be hungry. I will call Dad and make you some breakfast."

"Don't bother," Zev said. "I just need some sleep." His mother looked disappointed. He forced himself to get up and hug her.

It did the trick, and she smiled, mollified. "Okay, my Zevelah, you should sleep."

In his dream, Zev found himself inside the ancient temple in Jerusalem. The Maccabees stood watching the miraculous oil that burned for eight nights. A rabbi dressed in biblical clothing passed him two coins. "Put these on a dead man's eyes." The priest spoke to him in Hebrew, but Zev couldn't understand him.

He awoke covered in sweat. He could smell Rachel's scent still lingering on his skin. He smiled with pleasure at the memory of her and wondered how Aaron was doing. He considered how he might have felt if he'd lost his father at that young age, and realized that, in fact, he had lost his father and his faith when he was forced to tear up that baseball card. Spooked by the dream, he did something rare for him—he picked up his *siddur* and opened it randomly. Reading the Hebrew words aloud calmed him. But something was wrong. He couldn't seem to make out the words. He picked up another prayer book—no good. The Hebrew letters swam before his eyes. He got up and walked over to the bookshelf opposite the bed next to his desk. He opened one tome after another. The English was clear, but he could not form the words in Hebrew. He could no longer hear the ancient language in his head. He tried to remember the blessing for awakening, or for seeing the sun, but nothing came. He felt sick and lay back down. The room spun. He had lost the ability to read or understand Hebrew. Was this his punishment for having sex outside of the faith? He found himself curled up in a fetal position sobbing into his pillow, trying to be silent, until he fell asleep.

CHAPTER 9

Zayde Hal's Miracle

HEN HE WOKE UP, Zev felt as if his whole body had been smashed with hammers by angels. His mother and father sat by his bed. He fell asleep again, and when he awoke this time, Rabbi Cohen, a fat, grizzled man in his sixties, with yellow teeth, salt-and-pepper hair, and the regulation beard, was sitting by his bedside. The rabbi spoke to Zev in Yiddish—and he didn't understand a word.

I have lost my languages, Zev thought. He paid no attention to the rabbi. Instead, he thought of the liquid velvet of Rachel. There was a shooting pain in his lungs, and his whole torso suddenly shook with spasmodic force. It was not until that moment that he realized he was very ill.

Rivka Samuelson came to visit him. Rivka was his mother's choice, a pretty girl of eighteen, too young for Zev, but in the eyes of the community a highly marriageable girl. She had a voluptuous figure—perfect for making babies—a pretty face, soft, brown eyes beneath a high forehead, and a sweet smile. Zev watched as she maneuvered her shapely hips and heavy butt into a straight chair. Zev lay propped up on the living room couch. He could manage only whispers before lapsing into a horrific cough that made him think his left lung would rip from his body and project itself out of his mouth. He felt himself fading in and out of a delirium that he oddly welcomed in the hopes that it would help him fend off this hapless girl. "Rivka, I am probably very contagious. You should go."

"I am here for you, Zev," she insisted, shaking her head to indicate she wasn't about to be dismissed so easily. In the midst of his fevered delusion, he imagined that Rivka was Rachel. *Suddenly her little boy peered over the side of his bed, a worried look overtaking his sweet features. Zev turned and looked at the ghost-boy.*

"Don't worry, Aaron," Zev mumbled. "I'll be fine."

Rivka blinked and glanced down the length of the comforter, perplexed. "What?" she asked, leaning forward. "What did you say?"

Zev struggled to remain conscious. "Life is so unsure that it's best not to make any plans."

Her eyes filled with tears. He knew she had liked him for a long time, and his father's grudging admiration for her had added to her value, but Zev saw in her nothing other than the end of what little self he had left. He saw four kids, a tether to a meaningless job he did well but had grown to hate, and an increasingly unwanted involvement with the *shul*, since her father was the cantor. He knew he just couldn't do that.

"I want to take care of you," Rivka said as she wiped his forehead with a cool, damp cloth and smoothed back his hair.

He felt her warmth and love for him. Tears rolled down his cheeks. "No," he whispered as loud as he could. Inwardly, he screamed, *No, no, no!*

Rivka looked at him with hurt eyes. He felt a pang of guilt, but it was overpowered by the image that filled his mind—of being chained in old-fashioned leg irons on a ship, his wrist shackled to the oars like the Romans and Greeks in those old movies, one of many slaves rowing to power the boat down the Nile. But in his fantasy, the men wore classic black coats and hats as they pulled to the beat of the female nobility in charge, pounding the drum to keep them in line.

"Rivka, you deserve better. You deserve someone who truly wants to live this life."

She looked at him, startled.

"You don't mean that," she said. "You have a fever. I should go." She left the room, but he heard her sobbing in the hall.

Aaron was back at the side of the couch. "Have you seen my daddy?" Zev considered it. The little boy climbed onto the couch and curled up in Zev's arms.

"Not yet, little man, not yet."

For some reason that he did not understand, the remembrance of the boy made Zev smile and tear up at the same time.

When he awoke later, his pajamas and the blanket were drenched in sweat, and he clutched a pillow. Zev somehow got his soaking-wet PJs off and dragged himself upstairs to the shower, trying not to breathe because each gasp cut him like a knife.

His mother spoke to him through the bathroom door. He didn't understand a word of the Yiddish, but he couldn't let her, or his father especially, know that he'd lost his languages. When he came out of the shower, wrapped in a towel, her usually stern, disapproving face softened with motherly concern and worry. He staggered, and she rushed to his side, helping him into bed, propping him up on several pillows. She'd made him broth. The aroma turned his stomach, but he drank it obediently.

"Where's *Zayde*?" he asked in anguish. "Why hasn't he come to see me?"

Ruth didn't answer, but in a mixture of words, Hebrew and English, she berated him about his rudeness to Rivka.

He drifted off and slept, and woke up again to find his father sitting next to him in a robe. Alternately praying and reading, he smiled when he saw Zev open his eyes, then he continued his prayers. Zev floated back into slumber. He dreamt that he was searching inside his own lungs, which were etched everywhere with Aramaic graffiti, as if they were the walls of a cave.

Zev sat at a campfire warming his hands, dressed in white. He felt a sense of peace and said aloud, "Am I going to die?"

The scene seemed nice and comforting, and he was about to lie down and accept his fate when: "No." A voice said, "No."

Although his high temperature made him delirious, he was dimly aware that Rivka came to visit him several more times, and that his mother was constantly babying him and whispering to him in Yiddish, none of which he understood. He knew also that his father and the rabbi came in often and prayed for him, although he didn't understand a word of that either. He kept wishing to see his *zayde*, but he never came.

Then when Hal finally did come, he shouted, "Zev! Wake up! Wake up! Aaron's in danger! Wake up!"

Zev awoke and looked around, but no one was in the room. The clock said five thirty A.M. He sat up, carefully. He felt better, although his lungs felt tender when he breathed. He realized he'd been dreaming and was relieved until he remembered what *Zayde* Hal had said. The boy was in danger! He should call, but he remembered that he hadn't taken Rachel's phone number. *What was her last name?*

An image appeared in his mind's eye of Aaron rummaging through the medicine cabinet. He took some pills from a box marked with a big "X" and the word "poison" stenciled on it. What had to be done was clear. Feeling feverish and terribly weak, Zev threw on his clothes, got himself into a jacket, and staggered downstairs. He went outside, got into his car, and drove. Every few minutes, he shifted from sweating to freezing and back again. It was a forty-five-minute drive to Rachel's apartment, but he finally found it. He banged hard on her door, and Rachel opened it after a short delay.

"What the hell are you doing here? You scared me half to death!"

Zev barged in. "Where's your son?" he demanded.

Rachel was alarmed. "Aaron? He's in bed, of course."

"Better go see." Zev rushed past her and up the stairs.

Aaron had managed to climb on top of the tall wardrobe next to his bed to tie the end of a rope to the ceiling-light fixture and was just about to jump off the bed with the cord wound tightly around his neck.

"Stop!" Zev shouted, causing Aaron to pause long enough for Zev to step up onto the bed and grab him.

Aaron fought him with surprising strength. "Let me go!" he shouted, clawing and kicking. Zev wrestled with the hysterical boy, clamping him between his knees long enough to free his neck from the noose.

Rachel hovered, tears streaming down her face. "Aaron, calm down!" Her shuddering voice was rough from crying. He stopped fighting for a moment and looked at her.

Suddenly a stocky, gray-haired man burst into the room, hastily tucking his T-shirt into his jeans as he zipped them up. "What the hell's going on here?" he demanded.

He looked at Aaron and Rachel briefly, then stared at Zev. He flinched when he noticed the rope hanging from the light fixture, his shock turning to consternation as he peered back at Rachel pleadingly, as if for answers.

"Not now, Frank," she sobbed, whereupon he paused, unsure of what he should do, and finally shook his head, threw up his hands, and walked out of Aaron's bedroom.

"Who was that?" Zev asked.

"Uncle Frank. I should go tell him what happened."

She exited. Aaron clung to Zev fiercely.

"Are you okay?" Zev asked.

Aaron looked at Zev and demanded, "Why did you have to save me?"

Zev stroked his hair. "Life is God's greatest gift. Even if sometimes it doesn't feel like it."

Aaron thought about this. "I want to be with my daddy."

Rachel entered as Aaron spoke. Her eyes filled with tears, and she held out her arms to Aaron. "Oh, my darling, Aaron! Me too!" She stepped toward him but he recoiled, clutching Zev tightly. Rachel kept coming.

Aaron turned away from her and began shouting, "*No, no, no!* The other boys say you're a whore!" Rachel's hand came up to slap him, and Zev caught her wrist. Uncle Frank returned and stepped forward to intervene.

Zev gave him a cold look and said flatly, "Back off." The man stepped back and mumbled, "Maybe I should go, Rach."

Rachel nodded. "I'll call you later." Frank left. Now it was just the three of them. Rachel moved again toward Aaron. The pale boy became hysterical.

"Don't touch me! Don't touch me! Don't touch me!" he yelled. Upset and defeated, Rachel sat in the easy chair that faced the bed. Tears ran down her cheeks.

"Aaron, why would you try to do this? Daddy wouldn't want you to leave me alone. You are my little man." Aaron looked at the floor.

"You have lots of men. You don't love me."

"Yes, I do! Of course I do—I love you more than life itself."

"I don't like Uncle Frank!"

"Okay. I won't have him come over anymore, okay?"

There was a long pause.

"Okay. I'm tired now, Mommy. Can I go to sleep?" Zev looked at Rachel.

"Doesn't he have school?"

"No, it's Saturday."

Zev realized it was *Shabbos*. He was not in *shul*, he was not in his bed, he had driven his car, and God had not struck him down. Yet. *Zayde* Hal would approve. He realized, however, that not only would his parents condemn this behavior, they would be frantic as well.

"Aaron, I've got to call my mommy and daddy, okay?"

"Sure. I feel so tired."

"Of course you do. Let me—" Rachel said as she stood up.

"No, Mommy! I hate you! I want Zev to do it."

Zev's chest hurt and his bones ached. He suddenly felt very dizzy. He coughed, and a pain shot through his right lung. He dropped immediately to his knees on the floor.

"Oh, my God!" Rachel exclaimed, and she put a hand on his shoulder and leaned down next to him. "What's wrong? Are you okay?"

Aaron hovered nervously and began to cry. "What's wrong? What's wrong, Mommy? What's wrong?"

Rachel hugged her little boy. "I don't know."

Aaron sobbed and stuttered through his gasps, "I miss Daddy . . . I want to be with him!"

"God makes that plan, not us."

"Then I hate God! He's a bad man!"

"God doesn't do things to hurt us, baby. Things happen to make us grow."

Zev opened his eyes and all he could see was Rachel in her disheveled state, her curls cascading to the shoulders of her red silk robe.

"Do you really believe that?" Zev asked.

"Yes, I do," she said. "If I didn't, I couldn't go on living." She fought tears.

"I am just getting over pneumonia," Zev whispered hoarsely. "I should go."

"Thank you," Rachel said with a sweet smile that made her seem like a young girl. The tone of her words pierced Zev's heart, and he realized at that moment that he'd been emotionally dead long before the I-beam had grazed him. He slowly stood up, with Rachel's help.

He looked at Aaron. "I'd hug you, little man, but I don't want to make you sick. You be a good boy, now, okay? And no more acting *meshuga*." Zev rolled his eyes wildly and made a circle with his index finger by the side of his head as he said that last word. Aaron, in spite of everything, giggled.

"Mashaga? Mushagoo?" Aaron mimicked, then laughed even harder.

Zev giggled and said, "No, no! *Meh-shoo-ga*," sounding it out. "Like 'sugar.' "

Aaron tried but he could not get it. The more he worked at it, the more he laughed and the sillier his subsequent attempts became. Then Rachel tried to pronounce it and she was even worse, perhaps on purpose. Suddenly they were all laughing, and to Zev it felt like bright sunshine bursting through thick black clouds after a frightening and dangerous thunderstorm. He felt stronger, let go of Rachel, and pulled himself upright. She walked him to the door. "Will you be okay? Thank you so much again! I have no idea how you could have known . . ." Her voice trailed off and she looked him in the eyes.

He shrugged. "I don't either."

"Then I suppose you also 'don't know' why you said your name was Jim and you were here on business from Chicago."

Zev's new talent for lying failed him. "I'm sorry."

Rachel pressed him. "So why *did* Aaron call you Zev?"

"That's my real name. It's a long story. If you'll please let me, I'd like to explain it all to you. But not now . . . maybe when I'm well again? Perhaps over dinner? If you want to think about it, I understand. I'd like to know how the boy is doing anyway."

She thought for a moment, then without taking her eyes off Zev, she pulled her cell phone out of the pocket of her robe. Zev started to recite his number, but Rachel's hands were still trembling, so he took the device from her, put in the numbers himself, pressed SAVE, and handed it back to her. As she took it from him, she turned her head, tears streaming from her eyes.

"What's wrong, Rachel?" Zev asked.

"I . . . if you hadn't come . . . I . . . Aaron—"

"But I did."

"Drive safe."

"I will."

☙

Zev's Toyota was the only moving vehicle on his street. Jews did not drive on *Shabbos*, and there was a neatly parked car in front of each house. This was a sin that could not be hidden, and he realized that the fabric of his life had ripped, perhaps beyond repair.

His parents were in temple, so he was able to get out of his clothes and into bed. He texted his father and fell asleep, phone in hand.

When he awoke, his parents were sitting by his bed, looking very grim. "You're quarantined until your temperature gets back down below one hundred and three," his mother said. His father shook his head and sighed heavily. He spoke in Yiddish, but Zev could feel the guilt even if he could no longer understand the words.

"I'm sorry, Papa," he said. "I drove on *Shabbos*. It was an emergency for work!"

"Work? You've been on sick leave for three weeks—how could they call you like that?" Chaim was indignant.

"I don't know, but they did."

His father swallowed hard. "Don't they know you're observant?"

Zev nodded, and fell asleep.

CHAPTER 10

A CONDITIONAL FREEDOM

ZEV AWOKE. DOWNSTAIRS HIS parents argued over him in heated, unintelligible words. Rabbi Cohen arrived along with *Zayde* Hal, who had clearly been ill. They went into Chaim's book-filled study.

"What am I to do with this son? He won't marry, he won't study books. Now he's shamed me on the *Shabbos.*" Chaim paced, clasping and unclasping his hands.

"Let him be," *Zayde* Hal said. "Let him have a time to go out and see the world."

Chaim was furious. "Dad, you just encourage the boy!"

"Let me correct you, son. He's a thirty-two-year-old man."

The rabbi said, "When he was my student, he questioned everything. Now he's a scientist who does that for a living. I see him at *shul*—he's there in body but not in spirit. There are many ways to serve God. Maybe his way is not here."

Chaim slammed his hand on the desk angrily. Ruth had tears in her eyes—this was her only son.

The next thing Zev knew, Chaim, Ruth, *Zayde* Hal, and the rabbi all filed into his bedroom, and once again he felt like he was the problem child of the whole community. The rabbi walked around the room. It seemed ordinary enough until he spied the Converse sneakers. He bent down and picked one up by the laces.

It twirled in front of his face as he examined it—like he'd never seen one before—and put the sneaker back on the floor.

The rabbi sat down heavily. "Your son needs to leave the community."

There was a shocked silence. Ruth got tears. "You are banishing him because he drove on *Shabbos*?"

The rabbi shook his head. "Not banishing. Your son is highly intelligent, a scientist. However, he is not married, although pursued by our most eligible daughters. He listens to rock-and-roll music in his car. And he wears these things . . ." He bent over and held up the sneaker again. "He works outside the community—what can you expect? Let him have a little rope. Some freedom to explore—then perhaps he will come to appreciate what we have here and return to us with an open heart."

Zev nodded, though he could not understand a word. "English, please?"

The rabbi looked at him as if to say, "You see?"

Ruth, mercifully in English, said, "Zevelah, is this what you want?" It was clear from her intonation that she believed the correct answer was "No."

Zev nodded. "Yes," he said.

His father nodded. "Yes," he echoed.

"So!" said the rabbi emphatically, clapping his hands on his thighs as he stood. "It will be so."

"Where will he go?" asked Ruth, worried.

"Ahh! That's the point! Zev must choose his own life. For himself."

His mother asked, "But for how long?"

The rabbi shrugged. "How long does it take a broken arm to heal?" He looked at Zev. "But I want you to promise me one thing: You'll go to *shul* on *Shabbos*. Any *shul*."

Zev wanted to scream, *But I can't read Hebrew anymore!* He looked at *Zayde* Hal, who nodded. "Yes, I will," Zev said.

Zayde Hal spoke. "Let him ponder. Let him sleep. Let him get well. He will find his way."

The rabbi said, "There are several nice communities within

a few hundred miles he could visit."

Chaim nodded. "At least there they would be able to help him."

"Community? Bah!" *Zayde* Hal said. "A chain made of gold is still a chain."

Zev nodded, terribly tired, but happy knowing that he would soon be free. He fell asleep.

When Zev awoke, *Zayde* Hal was in the chair watching him rest. Hal smiled at him. "What's with the English? Are you making a statement?"

"No, *Zayde*." Zev gestured for him to come close. As Hal leaned in, Zev spoke softly, almost in a whisper: "I lost it. Hebrew, I mean. I don't speak it anymore. I can't read it." His eyes teared up.

Hal nodded. "You've had a shock. It will come back."

"What happened to you? I kept calling you, but you never answered."

"I'm sorry. I was sick, too exhausted to answer the phone. My time is coming soon!"

"No, *Zayde*. Then I won't go."

"Never mind that. What happened to you that night you didn't come home? And don't tell me you were in the office."

Zev gestured for *Zayde* to come close and whispered the whole story in his ear.

Zayde was silent, then gave a short, loud snort of laughter.

"So, I was in your dream?"

Zev nodded. "What should I do?"

Zayde sighed. "It's the story of the prisoner who is so long in jail, when he finally gets out, he wants to stay because he can't remember anything else!" It was true. "So don't rush, only know—this is your one life." *Zayde* Hal suddenly looked old and ill. "I'm going home."

He walked slowly to the door, then turned and looked at Zev

with a proud smile. "You have changed the world, my Zevelah. The Talmud teaches us that when you save the one, you save the many. You did a *mitzvah*. But now you are responsible for that boy. He has no father, and that nogoodnik brother-in-law sounds like bad news."

"And Rivka, am I responsible for her too?"

"No. You two are not a match. Leaving is the best thing you can do for her. She will give up waiting for you and find another."

Zev imagined his life if he stayed and married her. "You're right, *Zayde*."

After Hal left, Zev got on the computer and looked at his bank account. Since he lived at home, with few expenses of his own, he could get by for a year or two without worrying. He enjoyed his work, analyzing original inventions to see if they were seaworthy. While he would miss the intellectual stimulation, there were so many political games going on lately that it had become difficult to get any meaningful work done.

What would he do? He would have to work at something. He suddenly smiled, because it didn't matter yet—he'd send out his résumé and see what kind of fish he could catch. He dialed Rachel's number. She answered on the second ring. "Hello?"

"Hello? Rachel, it's me, Zev."

Aaron tried to grab the phone. "Mommy, Mommy, please. Can I talk to Zev?"

Rachel smiled and ruffled his hair.

"Hi, Zev. Aaron wants to talk to you."

"Oh, all right. But just for a minute."

"Hi, Zev!"

"Hi, little man. How's it going?"

"Okay. When are you coming over? I made you something."

"You'll have to ask your mother."

Rachel took the phone from Aaron, hushing him. "I don't know."

"Rachel, please—I'd like to see the boy."

"What? You don't want to see me?"

"Of course I do, but you seem to have a steady—"

"Oh, that. Long story. Okay, you can come by. Stay for dinner—it's only going to be mac and cheese. Can you eat that stuff?"

"Yes. I'll be there at six." He hung up, smiling. What did "kosher" mean to him any longer? He thought about it and decided that he wanted to try new things. The dietary laws had been created in the biblical era to save people from eating food that had gone bad, but these were now modern times. "Mac and cheese" didn't mix milk and meat, so he was still safe.

And what about work? He was on sick leave, but he could take a leave of absence and see where it took him. He began to compose the letter. What did he want? Where did he want to go? All the communities were pretty much the same. More pressure to get married and fit in. Much as he liked Aaron, he didn't want to have kids if he didn't know who he was himself. He felt longing and wished he could read his prayer book.

He got dressed in his new clothes, opting for the sneakers, and came downstairs. His mother was baking. "Where are you going, Zevelah?" she asked. She wore an apron that he knew said in Hebrew: *Let all who are hungry come and eat.* "You are not well yet."

"Thank you for taking care of me," he replied gently.

"What's with all the English?"

"I prefer it."

"Since when?"

He smiled but didn't answer, because anything he said might start an argument. She looked at him. "Since when?" She waited, and finally he risked speech but ignored the question.

"I have to do a *mitzvah*, Ma. Visit a sick little boy. Friend from work's kid."

His mother's face brightened. "Wait a minute," she said, and turned and immediately put some *rugelach* in a bag. "Here."

He remembered that he loved her, and gave her a big hug.

"Oh, Zevelah, if you leave, promise me you'll come back

someday—you're all I have." She was tearing up.

She moved him. He understood that she meant no harm—quite the contrary, she would do just about anything for him, and, of course, that was part of the problem. He had to do for himself. So he kissed her goodbye on the forehead.

"Zevelah—where are you going to go?"

"I don't know, Mom. Nowhere right now. I'll be back soon. Don't worry."

"For dinner?"

"I don't know. Probably not."

She looked worried, as always. "Okay, but dress warm and wear your scarf."

How old am I? he thought as he headed for his car. He had no idea where he wanted to go. He turned on the classic rock station and sang along to "Nothing Else Matters," a ballad by Metallica.

He bought Rachel some flowers. He parked in the street, went up to her apartment, and knocked. She was in better spirits—she smiled at him, but before Zev could speak, Aaron ran up and hugged him. Zev lifted him up and twirled him around. "Come inside, you two!" Rachel scolded.

Zev came in, carrying Aaron and feeling very awkward. How to feel about Rachel? He noticed that she'd cleaned up the apartment and she looked demure in a white turtleneck sweater and jeans. He smelled coffee and baked goods. With his free hand, he offered the flowers and the *rugelach*.

Uncle Frank was sitting at the kitchen table drinking coffee. Hadn't Rachel promised Aaron she'd get rid of him?

He couldn't understand Frank's presence there, in the apartment, at this time, but hoped he was friendly. Zev paused, with Aaron still clinging to him.

"So, um, it's nice to actually meet you. I'm Frank." Frank stood up, revealing a short, muscular body encased in jeans and a gray sweatshirt that read: IS IT TIME FOR BEER YET?

"Uncle Frank, this is Zev," Aaron said. "He saved my life."

"I know that. I was there, remember?" Frank's cold eyes

filled with sudden tears, throwing Zev off guard. He shook Zev's hand too hard and for too long.

"I don't know how to thank you, man. My late brother, John, left me in charge. I'm the oldest, you know? Can't believe it was happening in the next room." He gestured for Zev to sit. Rachel returned carrying a tray filled with coffee cups and saucers, sugar and cream, and a selection of Zev's *rugelach* on a plate.

Frank grabbed a cookie. "Gotta take off." He smiled at Zev, then reached over and gently patted Aaron's hair. Aaron flinched and looked at Zev. Rachel excused herself and walked Frank out of the room and toward the front door.

Aaron said, "Can I have a cookie?"

Zev replied, "They're called *rugelach*."

"*Rugelach*," Aaron repeated. "Can I have one?"

"It's up to your mom."

Aaron pouted until Rachel called from the hallway, "Okay, take one," then grinned as he grabbed a cookie and shoved it into his mouth.

Does Frank know I slept with Rachel? Aaron looked at Zev. "Come play Legos with me!"

Zev nodded and started to get up, but Rachel reentered the kitchen and said, "Zev will come in a little while—why don't you go clean up your room for him?" Aaron ran happily out of the kitchen.

Rachel sat across from Zev and twisted one of her blond curls. "Frank doesn't know about us. I told him you were a fellow teacher and that you were psychic."

Zev laughed. "Psychic? Really! So how'd that go?"

Rachel laughed slightly, then shrugged. "He's not leaving Marie and the three kids anytime soon, so—"

"Do you want him to?"

Rachel shrugged again. "Not so much. He's a great guy—reminds me of John a lot. But at some point I want to leave all this behind me and make a fresh start."

"Me too. You know I'm Jewish, right?"

"Not until Aaron called you Zev. So, truly, how was it that

you knew to come here?"

"I told you. I had a dream and I acted on it."

"Have you had them before?"

"No."

"Aaron really likes you. He talks about you all the time. All of a sudden he doesn't want to be a fighter pilot anymore—he wants to be an engineer, like you."

Zev nodded sadly. "That's why I came, Rachel—I have to go away for a while."

"Why? Is it me? Is it Frank?"

"Rachel, we aren't having a relationship. We aren't meant to be. We shared one night together. You have another man in your life."

Rachel got tears in her eyes. "Frank has been so good to us."

"I don't think sleeping with you when he's married is really nice." Zev's face got a little red at this. He stood up, stuffed his hands into his pockets, and leaned back on the kitchen counter.

But Rachel didn't react. Instead, she sighed and said, "I can stop seeing him if you like."

"It's none of my business—but you did promise Aaron."

"Why don't you like me?" Her eyes were sad. "Most men consider themselves lucky just—"

"Yes, I was fortunate. You are beautiful and sweet—"

"But what? I'm a slut? I'm a whore?" Her lips twisted in disgust. "My mother thinks so."

Zev was completely taken aback. "I don't judge you. I slept with you also. We had a great time, that's all. We are really the same."

"But you have an opinion about Frank."

"Yes. He's a fox in the henhouse. He's a predator."

"What makes you think I didn't initiate it?"

"Because I just do. Because I know men. You won't find what you want as long as he's around."

"But you don't want to take his place?"

"Don't sell yourself short. I'm just a guy."

She started to cry. He put his arm around her and she wept

into his shoulder. Aaron called from his room, "C'mon, Zev! I'm ready!" Her face still buried in his shoulder, she waved for him to go to Aaron. He walked to the child's bedroom with a heavy heart, his collar wet from her tears.

Aaron was in the middle of constructing some sort of tower. Zev smiled as he entered and asked, "What are we building?"

"A new house where we can all live together."

Zev inspected. "It looks like an apartment complex."

Aaron nodded happily. "Yes! I'm making it in New York City."

"Why New York?"

"Because Batman lives there, silly—everyone knows Gotham is really New York City."

"Why do you want to live near Batman?"

"Because Uncle Tom says he knows him!"

Rachel entered and saw the tower, then sat on Aaron's bed. "Nice work, Aaron. You've been busy! Aaron's going to be an architect. Aren't you, sweetie?"

Aaron nodded happily. "An engineer!" he corrected her. "I'm going to build my mommy a big house," Aaron said, then climbed into her lap.

Zev cleared his throat. "Who's Uncle Tom?"

"John's younger brother. He's an actor in New York. You could visit him. He loves Aaron."

"We should *all* go," Aaron said, excited.

"We're in the middle of the school year," Rachel said flatly.

"I don't care about school! I want to go with Zev!"

"Even if you came, Aaron," Zev said, "I would have nowhere for you to stay." Then he looked at Rachel and added, "My community doesn't take well to outsiders."

"You'd go to New York and stay with your relatives?" She looked at him quizzically, smirked, and said, "*And how old are you?* Didn't you hear me? You can stay with Tom until you figure it out."

"What would I do for work? Jobs aren't so easy these days."

Rachel looked him over. "If it isn't too low for you, Tom

drives a cab and sometimes works as a bartender. He does well enough, and every so often he gets a big job on a TV show."

"A cab?" Zev thought about it—*Why not?* "Do you think Tom—"

"You saved his nephew's life."

Aaron had lost interest in the conversation and continued to play with his Legos. Zev and Rachel stood up and proceeded back to the kitchen.

"I like it! You know, Rachel, I don't know anything but my own world. I even lived at home during college. I want to meet people. Driving a taxicab in New York—imagine the people you'd meet!"

"The nutcases, you mean," Rachel said, giggling. Then she added, "Seriously, you're going to drive a cab in New York—and do what?"

He thought of the Torah portion he had read at his own bar mitzvah, but he could not remember which one it was. Were all traces of his past disappearing?

"Would you like to stay?" she asked, and smiled as her son entered.

Aaron gave him a pleading look. Zev nodded.

God hadn't struck him down for driving on *Shabbos*. He wondered what would happen when he ate nonkosher food. Dinner was actually delicious. Rachel made a pretty salad and had bought fresh rolls. Zev would always associate this meal with freedom. After dinner, Aaron went back to his room. Rachel washed dishes as Zev cleared the table.

"I called Tom while you were with Aaron. You are welcome to stay with him for as long as you would like."

Zev smiled. Clearly, it was *bashert*—meant to be. "I will pay rent, of course."

"That's good, because he's always broke. Funny, you look a bit like him, same build. Tom always needs a roommate, so you never know."

A roommate! His parents wouldn't be able to argue so much. It would be like the college-campus experience that he'd longed for but never had. Rachel smiled at him, and he grinned.

"It would be good for you to go. I feel like I was your sister in another life."

"Are you saying we committed incest the other night?" She looked startled, then realized he was joking.

"In another *past* life." She smiled.

"Oh, you mean the one where I was Ramses and you were Nefertiti? I hope we didn't poison each other."

"Can't you take a compliment?"

"Compliment? It's a compliment that you're not attracted to me?"

She nodded. "True, but I do care about you."

"Because I helped you with your son. That's not caring, that's a feeling of obligation with sugar coating."

She looked hurt.

"I didn't mean that harshly. I know you meant well, and I will accept your offer to connect with Tom in New York. But you don't need to pretend that there is more than friendship between us."

She opened her mouth to protest.

"No, Rachel, please. I'm weighed down by every emotional obligation. I want to avoid new connections. There's a proverb that says if you save someone's life, you become responsible for them, so in my mind, for better or worse, Aaron and I have a bond for life." Rachel looked relieved.

"What does that mean?"

"It means that I am now and forever Uncle Zev. I'll write to him from New York. He can call me, and if there are further problems, I'll try to help. Do you need money?"

"No, thank you."

He stood up to go. Aaron appeared in the doorway in his pajamas. "Will you read me a story?"

"Yes, and then I must go."

"You have to take a long class," Rachel told Zev, "and pass a hard test that proves you know the city. Tom has the information, and he's sending you a link on your e-mail." She handed him a piece of paper. "Here's his number—Tom Dooley."

Zev frowned. How was he going to get the rabbi to convince his parents to let him go? He had shamed them enough. Still, he felt like he was trapped there, choking, suffocating—he had to do something.

As they stood in the doorway, Rachel said, "Would you stay if I asked you to?"

"Why? For Aaron?"

"No, for me."

Zev shook his head. "You are the most confusing person I have ever met. You already have one lover, who seems to take care of you even if he isn't free. You just told me you think of me as a nonincestuous brother, you got me set up in New York—and now you want me to stay? You're like a cat that purrs one minute and hisses and scratches the next, for no logical reason."

Rachel suppressed a giggle. "Trying to analyze me may have been what killed my late husband." She gave Zev a crooked smile. "Please keep in touch with my baby. He needs you."

They hugged, and Zev left to face his family.

※

When Zev got home, his parents were waiting for him. More and more, they seemed to have become one person—an "octo-parent" with eight limbs and two heads that walked, talked, and thought as one.

His mother burst out: "Rivka's father called to arrange—"

Zev held up a hand to stop her. "Oh, for heaven's sake! This is the twenty-first century, isn't it?"

"So you don't want to be married to her?"

"I don't want to be married to anyone! I'm leaving, remember?"

His parents started shouting, but he couldn't understand

"their" language, so he turned and climbed the stairs to his room and went to bed.

※

Zev slept fitfully all night, the last of the congestion in his lungs coming up with his coughing. By morning, he was a limp version of himself, his aching head filled with fragments of unresolved dreams starring himself, his few friends, and his family.

He got up to pee and hocked green phlegm into the toilet. He regarded himself in the bathroom mirror and angled his long body so that he could look down its length. He hadn't seen himself fully in quite a while, and was surprised, even somewhat shocked, by what he observed. He was rail thin, having lost weight from his illness. His ribs were quite visible, his hipbone pointing sharply through pale, waxy skin that sported a variety of birthmarks and scars. He had a hairy chest, and his muscles, while certainly not bulging, were taut and sinewy. He looked at his penis and scrotum. He'd learned early in school that he had what the other boys called "a big *schlong*," for all the good it had ever done him.

A sudden, uncontrollable grief filled him, making his knees shake. He sat down on the bed. How was he going to tell his parents he was about to leave for New York City to live with non-Jews outside their little community? He had no idea how that was going to go, and what's more, he really didn't know what he was going to do afterward.

CHAPTER 11

WHEN ALL ELSE FAILS, YOU GOTTA HAVE FAITH

HE NEXT MORNING WAS the usual hell, but at least Sarah had made it into her bed the night before. It was early, and she really needed to take a yoga class. She got out of bed and looked in the mirror. She felt like she was living in her own version of the movie *Groundhog Day*, where the protagonist is forced to repeatedly relive one particular day until he corrects his mistakes and can move on. She'd read somewhere that if you admitted you were in hell, you would instantly be released. Well, here was her admission. She waited for a moment, but nothing changed. It was all so utterly pointless. She had punched a client in the jaw!

Sarah never made it to yoga class. Instead, she had a glass of wine, and a second one, well aware that drinking alone in the morning was not a positive choice. She toasted the poster of Ganesh. Perhaps he could right the situation with Hirsch. She wondered why there was no conflict in her mind between believing in God and cultivating the various yoga deities. She admitted to herself that she knew that God knew that she knew they were all expressions of Him.

The bell rang, and she unwillingly got up and opened the door. As was his wont, Carlos entered carrying food—this time a small ramekin full of brown froth. He wore expensive jeans and a tight black T-shirt. He had recently grown a goatee that made him look demonic. Sarah didn't care for it.

"Where's your pitchfork?" she said sourly.

"I traded it in for my latest concoction: flan soufflé."

"Sounds like a case of confused ethnic identity," she said but accepted a small spoonful. The flan was rich, nutty, and gooey all at once. Carlos crossed his muscular arms, looked around, and saw the wineglass and the open bottle. Sarah nodded.

"How did the new butcher work out?"

"Well. And I went with red wine, not sherry."

"Good choice."

He opened the fridge, pulled out the leftover lamb, took a giant bite, and chewed.

"Good, really good." He got a napkin and spit out the remains.

"Carlos!"

"No, really delicious—but I feel fat."

"You are such a girl."

"That's why you are my little sister."

Carlos plopped himself down and swigged her wine. "You're the yogini. What are you doing swilling vino at this hour? Aren't you supposed to be in class?"

Sarah looked down, gnawing a cuticle.

Carlos stood up. "So why so low?"

Sarah shrugged, and Carlos laughed. "Oh, sweetheart, you are so transparent. You're feeling sorry for yourself, worried that you won't find someone new. What happened with the eligible plastic surgeon?"

"I don't want to talk about it."

"That bad? Tell me—Laura made the connection."

"Jesus, Carlos—he put heavy moves on me. He attacked me in the kitchen."

"Are you okay? He didn't—"

"No."

"Okay, so how did it end?"

"I punched him in the jaw."

Carlos looked serious. "You punched him?"

"Yes, I hope he doesn't press charges." Sarah waited for a rebuke, but Carlos laughed—a real belly laugh.

"You are too delicious. Laura is going to love it."

"You're kidding. What if he does something? He could mess up my reputation."

"You were alone with him?"

"No, the twelve apostles were hanging out with me."

"No need for sarcasm. Just trying to get the picture."

"Sorry. I was just finishing packing up, and thank goodness Santiago came in."

Carlos was already texting. He stared at his phone, ignoring her. A moment passed, then he smiled. "Your would-be rapist just called Laura to thank her for the terrific referral. I think you're off the hook."

Sarah poured herself some more wine. "Not even cooking is safe. What do I do, Carlos? I just feel so lonely."

"Look at you—you're beautiful. I mean, not right now. At this moment, you look like shit . . . but you'll find someone. You got to have faith. Look at me. I have Laura."

Sarah rolled her eyes. "Faith is the biggest racket in town. Ask the Catholic Church."

Carlos nodded. "Maybe, but it's like wine—takes that pain away."

Sarah found herself fighting tears. "Maybe for everyone else. I know it's bullshit, so, no, it doesn't. Nothing does. I feel like every day is a repeat of the day before."

He poured her more wine, sighing. "Drink. You can never go the easy way, can you?"

Sarah shook her head. "No. It's true."

Carlos dug into his jeans and produced his phone. "I'm e-mailing Gwydion."

"Your psychic? Why would I use a psychic? Yoga is about living in the present, not looking into the future." Sarah stood up and felt the wine hit her.

"Aren't you the one that told me last week that there's no such thing as the present, Sarah? That by the time we recognize it, that time has passed? That we really live in the immediate future?"

She shook her head. "I'm complicated, okay?"

Carlos laughed. "C'mon, little sister. I just outsmarted you with yourself." He composed the e-mail and sent it. "Too late, it's done. I copied you on it. You can't keep doing this over and over."

The poster of Ganesh suddenly fell off the wall, but Carlos caught it before it hit the ground. They both laughed.

"Okay, maybe he'll give me some hope." It occurred to her that at least her anger at God was a comforting sign. You can't be that angry at something that doesn't exist. Ganesh falling off the wall at that precise moment was surely a sign that Sarah was on the right track, or that the obstacle was too big to be removed and Ganesh was bowing out.

CHAPTER 12

YOU CAN'T GO HOME AGAIN

EV NOT ONLY SHARED a cab with Tom but also an apartment that actually belonged to Tom's ex-girlfriend, Heather, who owned the bar downstairs. It was a three-bedroom space overlooking the Hudson River in the area known as Hell's Kitchen, on the corner of 10th Avenue and 43rd Street. Heather had decorated it in what she called "shabby chic," an eclectic mix of modern and antique furniture. The casual intimacy of living in a shared space exhilarated Zev, and he loved his room. The only drawback was that he was not allowed to bring women there, but the windows looked out on the river, and there was a lock on the door. The bed was a double—a symbol of freedom. His parents slept in separate beds, according to Jewish law. His own twin bed had always been too short, but this upgrade was a perfect fit.

He had angled the wall mirror so he could see himself, and the hatless stranger in the glass who was living his life often surprised him. The mirror hung over a beat-up bureau, which faced the bed and supported a small flatscreen TV. Zev had hooked it up to his computer so that he could watch movies while lying down. There was a battered desk with a comfortable chair. The carpets, walls, drapes, and bed were all shades of pale blue. On one wall was a poster of Albert Einstein. The caption beneath the black-and-white photograph of the middle-aged physicist, with his silvery flyaway hair, read, I WANT TO KNOW GOD'S THOUGHTS. THE REST ARE DETAILS. The quote amused Zev—a scientist with faith. It seemed so ironic.

His old clothes and books were still in the suitcase with which he had arrived but never opened. He had accumulated so much vacation time at work that he had been able to negotiate a ninety-day leave of absence, during which he was sure that he would attain some kind of clarity. He'd been in New York for nearly two months now. There had been no culture shock, no adjustment period, but rather a sense of coming home. His old life seemed like a distant memory, and when he spoke to his parents, he felt as if he were an impostor inhabiting the body of this other person who was their biological son.

After one particularly profitable night, Zev dropped off the taxi and fell asleep in his clothes. When he awoke the following morning, he waited until his father would have gone to *shul* and called his mother on the home landline. She picked up, heard his voice, and launched into a tirade of Yiddish mixed with Hebrew. Zev waited, knowing the basic gist. But he realized rapidly, really truly, that he no longer understood her. He waited until her barrage subsided. "Mother, please speak English." Finally she complied, and said, "When are you coming home?"

"I don't know, Mama, I don't know. How is Rivka?" His mother launched again. He waited for her. He imagined her in the kitchen in her housedress, thick stockings, and terrycloth mules peeling potatoes while she talked, the yellow morning sun pouring in through the flowered curtains over the double sink— one for milk, one for meat. He could almost smell the onions browning, which was the basis for most of her cooking.

"Rivka has taken to her bed."

"Oh, my, I want to call her. Can you arrange it?"

"Call her?" Ruth wailed. "Come home and see her. You made her a promise."

"No, Mom, I didn't. That's the point. You and Papa made that deal, not me." Again the foreign-language tirade. He wanted to tell her he wasn't coming back but couldn't, at first. He did not want to open himself up to that discussion.

"I'm not coming home," he said finally, and his mother let out a howl that broke his heart. He wavered, but then grew strong. "I want to talk to Rivka. Please arrange a phone call. Can you do that for me?"

"It isn't possible. You know that."

"Then can you do it for her?" he said.

More silence.

"Mom, please."

"Are you going to marry her?"

"I don't think so, but I don't know."

"What's there to know?"

And again into Yiddish. Zev found himself getting angry. "We went over this. Speak English," he said more sharply than he'd intended.

"That's what the German Jews said in 1939. If we'd spoken German, we'd be—"

Zev grew furious. "There are no Nazis waiting to put us into camps. What are you saying? That America is like the Third Reich?"

"No, it's just their language—"

"Their language? What are we? Space travelers? Great-grandpa Joe came to America in 1892. We've been here awhile!" He paused. "Ma, it's my fault. I should tell her myself. I don't want to write, and I am not coming home. At least on the phone . . . can you arrange it?"

"Your father—"

Zev sighed. "Okay, I'll write to her. Thanks for nothing."

He heard his mother begin to cry. This was too awful. "I love you, Mama." He hung up.

Zev found himself suddenly, inexplicably angry with God. He wondered what his mother had ever done to deserve such a son. *Why can't I be good? What is wrong with me? What is wrong with this world, where there is always a winner and always a loser? Or two losers? Why can't the world be happier?*

Why don't I want children? The safety and security of a wife? He tried to begin the letter in Hebrew but couldn't remember a word or a letter. To his surprise, he felt no desire to relearn the language.

Dear Rivka, he wrote in English.

I wanted to explain my inexcusable behavior toward you. I know that our parents were concocting a plan for us to marry, but I think it would be unfair to you. You are 18 and I am 32. You deserve someone your own age and someone who'll be the right man and wants to give you the world. I tell you I am not what you are seeking. You are a wonderful, beautiful woman. I wish you love and happiness.

He signed it and, dissatisfied with the plain paper, went to the store. He bought a card with pink and purple flowers on it and no phrase inside. He walked slowly to the mailbox. He paused for a moment, then mailed the letter. Instead of the relief he'd imagined feeling, Zev felt sad and wanted to call his parents again.

How old are you? he asked himself, and went to the bar. It was eleven A.M, and the wait staff was busy setting up for lunch.

Heather was sitting at the bar, looking a little worse for wear. She was cursing about something. "Motherfucking cocksucker, goddamn dick . . ." She looked up as Zev emerged. "Hey." He pretended he hadn't heard.

"*Shalom,*" she said, smiling. "A little early for a drink?"

Zev nodded.

"Sit," she said, patting the barstool next to her. "Tell Mama what happened."

"Ended a relationship."

"Oh, boy. You want a drink?"

"Maybe some tea."

"Oh, shit. You need a real drink." She went around to the business side of the bar and poured him a shot of whiskey. He looked uncertain.

"Drink," she commanded. He gulped it and coughed. Heather laughed and continued to set up the bar.

"Hey, Tito."

The Mexican busboy, who was over six feet and two hundred and twenty pounds, appeared, carrying a full case of beer as if it were a single mug. "Yeah?"

"Get our friend here some Mexican *matzah* and eggs. Pronto."

He disappeared and returned quickly with a plate of huevos rancheros. In a mockery of the classic Jewish mother, but in a very accurate accent, Heather cut a lime into garnish and said, "Eat, eat, it's good for you." Zev laughed. "That's better. Now eat and tell me."

Zev dug into his eggs. "Thank you. They're good. She was my *bashert*."

Heather said, "Yeah, yeah. The one meant for you. Or so you were told."

Zev looked at her curiously. "You don't believe in there being The One?"

Heather shrugged. "I've had several, and they all felt like The One—at the time."

Zev laughed out loud. "I'm sorry, it's just that—"

"I know—it's the delivery. I'm a standup comic." She was serious and leaned over the bar. "Zev, do you love her?"

He shook his head.

Heather nodded. "Then you're free—she was not The One!"

Zev looked skeptical. "I'll think about it."

Heather roared with laughter. Zev got the irony. "Thanks for breakfast," he said, taking out money and laying it on the bar.

"No extra charge for the therapy." She smiled.

With the Rivka issue resolved, it surprised him how disconnected he must have always been from his community, since there was no one else with whom he wanted to stay in contact. He hadn't been near a *shul* since he arrived. Nor had he any desire to pray or get his languages back. He'd been given an amazing opportunity. He was young, had some money, was attractive to women, and he had escaped from some kind of prison relatively intact. *If there was a God . . .* He stopped in his tracks. When had his doubt become so firmly lodged? Looking at the bustling lunchtime world around him and up at a brilliantly blue morning sky, he caught a delicious whiff of street-vendor hot dogs.

Zev was confused by a crazy happiness. Suddenly, it was hard not to believe in something, something larger that could make you feel this good. Life had always been a chore for him— a boulder endlessly pushed almost to the top of a hill but never reaching the peak. He felt a sense of freedom he had never known. Was this a freedom with God, or from God? Either way, he knew he had to talk to his parents. He went to hit the speed dial on his cell but stopped the call. The listing for the number was HOME. That was no longer correct, so he changed it to CHAIM AND RUTH. He called and mercifully got the machine.

"I just wanted to let you both know that I am fine, and I love you." He hung up, and wondered if he still did.

CHAPTER 13

Church of God

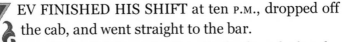EV FINISHED HIS SHIFT at ten P.M., dropped off the cab, and went straight to the bar.

He hadn't been in the city for long before he made a name for himself as a red-hot lover, and he was ecstatic, figuring he had about fifteen years of lost time to make up. His humble, self-deprecating style even had hardened New York transplant Tom taking notes. Zev's physical prowess, which meant nothing among the innocent women of his own community, counted for a lot in New York City. At home, Zev didn't drink except for on Passover, when four cups of wine were part of the ceremony. Tom said that it was a sin not to partake of the fruit of the vine at every possible opportunity. He'd taken Zev under his wing with the promise that he would show him how to drink and get women, but it was only the former with which Zev found he needed help.

Tom went right to beer and shots—boilermakers. Zev was thinking tea until Tom raised a disapproving look and handed him a shot of Jameson. Zev felt his mind go limp as he forced the drink down his throat, then he quenched the burning with cold Guinness. Tom laughed and said, "Good, now you've got some color in your cheeks, Jewboy." Zev still wasn't sure how to take Tom's nicknames, which could have been a sign of anti-Semitism, except that somehow Tom said it so matter-of-factly that it seemed more like calling a left-hander "lefty" or "southpaw."

Tom put a hand on Zev's shoulder. "So, what will it be tonight? Blonde? Redhead? Brunette?"

Zev shrugged. "As long as they're kosher."

Tom laughed uproariously. "I get it—no pigs!" He gestured to Heather for another round. Zev saw the hurt in Heather's eyes.

The entrance of a pair of pretty women in sunglasses quickly interrupted Zev's reflection about Tom's reprehensible behavior. When the taller one saw Tom and Zev, she squealed with delight and waved to them as they navigated the crowded room. Heather's Pub featured an old, polished wooden bar that ran the length of the railroad-station-style tavern. The bar had been built in the mid-nineteenth century and had beautiful brass rails and fittings. There were no peanut shells on the floor—not anymore—but one could easily imagine the days when that had been the case. Since Heather had taken over the place, she had replaced the nonstop Irish-Celtic music with some lite FM that played in the background.

The two women were obviously actresses—Zev had learned to spot the signs. The redhead looked to be in her mid-thirties, in a sexy green, satin slip dress and heels. The other girl was a natural blonde about the same age who wore black leggings and a tight T-shirt. Mindy, the redhead, threw her arms around Tom's neck and said, "I haven't seen you since *Law & Order*," a TV show for which, the previous year, Tom had been cast in a recurring role as a cop. Mindy's companion was Jessie, a lawyer and childhood friend of Mindy's, who was in New York visiting for a few days.

An hour or two later, Zev found himself drunk, dancing to some inane pop song with Mindy.

The next morning, he woke up in a strange bedroom with a vague memory of some wild sex, though he could not exactly piece together the sequence of events. The bed was empty, but the green dress that the redhead had worn—he realized he couldn't remember her name—was draped over the bedpost. He pulled on his underwear and jeans and found his shirt and socks. Tom came into the doorway. "Got to go. Come on—"

Zev looked at him. "But—"

"They're at the gym . . . we'll see them later."

Zev followed him, pulling on a sweater as they walked.

Tom clapped him on the shoulder. "Now, let's get you some balm. I'm starved. My treat." As they walked to the Westway Diner where they often ate, they passed a street vendor selling *halal* food. "Unless you'd rather have that—"

Zev laughed as they entered the restaurant. It was a bright place with gleaming, bright linoleum floors, 1950s chrome trim, and leatherette booths. In the well-lit, revolving glass case near the entrance, huge elaborate pies beckoned. From the time Zev first saw these confectionaries, he'd felt there was finally a place to suit his size. They ate in contented silence until Tom said, "Wish me luck—I got an audition in two hours."

"Good luck."

"Do you think Heather saw me leave last night?"

Zev nodded. Tom buried his head in his hands. "What the fuck is wrong with me? She's the best woman I ever had."

Zev was quiet and concentrated on his pancakes.

"What should I do? Do you think flowers would work?"

Zev had no experience with this—in his world there was no courtship, no dating, and the rules were clear. In New York, everything seemed chaotic. The three of them shared the apartment, though Tom and Heather had slept in separate rooms since their breakup.

"I don't know, Tom. If you two were married, you would be committing adultery night after night, right in her face. How could she forgive that?"

Tom hung his head. "I guess we need to find a new bar." Zev was incredulous. A person had to work hard to miss that kind of a point.

Tom excused himself, and Zev checked his messages. Chaim

had called: "Your mother is sick. You should come home."

Tom rolled his eyes when Zev told him. "Don't fall for it. Remember we grew up a few miles apart in D.C. They suck you back in."

Zev saw for the first time in Tom a sudden seriousness, a striking depth. "Don't you feel you owe your mother?"

Tom looked bitter. "What? For bringing me into the world?"

"Yes. And for raising you . . ."

Tom nodded. "Yes, I do."

Zev was confused. "So, you wouldn't go back?"

Tom shook his head. "No."

Zev was shocked. Tom continued, "Who asks to be born? What's so great about life? Even if I get what I want, I'll age out, get fat, and end up playing character roles or villains. I'll fall in love with some girl and get married. Two years later I'll be bored and unhappy . . ." Tom's voice trailed off. A pretty, busty girl entered, looking lost. Tom flashed a sharklike grin at Zev. "Come on. New meat."

Tom finger combed his wavy hair and put on his best smile. "Don't. Go. Back." He left the table and the check, heading for his new prey.

Zev gazed out the window as he took out his wallet to pay. A white truck stopped outside the restaurant. Written on the side in black block letters was CHURCH OF GOD. The words seemed to scorch Zev's eyes. *Is this the way gentiles suffer? In this church that feels a lot like hell?* For the first time, he could understand why his father would want to learn his lessons in the *shul* from books—so much cleaner and neater than this mess called life.

CHAPTER 14

A WELL-CONNECTED CLIENT

ETWEEN THANKSGIVING AND NEW Year's, Sarah was so busy that she could usually outrun her sadness. There were cocktail parties, dinner fêtes, brunches, Christmas Day feasts, and New Year's Day celebrations. Santiago would come and assist so that she could prepare. He rarely spoke, except to ask a pertinent question, and he was eager to learn. The list of events was up on the whiteboard above her filing cabinet. There were fifteen jobs in the next ten days, including a New Year's Eve bash she did every year for a Jewish family on Park Avenue.

Santiago was late and came in apologetically, followed by Carlos. It was clear what had transpired. She sent Santiago on some errand. Carlos helped himself to coffee and a bagel.

"Do you have to fuck everything that moves?"

"As long as I can't be with you."

"Oh, please. It's not me. You just want what you can't have."

"No," Carlos said. "It's because you're my sister."

"Creep!" But she smiled. "No emotional drama until after the first—I need Santiago in mentally good shape. I have enough work for three people."

"That's what I wanted to talk to you about. I need a favor."

"You *shtup* my best helper, and you have the nerve to ask

for a favor?"

"You always said that you liked my *chutzpah.* I need you to take over my job for a couple of weeks."

"I am a freelance cook. I do not work for any one person, ever. You know that. And this is the middle of the busiest season—how can you even ask me?"

Carlos looked at her. "My mother is really sick, okay? You can cook ethnic, right? It's all veggies and rice—actually, she likes Indian and Thai. Breakfast is simple: steel-cut oats, raisins, semolina, and water. Sometimes pancakes. When she has a party, people stay over, then it's a spread—soy eggs, etcetera."

Sarah shook her head. "You have no mother. I have fifteen jobs coming up."

Carlos looked at her. "Maybe you can just do dinners. She entertains many diplomats and celebrities. The dinners are relaxed and informal."

"But I have already committed to my clients. Most of them are repeats. I can't just blow them off."

"Okay, but there's one dinner—on December fourteenth. Please, at least do that one. Please interview. She is having some heavy-duty politician, and it needs to be masterful."

Sarah checked the whiteboard and nodded. She was free.

"Okay, but just the fourteenth. What kind of food?"

"No idea."

"Okay, I'll go see your lady."

"Great—you're due in an hour and a half."

"Are you kidding me?"

"Why waste time? By the way, my mother really is sick. Otherwise do you really think I'd leave Laura in the lurch?"

While Sarah was adding the date to her cell-phone calendar, a message from Gwydion came in: *Last-minute cancellation— are you free at nine p.m. E.S.T. tonight?* She hesitated. Carlos saw the e-mail. "C'mon—you know you're available."

"Okay." She confirmed the session with Gwydion and changed into her interview pantsuit. She collected a few random menus and walked down East End Avenue so she could be near the river.

Laura lived in an elegant brownstone on Sutton Place. "Carlos said you look like me," she said as she opened the door of the building in a row of similar homes. "Come up to the parlor floor." It was true. Sarah felt as if she were looking into a mirror, except that Laura was Italian and at least twenty years older.

The hallway was magnificently Victorian in style, like something out of a movie, with wine-colored watered-silk wallpaper, a marble bureau, and a patterned carpet runner up the alabaster stairs. A mirror hung over her hall table, ornate and dripping with gilt. A set of caricatures of Oscar Wilde and George Bernard Shaw completed the sense of a past time. The parlor-floor landing grew into a set of lace-curtained French doors that opened onto a Victorian living-room set resting on a magnificent Oriental rug, which was wine with turquoise accents. A massive Victorian dining table with twelve chairs, six per side, stretched away, ending in a fabulous faux Chinese screen. Priceless Impressionist art covered the walls, and there was Greek pottery everywhere. Laura carefully picked up a pitcher and handed it to Sarah, who froze for a second before taking it. She realized it was covered with images of an orgy!

Laura laughed. "Yes, this piece is from Greece during the third century. They obviously had a lot of fun back then."

Sarah had dabbled with lesbian sex when younger and could tell Laura found her attractive. She swallowed. "Third century? And you have this stuff just lying around?"

"No," Laura said indignantly, "I use these every day. Otherwise, what's the point? Everything in here is antique—including me." She cackled and gave Sarah a sly wink. Sarah just smiled politely.

Laura wore a golden Om symbol around her neck. Her hair, the same shade as Sarah's, was cut shoulder-length. Laura was slender, perhaps an inch taller than Sarah. She wore an oversized white shirt tied at the waist over a man's white undershirt and expensive designer jeans.

There was a red string bracelet with charms attached. She caught Sarah staring at it. "Yes, this is a *Kabbalah* bracelet. Sarah Hirshbaum—Jewish, right? Do you cook kosher?"

Sarah nodded.

"What kind?"

"Mostly Ashkenazi—Eastern European."

"Know much about Sephardic kosher food?"

"A little. I've cooked plenty of Middle Eastern meals. I will definitely look into it. Are you—"

"No. Italian, Catholic. When I was in school, the nuns would tell you that if you touched yourself 'down there,' you were putting another nail in Jesus's coffin."

"Wow. That's pretty—"

"Yeah. So I take what's appealing from all the religions. In Kundalini, it's definitely the mantras, and in Islam, it's definitely the food. Especially Persian. Are you familiar?"

"Somewhat, from the Sephardic Jewish side."

"There's a lot of overlap. So, do you feel vengeful?'

"About what?"

"I mean, since you're Jewish, do you wish for revenge?"

Sarah laughed. "That's a waste of time. But you make me think of a great film—*Inglourious Basterds*—where they get all the Nazi bad guys and kill them in a movie theater. I admit that was kind of a satisfying fantasy. But that's all over. Ancient history."

"What about in the old movie, you know, *The Dead Zone*, where the shrink asks Christopher Walken, 'If you knew in advance that Hitler would be Hitler and you had a chance to kill him, would you have?' "

Laura certainly had a peculiar line of small talk. "Would I have escaped afterward?"

"No."

"Then, no. What about you?"

Laura agreed. "I enjoy living too much."

Laura walked her behind the Chinese screen into a sumptuous gourmet kitchen with a freestanding island and professional-quality appliances. It was like a movie set, but the butcher-block top of the island was pitted and covered with stains. "No, we don't use it for human sacrifices"—Laura smiled—"but one night a chef decided to show us how to 'correctly' butcher a side of beef, and the stains have never come out. So I'm having a dinner for eight on the fourteenth. I have very unusual friends. Attending this dinner will be a Persian diplomat. You might say I'm sleeping with the enemy, but you know the old maxim: *Keep your friends close and your enemies closer.*"

Sarah was overwhelmed but said only, "Persian food can be wonderful."

Laura looked pleased. "What would you cook?"

"Are you vegetarian?" Laura raised an eyebrow in response to Sarah's question. "I mean, after seeing butchering, it could turn you off."

Laura considered. "Good point! He is not vegetarian, but he's Muslim, so it would have to be *halal.* Is that similar to kosher?"

"In a way. What might be interesting would be to explore the overlap of Persian cuisine with Sephardic kosher food."

Laura nodded. "It just proves that we're all the same underneath. So, what might you cook?"

Sarah remembered something she had read, and she quoted it, not remembering the source. "Roast chicken, peppered rice, sausages, stuffed cucumbers, vermicelli with broken almonds, fritters, and almond cakes—and I would serve the roast chicken with rose petals." Sarah was surprised. The menu had come to her mind completely from that same inner voice that had revealed her true name was Judith. She felt the hair on her arms prickle.

"My guests will love everything you've mentioned, but skip the rose petals." Laura looked pleased. "Carlos told me you have fifteen events coming up and that they are loyal customers. It's quite simple—I will pay you triple for each of Carlos's jobs that you take over."

"I will have to think about it, but we're set for the fourteenth." Sarah was feeling smothered. She had never put all of her eggs in one basket . . . and what if Carlos's mother did not recover right away?

"If you are not going to take Carlos's job, please let him know." Laura led Sarah to an antique Victorian desk and took out an envelope. "Fine, here's three thousand dollars on account, plus five hundred dollars for shopping. Do you mind being paid in cash?" Laura's cell phone rang. "Excuse me." She walked out of earshot, took out her phone, and began talking in rapid-fire Italian. She then covered the phone and walked Sarah to the door. *"Ciao, bella,"* she said, kissing Sarah on both cheeks. "Please see yourself out." Sarah turned to go, and Laura said, "By the way, Ed can be a real shit, and you're just his type. I am sorry you were not warned, but I'm relieved you were not harmed. On the other hand, he keeps me young."

CHAPTER 15

LOVE IN THE REARVIEW MIRROR

HERE WAS A FREAK blizzard in late October. A mixture of snow and sleet coated the streets. The snow was coming down so hard that it was barely possible to see even five feet in front of you. The Jewish holidays had come and gone, without Zev setting foot in a *shul*. He fasted on *Yom Kippur* (the Day of Atonement) because the core of the holiday was the opportunity it presented to rectify one's sins against God. Traditionally, one made peace with his or her fellow man during the ten days leading up to the holiday. To this end, he had given out money to all who asked, as was the custom, and hoped that he was doing the right thing. However, on the day itself, one talked only to God. On the day of *Yom Kippur*, every Jew was allowed to speak to God. He had passed and yet had not been struck down.

Zev was driving a cab up Sixth Street and Eighth Avenue, bundled in a down parka and a navy knit watchman's cap pulled low on his forehead. A pretty red-haired woman in a pink beret and coat hailed him. She was with a tall man in a red parka who possessively had his arm around her and appeared to be pulling her in for a kiss. She in turn was clearly trying to avoid the embrace and opened the door of the cab quickly. The snow was coming down so heavily that the seat of the taxi became instantly wet.

"Hey, you can't keep the door of my cab open like that!"

"Okay—sorry!"

The woman pulled from the man sharply. "I gotta go. See you." She quickly climbed into the cab and slammed the door, leaving her companion standing there, befuddled. "Let's go," she said. Zev put the cab in gear and pulled away from the curb with as much speed as he could muster. A slippery mixture of snow, ice, and slush covered the ground, so he was able to drive only about ten miles an hour. They traveled a block or two in silence. "Thanks. I really didn't want to kiss that guy."

"Why? Because he's your husband?"

In the rearview mirror, Zev could see her smile. She pulled off her beret, revealing a mass of curly hair, and settled back in the seat. "Yeah, good one," she said cynically. "What are you doing out on an awful night like this?"

"Making a living. What about you?"

"Making a mistake."

What could Zev say to that? It occurred to him that maybe he was doing the same.

The cab skidded, but he was able to bring it under control. "I can't see a thing. Do you mind if I pull over and scrape the windshield?"

"Fine, but it won't help the tires."

There was a scraper in the trunk. Zev cleared the windshield and noticed that his fare had taken out a notebook and was writing something down. He got back in and started the cab. They moved off slowly up Eighth Avenue.

"What are you writing?" he asked.

"I'm a cook, and I had an idea for a new recipe while I was having drinks with that loser."

The reason that driving a cab had worked out so well was that, oddly, Zev and Tom resembled each other. Tom was also tall with dark hair, and both men had large, well-defined noses— Tom a Roman one, Zev a Semitic one. This enabled Zev to get away with driving the cab using Tom's identification, and every so often some drunk called him "Tom" and revealed a few un-wanted secrets. He stole a glance at his lonely passenger—she was very pretty.

For a moment, Zev felt content, and realized that he had been very fortunate. Presently it was as if he had walked out a door marked LIFE AS I KNEW IT and through another door marked THE LIFE I SHOULD HAVE HAD, in the blink of an I-beam. He smiled to himself at his humor. Here he was driving a cab in New York City with a beautiful young woman in the backseat. The moment formed into a memory he knew he would call upon in future moments of despair.

"What's funny, Tom?" she said, breaking in on his reverie. He longed to ask her if she had ever had an experience like this one.

They pulled up to a red light. He turned on the radio, and a tune by Madonna came on.

God?
Life is a mystery
Everyone must stand alone
I hear you call my name
And it feels like . . . home
When you call my name
It's like a little prayer . . .

Zev's passenger sang the words softly, sounding like an angel, and Zev found himself humming along with her. The light changed, and they drove through the white darkness singing, Zev fumbling some of the lyrics he didn't know. When the song ended, she laughed. "Do you like Madonna?"

"Yes, sometimes."

"Me too. But I just love that tune—it's a disco hymn."

"Really?"

"Yeah, think about it. The first word was 'God,' question mark, as if she is talking directly to Him."

Zev inwardly squirmed.

"You know she's into *Kabbalah*? That's a Jewish thing."

Jewish thing? Was he not . . . he realized she thought he was

Tom Dooley, and hence Catholic. "Yes, I've heard that. Are you into *Kabbalah*?"

She laughed. "No, but at least I'm Jewish."

He decided to play dumb. "Oh, yeah, didn't you celebrate your New Year's recently?"

"Yes."

"Make any resolutions?" She met his eyes in the rearview mirror. They were intense and serious.

"Oh, you mean like regular New Year. No, the Jewish New Year is about making peace with people, and then making peace with God, who will forgive all of your"—she made quote marks in the air with her long, slim fingers, one of which had a Band-Aid taped around it—"sins, but only the ones against Him."

"Wow," he said. "That's cool. Did you commit any biggies?"

She was silent, and he saw something dark flash through her eyes. The cab skidded again, and he turned his attention to getting them back on track. "What do you define as a sin?" she asked seriously. It was a great question.

He was about to quote from the Talmud but remembered he was channeling Tom, who would no doubt say that *any* missed chance to bed a beautiful woman *was* a sin. Heather had once asked Zev about the Jewish definition of sin versus her traditional Catholic one. According to Heather, Catholicism viewed sin as "committing wrong against God's law," so Zev parroted her words now.

"Oh, that's the classic Catholic definition. It would work for me if I could be sure those laws were God's laws and not some man trying to get control so he can charge a toll to get into heaven."

Zev stopped at another red light and turned to look at her briefly. She was frowning. "Tom, so, if we don't believe in God at all, then there is no law, so we can't sin, isn't that right?"

Zev swallowed hard, for she had touched a raw nerve. "I don't think it's that easy." He turned back around as the light changed. He reached 34th Street. "Where are you going again?"

"Seventy-seventh and First."

He took a right on 34th because it was a main thoroughfare and seemed less slippery, but he was still crawling along at ten miles an hour. The definition of sin that he understood was that there were three types: *pesha*, doing something in deliberate defiance of God, *avon*, doing something knowing it is wrong but not in defiance of God, and lastly, *chet*, something done unintentionally.

"So, did you do any biggies?" He was dying to know.

"Yes. You're Catholic, right?" She leaned forward earnestly and attempted to slide back the Plexiglas partition. She giggled, saying, "I've had too much to drink," and gave up.

"Right." As he rolled slowly down 34th, he was able to deftly reach back and slide open the partition.

"So, you can go to confession and repent," she sighed, "but we Jews can never be absolved." She sat back dejected and gnawed on a cuticle. "No, no point in boring you with my secrets. No point in trying to get you to hear my confession."

"You want me to act as your priest?" He felt suddenly as if he had drunk too much wine himself and shook his head to clear it. The cab skidded a third time, and Zev realized he had better focus on his job.

She sighed again and said, "I would, but it won't do any good."

He smiled—he liked this drunk Jewish girl. He did a passable imitation of an Irish priest that he'd learned from Tom, who could imitate anyone.

"Oh, and to be sure, a nice girl will benefit from a clear conscience. Confession is good for the soul."

She pondered this, and they drove in silence until, without warning, they were almost blindsided by a giant SUV that came careening toward them, wheels spinning, from the oncoming lanes. Zev veered sharply right, skidding toward the curb, and missed being hit by inches. The SUV whipped across the pavement and crashed into the plate-glass window of a clothing shop with enough force to shatter it, causing the store's burglar alarm to wail. The driver's door opened, and a black man dressed in high hip-hop-style clothing stepped out.

"Yikes! That was a narrow escape!" the redheaded woman said.

"No kidding!" said Zev. "Seems like I've had a few of those lately."

Zev stopped the cab and called out, "Hey! Are you okay?" The man, who was already on his cell phone, nodded and gave Zev the thumbs-up. Zev looked around at his passenger, who had a frightened look in her eyes. "You okay?"

She nodded ominously. "Good save. If he had hit us—"

"But he didn't."

"That was a miracle."

"Luck."

"Well, whatever it was, it has inspired me to confess, just in case I can get absolution." Zev registered that she was flirting with him, or rather with Tom.

"What do Jews get instead of forgiveness?" Zev couldn't wait to hear what she would say.

"You wouldn't want to trade for it. No forgiveness for sins, no afterlife, no freedom—though that's changed somewhat. We get a punishing God who judges—and terrible misogyny against women! Did you know a woman cannot be considered a first-born? Horrible! Being a Jewish woman is a lose-or-lose-big situation!"

He heard real anger in her voice. *Prejudice against women?*

"I thought women were considered better than men in your faith?"

She laughed bitterly. "*Ha!* Don't you see how condescending that is? It's the same damn thing in the yoga I study. Yogi Bhajan says we're better, but he is patronizing us, just like in Judaism."

"How can such recognition be patronizing?"

"Oh, c'mon! All right—then how about this? When I was about five or six, I overheard my grandfather—who was Ortho-dox—saying his morning prayers. I used to peek through the keyhole. I loved to watch him wrap the straps of the phylacter-ies around his arms and head. Anyhow, as he prayed, he said aloud—and in English—'Thank You for not making me a woman.' I was shocked—horrified! Why would a man thank God for that, unless it meant women were something less? Understand, I loved my grandfather and recognized he was a man of true faith. So when he came out I asked him, 'Grandpa, why did you thank God for not making you a woman?' "

"And what did he say?"

"He lied to me. He said, 'No, you don't understand—I was thanking God for sparing me the pain of childbirth.' "

"That sounds reasonable."

"But he was lying. I could see it in his eyes. He was lying! So I insisted, 'But Grandpa, you didn't say that. You said, *For not making me a woman*. And he belittled me, saying, 'It's not what you think.' So I persisted. I said, 'But wouldn't the greatest power be to actually be able to have children? You fight wars—which hurts more than having a baby, doesn't it? Why did you thank God? What's wrong with women?' "

"So what was his answer?"

"He had no answer. He gave me an angry look, called me a silly child, and disappeared. I remember feeling ashamed for no reason, like I was being greedy or something. Then I tried to pray to a woman God but realized that if I prayed to Her, it wasn't a true deity that everyone else acknowledged, which was how I understood God. So if God made men 'in His image' and Grandpa was a true believer, then God obviously thought less of women—He was certainly not androgynous, but male only. So how could I have faith?"

"It upset you that much?"

"Of course! I was already aware that because of my gender I was expected to sit with the women and children. But what I wanted to do was *kibitz* with the men and hear about business and important things."

"You don't think what the women and children talked about was also important?"

"No, because the men thought it wasn't. I could tell by the way they talked to their wives—horrible! Nothing I ever wanted.

They saw the women as broodmares. There's an old off-color joke about how the perfect woman has a flat head and no legs—the men see them as objects there to serve."

"All of them? And you were how old?"

"Mostly, yes. And I was six."

"I bet you were a cute little tomboy."

The woman was incensed. "I was not! I was always interested in cooking. I liked being feminine. I just couldn't tolerate the male attitude. And if God were male and we were made in His image, I believed that He would naturally prefer those that were male like Him. It made sense in a way, but I was still pissed off about it."

"Did you wish you were male then?"

"No—what? So I could get into fights, play football, abuse women, go to war, and be a civil engineer? No way, I just wanted men and women to have equal status. Different but equal. I was very angry with God. If He'd been female, none of this would have happened."

They were almost at First Avenue. The slushy snow was still pouring out of the sky.

"And now?"

She shrugged. "That's what I get for drinking! Babble, babble. Look, I think it's clear." Zev turned onto the avenue, which the plows had mercifully cleared.

She'd given him a lot to consider. He revved up the engine, and they resumed driving up First. They rumbled past 60th, seventeen blocks to go.

"So, if God were female, there wouldn't be wars?"

She responded vigorously, "Absolutely. Women might do other bad stuff, but since we give birth to things, I don't think killing is our first impulse."

Zev had never really contemplated any of this, while she clearly had given all of it a great deal of thought. He wanted to talk more. Maybe she really knew something—could teach him a thing or two. Knowing such a woman would be interesting.

"So, what's the sin you needed to confess?"

They were approaching her destination, and before they parted he was eager to learn about this egregious thing that she'd done.

"Okay, here goes: When I was bat mitzvahed—that's like a Catholic confirmation except that you give a speech about what you are going to do now that you have become a grownup, thirteen is the cutoff age—anyway, when I gave my speech, part of what I said was now that I was a woman, I could choose how to conduct my religious life, and that I would please myself."

"And?"

"And I never went back to *shul*—you know, church."

"Wow. Why not?"

"I guess I'd lost my faith because I had no respect for a god who could create such inequality and suffering. The saddest part was that I didn't even know I'd lost it."

"That *is* sad," Zev said, in shock. They were soulmates, *bashert*, destined to be together, but he had already lied to her. "So, your sin is that you no longer believe in God. Can't you go to confession for that?"

"No, it's that I *do* believe in Him, but I think He's an ignorant jerk. My sin is that, just like our current president, I believe that the whole shebang is being run by a hypocritical loser, but He's the only game in town."

Zev had never heard anyone talk about God with such familiarity and so much fury.

"So, it's your attitude that's a sin?"

"Right. I'm a Jew, so I have to behave properly. That's what that 'chosen people' stuff is all about. Not that you get extra perks, but rather you must set the standard for moral behavior on the planet. So my sin is in my thoughts."

"And do you behave properly?" He hoped the answer would be *no*.

"Sadly, yes."

Sadly, indeed.

"Sadly?"

"It's not fun."

Zev longed to drop the charade and tell her about losing his Hebrew and Yiddish, but he couldn't blow his cover. Playing dumb suddenly wasn't quite as much fun as he'd expected. He suppressed the thought and made a silent resolution: *This year I will relearn my languages.* As if clairvoyant, the woman lunged, her face near the perforated plastic divider, and said excitedly, "That's it! I'll make that my Jewish New Year's resolution. I will get my faith back! Brilliant! Thank you!"

They were approaching her destination, a huge building on the Upper East Side of Manhattan. He pulled up to the fancy building on East 77th Street that was barely visible through the blinding snow illuminated brightly in glowing streetlamps, thinking, as he slowed, of the Hell's Kitchen bachelor pad he shared with Tom. He rolled the cab as close to the curb as he could to let her out and, with one hand on the wheel, turned to her in the backseat.

"How will you find your faith?" he asked.

"I don't know, but it's a worthwhile goal, don't you think? Thank you again."

She fumbled with her purse, looking for her wallet. Zev saw his window of opportunity quickly closing.

"I, I never do this . . . but do you suppose we might have coffee sometime? I'm new in town and . . ."

She stopped fumbling, looked up, and smiled, seeming surprised but not offended.

"Why not, Tom Dooley?"

Immediately he was horrified to remember how he had initially offended Rachel by pretending to be someone else—now he'd done it again. He feared that he could never call her now.

"Here's my card," she said, and she handed it through the Plexiglas partition. Zev read it aloud, "Sarah Hirshbaum, Executive Chef."

She tried to open the door of the cab, but it was stuck. "Can you believe this blizzard happening in October? The weather has gone mad."

"Here, let me!" Zev jumped at the opportunity for chivalry,

muscled the driver-side door open, and dashed around curb-side. He pounded the slippery door handle with a cold bare fist, sending shards of ice flying, then wrenched open the door for her. She got out and slipped on the icy ground. She grabbed Zev to break her fall, and he succeeded in wrapping one arm around her waist and another under her knees, breaking the momentum. For a moment, they were very close. Even in the swirling winds of the blizzard, her perfume was memorable and intoxicating. She extricated herself gently and hurried off.

Zev waved weakly, but she hustled into the building without a backward glance. He sighed, standing there collecting snow. He was smitten and impressed. Here was a woman who dared to be angry with God!

CHAPTER 16

MEETING WITH THE MENTOR

O LAURA KNEW ABOUT Hirsch—and hadn't told Carlos. She had sent Sarah into the lion's den without a shield. But three thousand dollars in cash was a good beginning. *Chicken with rose petals?* Still curious about where exactly that idea had come from, Sarah was nevertheless relieved that she wouldn't have to run around the city looking for edible rose petals, since Laura didn't want them. And Laura had offered Sarah triple what she was paying Carlos. Tempting for the moment, but the clients you keep are the future.

Sarah was too tired to go to class and worried about the time. She changed into white yoga clothes and did a little breath of fire and a meditation. Her timer went off—it was time to call Gwydion.

"Hello, is this Sarah?" She was struck by just how thick his accent was, like a drunk John Lennon. "Let me put the tape on." There were a series of clicks, then Gwydion cleared his throat and began. "The way this works is this: Everyone's got guides watching over them. They talk to me, and I talk to you. See this as an opportunity to talk to your guides. Are you ready?"

"Yes."

"The first thing they want to do is to clarify one or two recent experiences. There's a reason why past-life memories are blocked. Too often the past lives have been difficult or have borne witness to horrifying circumstances. If those memories were allowed to intrude on the current life one is living, the impact would be significant. For example, those who were cruelly treated in one or more previous lives might seek retribution against those who had inflicted misery upon them in times past. This would serve no valuable purpose, but indeed would only serve to visit upon the present life the same drama over again, creating a recurring cycle of suffering. It is for this reason that most people's memories are severely repressed. However, from time to time, certain objects, people, or, oddly, even smells can trigger those repressed memories to resurface, and in your case this has recently occurred. You have recently learned that you were once a renowned biblical figure, and we can assure you that, in spite of academic doubt surrounding her story, she did in fact live and act as the story reveals.

"What is not written was that she was an acclaimed cook, and it was more than cheese and wine that conquered the general in question. Do not hold on to the memory. We are fine if you want to acknowledge your experience, but do not delve into the details, because nothing valuable can come out of waking up those memories. Take two important things that relate to your soul's identity: Your faith has always been Judaic, and you have always been an artist, whether with food or with paint. The intellect you possess you have always possessed, and the truth you seek is nearer to being revealed than it has been in any other lifetime. Yet, in the end, the truth reveals itself whether we search for it or not. One of those truths is that life, under all circumstances, goes on. Another is that each lifespan is an opportunity to enhance, strengthen, and enlighten the soul's identity. Greater importance should be placed on the life one has rather than on any other existences she has had. You have been allowed to become reacquainted with a former identity so that you can find the courage to act appropriately in this one. In many lifetimes since that first one, your soul has shied away from conflict and failed to achieve its purpose. We are hoping that you will find a role model in this former self and complete the pattern of your soul's journey so that you can return home. This separation and endless wandering of the earth is why you suffer the way you do.

"In your case, however, if I may reiterate, you are being re-acquainted with a former self so that you can find the courage to act accordingly when the occasion presents itself." There was a pause.

Gwydion took a breath. "Questions?"

"How could you have known about Judith?"

"Who do you think that voice was?"

"And the menu for Laura?"

"Also the guides. As I said, everyone has guides from the other side who watch over them."

"Dead people."

"In fact, yes, and I'm like the guy in that movie *The Adjustment Bureau*, or the kid in *The Sixth Sense*."

"So, was Judith talking to me?"

"No, you were Judith. The one who's talking to you is your guide."

"So, not you?"

"No."

"So, does this guide have a name?"

"Yes, but that's not important."

"I'm receiving divine information from someone who's dead with no name?"

"No. He's a high angel, and if you must give him a human name, you can call him *Abe*."

"An angel, huh?"

"What's your question?"

Sarah found herself unable to talk because of the sobs that now blocked her throat. Gwydion's tone was suddenly kind.

"Your tears are about the separation from God. Those of us who do remember know that where we came from is paradise, and we want to go back where we are one with Him."

Sarah's tears spilled over, and she couldn't stop them. "I'm . . . sorry," she managed to blurt out in a moment of calm.

"Breathe deep, and let's count slowly back from ten to one. Ten, nine . . ."

They counted together, and by the time they reached one, Sarah had regained her composure.

"This will be a critical year in your life. You have been offered a job as a cook, an unusual one by your standards, and you will take it."

"But I could lose my business."

"Accept the three soonest jobs, call the others, and tell them that there has been a family emergency, and they will accept that."

"What is it I will be asked to do?"

"Deflect the intention of an antichrist."

Sarah laughed, ignoring the urgency in Gwydion's voice. "You're not serious! What could I possibly have to do with such an immense task?"

Gwydion said, "You feel that life is meaningless—a computer game for some bored deity. But it's not so. The guide feels that you are making a choice to be unhappy. Your soul does not delight in the ordinary but longs to bristle with purpose. You feel you must earn your way back to God."

Sarah felt hugely relieved but also confused. How could this man, whom she had never met, know her so well? How could he—and these "guides" he spoke of—know about what had happened on the yoga mat?

"As for your marriage," Gwydion continued, "we needed you to feel the possibility of happiness in the shared life. You did have some solid period of contentment. You were never at fault. It was just that your destinies led you in opposite directions."

"Why didn't you tell me it would end?"

"Would you have married him?"

"Fair enough. So, will I find love again?"

"Sooner than you think."

"If I take on this job with Laura, and risk losing half my clients, what will I get?"

"The chance of a lifetime."

"Now you sound like an ad for the New York Lottery. And what if I don't?"

Gwydion said, "There is destiny and also free will. Whatever you choose will be good. But we understand the deep sorrow you experience and invite you to take a chance to remove it, once and for all."

"How will cooking for Laura cure my sadness?"

Gwydion was quiet. Sarah continued, "If I have free will, why are you telling me one choice is better than the other?"

"I never said that decisions were equal or unequal—just different."

"Point taken. So, cooking for Laura is a better choice?"

Gwydion didn't answer directly but said instead, "Your guide wants you to know that your life will very soon change for the better, and you need to be prepared for something sudden. I will put the tape in the mail to you tomorrow. Please listen to it when you receive it. What is your address? And please give me a phone number for the courier company."

She gave him all the information he requested but felt like saying, *I thought you were psychic—shouldn't you know where to send it?*

"Thank you, and I'm sorry, but your time is about up. Do you have one last question?"

"Does God exist?"

"Silly girl, you talk to Him all the time. How can you hate something that doesn't exist?"

In spite of herself, she smiled. "Is my guide God?"

"Let's just say he has God's ear but is not God. As I suggested in the beginning, don't delve too deeply. Take it on face value to help you make sound decisions in your life. Bye for now."

"Bye for now," she echoed as the line went dead. Once again, she felt alone. It was strange, but while she'd been talking to Gwydion, she felt a sense of connectivity that was sweet and reassuring.

She went across the hall and banged on Carlos's door. Better find out what she might be getting into. Carlos appeared wearing nothing but an apron. He obviously was expecting someone else and held up his hand. "Wait." After a moment, the door to his dimly lit bachelor pad opened completely. He had added jeans and a T-shirt. "Come in."

CHAPTER 17

SEX, WHEELS, AND STREETS

om and Zev each drove a twelve-hour shift. When they met at the garage, Tom got out of the cab and said, "I'm done! All yours. What about your mom?"

Zev struggled. "She's never been sick before."

"Really? What convenient timing. Is it near some Jewish holiday or something?" Tom's cynicism seethed—Zev could feel it like heat radiating from a furnace.

He imagined his mother, wrapped in her flowered housecoat, lying in bed sneezing.

"No."

While waiting to gas up the cab, Zev's buddy, a tall Nigerian named Taibo, got out of his own cab and said, "Be on the lookout, man. The cops are on the warpath. Must be quota. Be careful where you drive."

"*It's a great day for love . . . ,*" Taibo sang suddenly in a startlingly beautiful baritone, and ended with a series of operatic trills that were clearly expert. "Wish me luck. I have an audition for a show today."

"Good luck," said Zev.

Taibo shook his head. "No, seriously, man, you're supposed to tell me to break a leg."

"Break a leg."

"How do you say that in Yiddish?"

Zev shrugged and smiled. He had no idea. It was gone. *Finito*—finished—gone. Not one word left in his memory!

∰

Zev's shift went well—five airport runs—no need to hit his savings this week. Then, on Eighth Avenue, he saw a woman in a dark-green coat cross the street quickly. His heart raced— she looked like she might be the redhead who had been in his cab that snowy night. As he pulled up to a red light, the woman crossed in front of his taxi and walked briskly into Central Park. To his own surprise, Zev followed her and turned into the park. It was empty—lucky him. He was able to follow her from a distance. She looked lovely.

Then, suddenly, there were flashing lights, and the park police stopped him.

"Don't you know the park is closed?"

He shuddered. If this guy checked his license and ID, it would take some explaining. "Sorry, officer, I didn't realize . . ."

He saw the woman cross and head toward the 86th Street exit. Dismay settled over him—he would lose sight of her. Why had he followed her at all? It was a stupid impulse—there had been no click or spark between them—but her intelligent angst had kindled something in Zev. The park cop was a pale, freckled redhead with crafty blue eyes and rimless spectacles.

"I'm sorry. I'm a new driver. I didn't know."

The park cop stared at him with snake eyes, but before he could speak, a white truck with CHURCH OF GOD written on the side sped past. The cop turned and saw it, then said hurriedly, "Your lucky day—drive out through the 86th Street exit. And don't let me catch you again."

The cop jumped into his car and sped off after the truck. Zev sighed in relief and drove away. He would have to be more careful, but his impulse had surprised him. As he pulled up at the traffic light at the edge of the park, he thought he saw her pink beret, but the light changed green. As he turned south on Central Park West, there was no sign of her. He felt the familiar ache of loneliness grip his heart. He was alone here in this great city, with no one to love.

He picked up a fare to the airport and drove, his mind blank. It was a Friday, four P.M. In his world back home, his mother normally would be in the kitchen frantically cooking in order to get everything done in time for *Shabbos*.

But if she were sick, who would cook the *Shabbos* meal? He imagined his house cold and empty. He got a lump in his throat, and bitter tears rushed to the corners of his eyes—which he pushed away. The rabbi had negotiated a deal and Chaim had consented to let Zev leave the community, provided he kept the *kashrut* laws. Another condition was Zev agreeing to attend *shul*. Back when he was putting his bag into his car preparing to come to New York, his father had said, "Repeat your vow that you will go to *shul*."

Zev had looked away and said, "I promise," not meaning it.

"Observing *kashrut* is a display of self-discipline as much as piety. To abandon religion is to abandon self-discipline." Chaim's voice was stern.

Zev suddenly felt like a small boy, full of unexpressed rage. He took a breath and decided to try to connect with his father one last time—there was nothing to lose.

"Dad," he said, turning to face him squarely. "Dad, I was almost killed by that falling steel beam. Then I . . ." His voice trailed off. He was going to tell him about saving Aaron, but it would be much more than his father could have handled.

"But you were spared—that should confirm your faith." Zev felt himself get angry. As usual, just when he thought he was making headway, his father changed the game. They had gone from going to *shul* to faith.

"What does observing Jewish law have to do with having faith?"

His father's face flushed red with anger, and he shouted in a stream of incomprehensible Yiddish. When this subsided, Zev said calmly, "In English, please. In case you haven't noticed, we've been in America for quite a while."

"Don't be a smart aleck! Going to *shul* and the other duties are a way of tending the garden of your faith."

The garden of my faith? Typical to use some ridiculous metaphor to talk about something that should be concrete. But as Zev thought about it now, he had promised to go to *shul,* and what with his mother being ill, he had an impulse to follow through on his promise.

He drove past a synagogue and stopped the cab. It was a rather grand house of worship, a lot like a church or cathedral. He sat outside for a while, then drove off. He felt lonely and called Rachel. She was delighted to hear from him, and, surprisingly, he felt a rush of warmth toward her.

"How's Aaron?" were his first words.

"He's fine," she said. "He's right here—one moment, I'll put him on." Aaron grabbed the phone.

"Hi, Zev!"

"Hi, little buddy! I miss you." Where had those words come from? He somehow felt *Zayde* Hal near him.

"Mom got me a book on arch . . . arch-it . . ."

"You mean architecture?"

"Yeah. I want to build buildings when I grow up."

"That's good—what would you build first?"

"Mom says you are Jewish. I want to make you a church."

"You mean a synagogue. A *shul*. It's different than your church."

"Okay. How? Does God come into a *shul* too?"

"Yes."

"How can God be in two places at once?"

Zev thought about that question and rued the fact that he had no immediate idea how to answer it. "Maybe He moves really fast."

"Like a hip-hop dancer?" Aaron giggled, amused at the idea of God as a break dancer, and Zev chuckled imagining the look on his own father's scandalized face at such an idea. "I want to come and visit you and see the Knicks," Aaron continued.

"We'll see. Maybe once I'm settled here."

"Okay. Mom wants to talk to you."

"Hi, Rachel. How are things? Any more stuff with Frank?"

"There is and will always be stuff."

"And for you too?"

Rachel said quietly, "Yes, for me too." There was a pause, then she continued. "Did I do something wrong?"

"No." He heard the lie in his own voice, and she did too. His head hurt. "Rachel."

"What is it, Zev? What's wrong?"

"I think I need guidance."

"Why?"

"I don't feel connected to anything."

"Maybe you're just homesick."

He shook his head. "I feel like in some weird way maybe I did die."

"What, what are you talking about?"

"Oh. Shortly before I met you, I was almost killed on my way to work. A steel beam almost hit me."

"You were lucky."

"Was I? At first, I thought so. Now I seem to have lost any sense of direction."

"But you're a hero! You saved Aaron's life."

"What does that have to do with anything?"

Rachel was silent. Then finally she said, "I read somewhere in your religion there's some saying about how if you save the one, you save the many."

"And?"

"You are so bitter. I thought you were a religious Jew."

"Not anymore. Now I'm a New York City cabdriver."

"What do you want?"

"That's my point. I have no idea. I got sideswiped last night."

"What?"

He recounted how he'd picked up a fare at Columbus Circle, a couple fighting about some transgression committed at the party from which they had just departed. A huge truck had tried to turn, smashing Zev's mirror on the passenger side.

"I got my first lesson in handling such things—the guy gave me cash to fix the mirror and claimed that if we called the cops we'd both have more trouble than either one of us needed. I mean, I was driving on Tom's hack license, for God's sake! But I worried that Tom's cab could be really damaged."

"What did Tom say?"

"Haven't told him. I'm just gonna get the mirror fixed quickly."

"Give it a little time, maybe. Aren't you having fun up there?"

He was, but it didn't matter.

There was a pause.

"Aaron wants to say goodbye."

Zev smiled.

"Hi, Zev! Bye, Zev! See you later, alligator!" Aaron laughed.

"Bye."

The image of Aaron about to hang himself came into Zev's mind. He understood Aaron—the wish, the hope that somehow his father would always be there waiting.

Zev hung up, feeling empty. He realized he should get back to work.

He stopped at a red light. He was suddenly a small boy again in his toy car. His parents were arguing in Yiddish. Somehow, he understood them.

"If you really loved me, you'd give me another child," Chaim said.

"I've done my duty to God and given you a son," Ruth retorted. "I almost died having him. What part of that don't you understand? If you really loved me, you wouldn't ask me to put my life at risk."

There was a slap, and tears. The sound of a bedroom door slamming, then the front door doing the same.

Zev had never felt loved and welcomed the way other children did. Perhaps that's why he never married. He remembered one day when he was about twelve coming home from school.

The teacher had excused them early. When he walked in, he heard his mother upstairs, crying. He knocked on the bedroom door and entered. Ruth was curled up in a chair, her ritual wig off, hair cascading down her back, clutching a teddy bear. He stood in the doorway for perhaps a minute and got tears watching her. Finally, she looked up and saw him and spoke sharply in Yiddish. "Zev! You are home early. Go downstairs. Make yourself a snack. There's rye bread and butter." He moved toward her to comfort her, but she held up a hand sharply, palm facing him. "No." Zev felt something inside him shrivel.

The blare of a car horn yanked him back—the light had changed. Another fare beckoned, a tall man in an overcoat talking heatedly on his cell phone. He wanted a hotel in Midtown.

Zev felt shaky. His mother was sick and aching for him. Was Tom right? If he went back, would he be reabsorbed? Would they suck him back in? Nevertheless, he was concerned—at that moment, he realized he'd been operating on automatic pilot.

Better focus. Zev drove the next fare—a large, officious woman in a fur coat bearing a lot of luggage—to the airport. Tom was always marveling at how Zev seemed to know the city as if he'd lived there before. "You been here in another life. Maybe you were a mayor—or a wino!"

Zev had laughed. "Do you believe in that—reincarnation, I mean?"

"I have to believe the next life will be better. Maybe I'll have my own television series."

"I remember Heather saying that you had to go to Los Angeles if you wanted that sort of work."

Tom had shrugged listlessly and stared into his beer. "Can't afford it yet," he mumbled, closing the conversation.

Jews didn't believe in an afterlife. They conceded that you die, and later, when the Messiah comes, if you've been good, you will be resurrected. Zev was pessimistic about his chances of being part of that particular "in crowd"—at least reincarnation as a concept was comforting! Not only did you get endless chances to be alive, you could take as long as you wanted to learn, and that seemed to be at the core of reincarnation—that earth was some kind of school and each round a lesson.

"Then how come everyone is always reincarnated as Nefertiti or some king?" Zev had asked Tom.

"That's easy," Tom had replied. "It's like in acting: You might be in one hundred plays, but you only remember the ones where you played major roles."

If Zev was in a play, and there was a lesson he was supposed to learn, what was it? He had looked at Tom doubtfully, but Tom had abruptly raised his glass and said, "You'll remember this one, buddy. It's not everyone who saves a kid! That will earn you a place in heaven for sure!" Tom had clinked his glass against Zev's.

A place in heaven? Such a gentile concept. Thinking about all of this made Zev dizzy.

His cell phone rang. It was Tom. He was drunk.

"I am at the bar with a pair of prize pheasants trussed and ready to go." Zev wondered if pheasants were kosher, then lit up at the idea of creamy gentile skin and light hair.

He checked to see if he'd made his "dollar," and he'd done well. So he went to meet Tom at the tavern. Tom was at the far end, working behind the bar, as he often subbed for Heather. The two ladies in question appeared to be in their twenties— newbies to the city from Des Moines. As Zev walked in, he could hear Tom pontificating, as usual. Zev could see from the doorway these girls—no, women—were on the hook. They giggled when they saw Zev, and chuckled even more when Tom made a lewd gesture demonstrating the extra-large adornment Zev possessed. One of the girls, a curly-haired brunette, smiled at him as he bellied up to the bar.

Melanie was a beautiful girl with freckles and eyes that seemed to change color in the light. It took the rest of the evening to get them into bed.

CHAPTER 18

You Can't Go Home Again, Again

nce again, Zev awoke in a strange bed, alone. He dressed quickly and left. Despair filled his throat until he felt he would choke on it. Loneliness consumed him.

Zev went to Penn Station, got on a train for Washington, and got right back off. He realized that "home" was no longer a place he knew. He called Ruth knowing that his father wouldn't answer. She did, going on in Yiddish. She wasn't sick—Tom was right.

"Mama, speak English." But she argued with him. He still didn't want to tell her he didn't understand.

"When are you coming home?"

"I don't know, I don't know."

"Are you eating?"

"Yes, I am. And sleeping well."

"It's been too long. Enough already."

"I don't want to argue."

"Rivka has come by several times. She was in tears. She said you wrote her a nasty letter."

"It wasn't nasty—I just want her to find someone else so she can be happy."

There was a pause. His mother coughed—a deep, phlegm-riddled bronchial hack, or so it sounded to Zev.

"Are you okay, Mom?"

"What do you care?" she cried. Through the tears, she added, "Your father is frantic. I've never seen him like this. You have shamed him in the eyes of the community."

Zev felt a cold rage freeze his heart.

"You can't measure yourself by other people."

"Easy for you to say."

She was right. "I'm sorry, Mom. What's wrong with you?"

She launched into Yiddish again. He couldn't understand a word.

"English. Is it bad?"

"No, just a chest cold," she sighed.

"Okay."

There was an awkward silence.

"I'm worried about you, Zevelah."

"Don't be. I am finding my way."

There was more silence.

"Zev, call me, okay? Just to let me know you are fine. You're in my prayers."

On cue, a lump big enough to make him cough filled his throat. "I love you," he said, and hung up. The worst part was that he knew he no longer did.

CHAPTER 19

How Can You Be Sure?

ZEV ASKED HIMSELF ALOUD, "I was spared death, and then I saved Aaron. What am I to make of all this?" Of course, there was no answer. He sighed.

Ask Heather, that was the answer. She seemed to be wise. He would go after his shift, which was unremarkable except for getting a bit lost out in the nether regions of Brooklyn in a place called Brighton Beach. By the time he got back, the bar was winding down.

Heather came over. "*Shalom*, sweetie. Have a drink?"

He smiled. "Can I buy *you* a drink?"

Heather looked around, saw everyone was temporarily at peace, and poured herself a shot of Jack. They clinked and drank.

"Thank you. How do you say that in Hebrew?"

"I don't know."

"I thought you religious types spoke the language . . ."

Zev shrugged. "Part of a long story. Question for you: Do you believe in God?"

Heather nodded.

"Do you pray to Him or Her?"

"Yes."

"Do you get answers?"

She laughed. "No, for that I go to Gwydion."

Zev frowned, confused. "Who?"

"Gwydion, the psychic. He's in some remote place in the U.K. You call him, he tells you the answers and more."

"Is he accurate? How does it work?"

Heather responded, "Really accurate. Scary accurate. It's a hundred dollars. Then you get a special message and you can ask questions. He'll send you a tape of the session as well."

Zev nodded. "So you pray to God, but you talk to some guy in England for answers?"

Heather nodded and gave Zev Gwydion's e-mail address. "Do it now," she said, and turned to serve another customer.

Zev considered how blasphemous this would be, and went to the men's room. When he returned to the bar, a big, bearded guy in a cowboy hat was hitting on Heather. Zev sensed something was wrong. As he approached the bar, Heather saw him and gave him a relieved *I am so glad you're here* look.

Zev leaned on the bar. The cowboy was about Zev's height, but burly. He was gripping Heather's forearm.

"Take your hand off her." Heather tried to pull her hand away.

"Hey, Zev, what'll it—"

The cowboy hauled off and slammed him in the jaw with his fist. Zev staggered back, stunned, and stumbled but did not fall. Before he could think, Zev punched the cowboy, knocking him to the floor.

"Call the cops!" Zev said.

But Heather shouted, "No! No police! No one saw anything. Drinks on the house!"

Tito, the barback, appeared and escorted Zev to the back office, which he'd never seen before. Heather came in with an ice pack and a big glass of whiskey. She said, "Tom's here, thank God."

Zev felt frozen, unable to say a word. Heather told him he had a black eye coming. "Thank you so much," she said, clearly unnerved. "You were wonderful!"

"Who the hell is he?" Zev managed through a heavy tongue

and swollen lip.

Heather sat down heavily. "My ex-husband. I don't like to talk about him too much. We had a child. She died. SIDS. He blamed me, he left me. I haven't seen that SOB since I can't remember when. He must have thought you were my boyfriend or something."

"What did he want?"

"Oh, the usual—money. He shows up every so often—he's a carpenter, a nomad. The death broke his heart . . ."

"What about you?"

Heather's eyes teared up, and she shrugged. "Lucy. Her name was Lucy." She picked up a little stuffed bear that was sitting prominently on a shelf. "This was hers."

Zev didn't know what to say, but he remembered his mother always remarking, "If you don't have something nice to say, don't say anything."

Zev's phone dinged, but he ignored it.

Heather lit a cigarette.

"He usually hits me," she said in an oddly conversational voice.

"And you just take it?"

Heather shrugged.

Zev protested. "SIDS is an accident of nature—it has nothing to do with the parents. They've proven that when a baby's serotonin level drops, it can die."

"He accuses me of letting her smother because I didn't check on her enough. We found her facedown. Her whole body was turning blue. I was on the phone, arguing with my mother instead of checking on her." Her voice trembled. "If only . . ."

Heather sobbed suddenly, a sound that cut Zev to the core. He hugged her, patting her back gently, averting his face so his sore jaw didn't touch any part of her. "I'm sure you did everything . . ."

She pulled away. "How can you be so sure?"

※

Zev had not been able to get the idea of Heather's psychic out of his mind. While on his way home from the bar, he was weighing the pros and cons of calling Gwydion when the CHURCH OF GOD bus passed, almost hitting him as he crossed the street. Once again Zev found himself on his knees, fumbling for a cap he no longer wore. He took this as a sign. He called Gwydion and requested an appointment. *This is like Zayde's pork chop,* he thought, and hoped that the God he didn't believe in would forgive a spiritually starving man.

CHAPTER 20

Cooking with Rose Petals

ARLOS HAD A SPACIOUS one-bedroom with a galley-style kitchen. The living room was navy and light blue with a sectional leather sofa, deep carpet, and a huge flatscreen TV. John Coltrane glided from hidden speakers. The surprising thing about the room was that there were dozens of family photos, making it somehow homey, belying the wild antics Sarah imagined went on there. It was a little creepy. Carlos handed her a glass of heady red wine. She toasted, "To Gwydion."

"Oh, tell me everything—what did he say?"

"Before I tell you, a few questions. Have you ever cooked Middle Eastern for Laura?"

"Yes, sometimes she has important guests from that part of the world. One guy traveled with six bodyguards at all times. They sat at the table and one of them tasted all of his food. I'm serious! He stayed in the kitchen while I cooked and tasted each dish before I served it. I'm not talking from the pot—I'm talking right from his master's plate! Can you imagine?"

"Who was it?"

"No idea. Laura served herself and made it clear that it was not up for discussion. It's happened more than once. This lady knows some heavy-duty people."

"Okay, so what is her deal?"

"You mean gay or straight? With me, she is straight and vice versa. Take love where you find it. You won't get free of Michael until you sleep with someone new."

"Okay. Okay. What should I be careful about?"

"Swearing. She doesn't like it."

"Fuck. Really?"

They shared a smile.

"I came up with a recipe with rose petals. She liked it but nixed the flowers."

"Makes it easier on you."

Carlos punched buttons on his phone and showed her a photo of him with his fragile mother standing proudly in front of a Sri Lankan temple. She was as beautiful as Carlos was handsome. "This was taken five years ago." He punched more buttons and showed Sarah another photo of his mother. This time she was in bed and looked terribly ill. "This is from last week. The doctors give her a few weeks at most."

"Damn you, Carlos. I'll take it."

"What about all the other gigs?"

"I'll handle it. If someone comes along who wants to pay me quadruple, then I might have a problem."

He leapt off the sofa and hugged her. "I love you!" Then he got businesslike. "How much did she offer you?"

"Triple for each job of yours I cover."

"Oh, now I get what you just said. Good, she's very generous. Be careful and keep good receipts. And by the way, she may hit on you too."

Sarah rolled her eyes. "When do you leave?"

"On the next flight. I owe you."

"I'll collect in the next life."

CHAPTER 21

A Psychic Reveal

EV GOT SUCH A swift response from Gwydion that he barely had time to process the whole thing. He was still nursing his sore face when he agreed to a nine P.M. appointment only a couple of nights after his boxing match with Heather's ex. He was in the middle of his shift as the time approached, and he looked for a quiet place to make the call.

Five hours ahead in Cornwall, at about one forty-five A.M., a sleepy Gwydion entered his study carrying a cup of coffee and a plate of cranberry muffins, wondering why the angel insisted on making so many of his sessions for the wee hours of the morning. He barely had time to finish his coffee before he felt the cold hand on his shoulder signaling it was time to go to work. "I'm coming," he grumbled, taking a last bite.

A moment later, Gwydion was ensconced at the desk of his virtual study. The angel sat across from him. "Please don't talk so fast this time," Gwydion said.

The angel nodded and said gravely, "And please don't interpret my words."

But this admonishment was accompanied by a smile that Gwydion returned. It was a conversation they'd had many times. Gwydion settled back into his chair, waiting quietly for the call from his new client.

Zev found a Greek diner somewhere in Queens and pulled in. He ordered tea and a piece of apple strudel as big as a dinner plate, but he was having second thoughts about this whole psychic business. He dialed the number on his cell phone. Of the many laws he had been taught to uphold, a big one was not worshipping false idols. The Jews who had worshipped the golden calf had been severely punished. Well, he was an atheist, right? Was he then not a Jew? There was no God, just a fantasy created by man to control his fear of chaos. Therefore, there could be no one to strike him down. And since psychics claimed to talk to the dead, and Jews did not believe in an afterlife, what kind of spiritual salvation could possibly be on offer? What was he doing? He was about to hang up when the phone clicked.

"Hello, is this Zev?" rang the smooth baritone with a thick English accent.

Zev nodded and said, "Yes." He realized he was soaked in sweat. He cleared his throat. "Is this Gwydion?"

"Yes. Okay then, here's how it works: I talk to your guides. They help me to talk to you. See this as a chance to have a conversation with your guides."

Zev had no idea what to expect but had thought to bring a pen. He wrote notes on the back of a napkin. *Who or what are the guides?* He made a note to inquire if he was allowed to ask questions.

"Okay. You were not hit by the beam or that bus because there's a job we want you to do." *How does Gwydion know this?* Zev sighed in relief—the clip about the I-beam had been broadcast on the news, and Gwydion could easily have seen it. He was a fake. But no one knew about the near accident with the bus. Zev felt a cold finger on his spine.

Gwydion continued, "Zephaniah means 'hidden by God' in Hebrew. Consider yourself a mole, a long-term plant in the Cold War. Please understand that free will plays a part, and you alone will decide if you want to be an actor in this play."

Zev squirmed and drank some tea. *This is complete mumbo*

jumbo.

"The Cold War is becoming hot. Those who would further the dark side are gaining power and using their wiles to enslave the earth. Before you came back this time, you volunteered for a dangerous job."

Oy, Zev thought, *this is exactly as pointless as I feared it would be.*

Gwydion continued, "You are not a believer, but it does not matter. As you know, faith is a man-made construct. God concerns Himself with behavior. Although you have lost your birth languages, you will soon find your true voice. Saving the boy is reparation for any past debt you were carrying, and you are free to make your own choices."

Zev was stunned. How could this lunatic know about the Hebrew and Yiddish and about Aaron? Zev had trouble breathing. He pressed his hand against his heart.

"You do not owe your parents or your community any further loyalty. They were the chrysalis, and you have emerged and are now finding your wings."

Gwydion sighed, audibly winded. Zev could hear him light a cigarette. It made sense—if you talked to dead people, smoking was probably not a big deal, since they knew there was life after death.

"But why was I spared?"

There was a silence, then Gwydion said, "Hold on, let me tell him slowly." Zev wondered who was there with him.

After a long pause, Gwydion spoke: "You were not spared. Death would have been an easy way out for you. We interfered."

"No, it was luck: a lucky coincidence."

"There is no such thing as coincidence. There are no accidents, only arrangements."

This was unnerving. "Who or what is my guide? Does everyone have one?"

"Yes. As in life, you find people who help you. In the larger universe, where the other side is as real as our earth, there are spirits who volunteer to help those on the earth plane."

"I have to be honest," Zev said, "I don't believe in reincarnation."

"That is because you have not studied the Zohar. This book affirms and explains your religious beliefs concerning such. You saved Aaron because you weren't able to save your own son many lifetimes ago."

Zev trembled, suddenly chilled. Tears stung his eyes. On a gut level, he recognized that somehow this was true, whatever "true" was starting to mean.

Gwydion continued, "The little boy needs a father. We recommend strongly that you call him once a week and let him know you care. His mother is still overcome by the loss of the boy's father and can't give the boy what he needs."

How can he or they know so much? How can this be logically explained? "What about—"

Gwydion cut him off. "Please hold further questions until I have finished. If you want to find a context to understand reincarnation in the Judaic tradition, please recall that the *Halakhah* is the body of all of your religion's commandments or *mitzvot*, six hundred and thirteen in all. The *Kabbalah* states that reincarnation occurs until a soul has fulfilled every one of those laws. The *Kabbalah* is something you may choose to study since you are well versed and were raised to travel this spiritual path. But for now there is no need for you to struggle with its veracity, merely accept what has been said as a way to explain the recent past and to prepare you for the future."

Zev had heard of this book, but his community strictly forbade its study.

"Zev, you will have an opportunity to prevent a major world crisis. You must act in accordance with your conscience, not your heart. Remember the essence of Judaism is to do justice, to love goodness, and to walk miles with your God."

Zev wrote, *Prevent Crisis.*

"Will I find love?"

"Yes, you will find your . . . *bashert*, but not in the way you might have thought."

"Question?" Zev interrupted again.

"Yes, go ahead."

Zev wiped his palms on his pants legs. "Is there a God?" All of Zev's doubt had suddenly condensed into this one question.

"Yes, of course there is a God. And you are a nonbeliever, yet this question has troubled you. Rejoice in knowing God does not care whether you believe in Him. He is sad that your human actions are based on the fear of consequences, earthly or otherwise, instead of on the most basic impulse, which is to love."

"But how can I have proof of God?"

"It is being proven to you all of the time. Why do you think that I-beam didn't crush you?"

"But I almost died—I lost my Hebrew—"

"As I said before, there are no accidents. Sometimes we need a shock to set us free. You were never meant to stay in the bubble of your parents' insular world."

Zev was pleased, then worried.

"What about my mother?"

"She might outlive you!"

"And my father?"

"Your father is a fool and a bully."

Zev smiled at this. "So, I will serve some useful purpose?"

Gwydion was empathetic. "You can and you will."

Zev felt better suddenly. "Well, what is it?"

"Man, that would ruin all the fun, wouldn't it?"

"How do I know you're not a *dybbuk*?"

"A what? Oh, wait a minute, the guide is telling me." There was a silence, and Zev heard Gwydion say, "Oh, well, that makes sense."

"What makes sense?"

Gwydion laughed. "Sorry, I was talking to the guide. Oh, no—I am no demon. I am one hundred percent human. Ask my wife!"

So this man had a wife. Zev envied him suddenly—here was a man who had real clarity.

"Should I stay in New York or go home to take care of my

mother?"

"Stay in New York. Accept this fact: The structure of your life has been altered and can never be the way it was. You feel lost because you don't yet have a new purpose, but you will."

"That's it?"

"*That's it?* Finding out your purpose is pretty big news!"

Zev was silent.

"What is the alternative?" Gwydion asked. "You're either a sheep or a shepherd. Your choice. That's our time. I'll put the tape in the mail—you should have it in a couple of days."

The line went dead.

CHAPTER 22

Unchained Melody

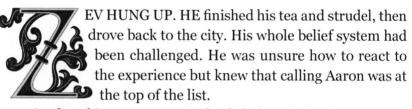EV HUNG UP. HE finished his tea and strudel, then drove back to the city. His whole belief system had been challenged. He was unsure how to react to the experience but knew that calling Aaron was at the top of the list.

So, first thing next morning he dialed Rachel and Aaron, and Aaron picked up.

"Hi, Zev!"

Zev felt his heart twist in his chest. "How's it going, little buddy?"

"When are you coming to visit?"

"Soon, soon. Is your mommy there?"

Rachel got on. "Hi, Zev. He's been asking about you every day."

Zev realized that he had been thinking of him too. "How's he doing at school?"

"Much better. He joined the choir and seems to have made some new friends."

"How is Frank?"

There was a pause, then Rachel said, "It's complicated. Now he wants to separate from his wife and come live with us. There's enough divorce in this world, Zev. We would all be living in sin—"

"According to some people who think that way, you already do."

Rachel giggled. "Thank you for making me laugh."

"Do you love him?"

Rachel sighed. "No. I like him. He's a sweet, decent guy. But, no, I'll never get over Aaron's dad. That was the big one for me. The real problem is that I like my sister-in-law, and it would destroy her if Frank left."

"Does she know?"

"I think she does, but looks the other way. They've got three kids, for Pete's sake!"

"Does Aaron like him?"

Rachel shed a tear. "No, Frank is tough on him—calls him a sissy."

Zev was surprised at the bitter anger that gripped his heart— it actually hurt. "How dare he!"

"Well, when a lion takes over the pride of another lion, it kills the offspring of the previous alpha male."

Zev was stunned. "We're not talking about lions here! How can you let him into your life if your own son suffers at his hands?" His voice was rough with anger.

"Who said anything about suffering?" she snapped. "I don't see you here helping me make ends meet, repairing my roof, paying for Aaron's school or the phone bill—"

"I had no idea you needed money."

At that moment, Aaron interrupted. "Can I talk to Zev, please?"

"Sure . . . here!"

"Hi, Uncle Zev. I built a castle for my school project. I used the stuff you taught me with Legos."

"Is everything okay?"

Rachel grabbed the phone, still upset. "Okay, look, Zev. I've got to get ready for work. Bye." She handed the phone back to Aaron before Zev could get another word in.

Zev could hear Rachel's footsteps clicking away and Aaron's breathing.

"Aaron, are you having trouble with Uncle Frank?"

Aaron stifled a sob.

"Does he hurt you?"

Aaron's voice trembled. "No, but they fight. It scares me. Uncle Frank threw a plate at Mommy because she won't let him live here."

"Has there been anything else like that?"

"No, but they shout late at night when they think I'm asleep. I wish you were here."

Zev longed to hug him. "My parents used to fight, and my dad threw things. But eventually it got better."

"What did they fight about?"

"Money mostly, and sometimes about me."

"Why you?"

"Well, I didn't want to obey them. In my religion you have to follow an awful lot of rules, and I didn't want to. Aaron, I am giving you my cell phone number. And I'm going to send you a cell phone that you can always call me on. Okay?"

Aaron brightened up immediately. "Okay!"

"If you don't feel safe or you just want to talk, you call me anytime. Okay?"

They hung up, and as soon as he finished his shift, Zev went right out and purchased a new cell phone, loaded his own number into it, and sent it FedEx to Aaron with a note to Rachel and five hundred dollars in cash.

⚜

Heather's Pub was near closing when Zev arrived. Heather and Tom were behind the bar, and as Zev took a seat, Tom shouted, "Hey, Christ-killer, how's it hanging?"

"Toward Jerusalem. And we didn't kill him," Zev said, amazed that he was about to attempt a joke. "We just had the contract for the lumber."

Tom laughed and offered his knuckles for a bump. "Good one!"

"Shut up, you racist loser," Heather snarled at Tom and said to Zev, "Don't mind this idiot!" Tom smirked like a schoolboy and exited behind the bar toward the stockroom. Zev shrugged. He was amused—and besides, there was a grain of truth in the accusation. The Jewish priests were the ones most eager to bump Jesus off in the Bible story.

"So, what did Gwydion say?" She poured him a drink and one for herself.

What could he tell her? He still wasn't sure about the information. "Well, he and a guide said I should study *Kabbalah*, and that I will find my *bashert*, my soulmate," he said skeptically.

"Oh, really? Is her name Madonna?"

Zev smiled. "Do you really trust this guy?"

Heather nodded. "I do."

"According to Gwydion, I never have to go back." He felt buoyant, absolved of the weight of feeling he had betrayed his family and excited now at the prospect of the future. At the same time, he was mystified as to how the disembodied voice of a person three thousand miles away could cause such change—but he was not inclined to question the matter right now.

"What about you, Heather? What has he said to you?"

She sipped her drink, wistful. "So many people in New York are refugees. Seems like when there's no resolution with their families at home, they come here. Take Tom."

"What about him?"

"You don't know about Tom?"

"No."

Heather laughed. "We were almost married three years ago."

"So, what happened?"

"I spoke to Gwydion."

"C'mon."

"Truly. He told me that I wasn't over that creep you punched out—if you can imagine it—and that I would break Tom's heart."

"And you listened?"

"Yes, I knew it was true. I broke off our engagement. Tom pursued me, but I refused to get back together. After a while, he stopped waiting for me. He fell in love with the makeup artist on the TV show he was in at the time—who did not return his love, by the way—but he gave up on me to go after her. Then she dumped him. So now we're both single. I am over that jerk of an ex, and Tom fucks anything in a skirt."

Zev heard the pain in her voice, and Tom's behavior seemed more understandable, if not justifiable. Zev wished they could find their way back together.

"Why don't you have another session?" Zev asked. "All of that sounds like ancient history already. And Gwydion told me that there are no accidents."

"Maybe you're right, but I don't know."

Zev got an inspiration. "There might be no need, actually, because he gave me a message for you."

"Really? For me?"

"I had to tell him who referred me."

"And he remembered me?"

"Of course, he recollects everyone," Zev said with a wink.

"So, what did he say?"

"That it would be okay now—I mean, if you two got together."

Heather's eyes filled with tears, smearing her mascara. "Really? He said that?"

Zev nodded and crossed his fingers behind his back like a child.

Tom returned, carrying six wine bottles. "Tito split, so I grabbed these." He saw Heather's tears and turned on Zev fiercely. "What the fuck did you say to her?'

Heather laughed and uttered, "It's good news, Tom. Not to worry."

Tom picked up a cocktail napkin, wet it at the sink behind the bar, and gently cleaned away the eye makeup. "Hey, me too—I just got picked up for a new series. Guess what I play?"

"A cop."

Tom nodded ruefully. "Zev, can you take over the shifts I'll miss?"

Zev silently agreed. He would be able to stop dipping into

his savings and could send Rachel some money. "Unchained Melody" by The Righteous Brothers began to play, and Tom said to Heather, "Remember? This was our song. From the movie *Ghost*."

Zev had the good sense to wander away to a table as Tom sang the words.

My love, my darling
I hunger for your touch
Alone, lonely time
And time goes by so slowly
And time can do so much
Are you still mine?
I need your love
I need your love
God speed your love to me!

They began to dance, and Zev had to concede that an amazing coincidence had occurred—a moment of confluence in which his lie and Tom's good fortune had created some kind of a portal that had allowed Heather and Tom to reunite. And the big lesson that Zev had just learned from Gwydion was that his opinion of God didn't matter one bit to God, and knowing that took a lot of the pressure off. He had lied to create a moment in time, and he felt happy knowing that he could affect positive change in the immediate world around him. Perhaps that was a solid working model of faith.

Okay then, he thought. *On with the dance!*

CHAPTER 23

GUNS AND ROSES

A WEEK PASSED AND the tape had not arrived. Heather and Tom were back together, which made Zev happy. Tom was taping the show, so Zev had been driving nonstop, except when he was sleeping. He worked straight through Saturday night and fell into bed exhausted as dawn broke.

He awoke groggy and was amazed that he'd napped through the entire day. It was time to go to work, but he was beat. Sunday night wasn't great for driving, and Zev thought about not working but knew that he could still do well at the airport.

The garage was subdued. He got the cab and gassed it up, listening to rock music.

But he was tired, and at ten o'clock he was about to turn in early when a fare practically threw himself in front of the cab as Zev was slowing for a red light near the Hudson River in the West Village. Zev hit the brakes hard, and the cab screeched to a halt. He narrowly avoided ramming into a fat man wearing a windbreaker and baseball cap who looked to be Middle Eastern. The man opened the passenger door and threw his bag in before Zev could protest.

"I'm off duty," Zev said. "Going home. I'm sorry."

The man flashed a hundred dollar bill. "Please, you must

take me to Kennedy Airport. If you don't, I will miss my flight."
Zev looked at the traffic, and there were a few cabs, but the ones
he could see, like his own, all had their off-duty light on. A hundred dollars was a hundred dollars. "Okay, get in. Kennedy Airport it is," he said, popping open the trunk.

The drive to the airport was uneventful and slow. Zev dozed
during a lull, and a battery of angry car horns and loud insults
came from behind, rudely awaking him. He stifled a yawn and
put the car in gear.

"Sorry," Zev said to his passenger. "Where are you going—
which terminal?"

"Air Emirates."

Zev stopped at the curb. The man gave him the hundred
dollar bill, and Zev opened the trunk. But before he could reach
for the bags, the man said, "I got it," took out his luggage, and
slammed the trunk closed himself.

Zev blasted rock music to keep himself awake. He turned
in the cab and began to walk home when he remembered that
he had left his jacket in the trunk. When he went back to get it,
he saw that it had been mashed into a ball. He picked it up—it
was strangely heavy. He unrolled it and stopped. An automatic
nine-millimeter Glock handgun, complete with a silencer and
fully loaded thirteen-round clip, had been hidden there, neatly
wrapped in the jacket. Did it belong to the fat man he had just
dropped off? No way to know. *A gun!* Whoever left it knew his
name and hack-license number, or, rather, knew Tom's. Would
that be significant? He sniffed the barrel as he had seen cops do
on TV shows. Zev shuddered and looked over his shoulder as he
wrapped it back up in the jacket. He called Tom.

"Just dump it."

"What if somebody comes back for it?"

"We can't leave it—we could be arrested."

"Why not call the cops?"

"Are you kidding? You don't have a license, Jewboy, remember? Besides, they won't believe either of us. Zev just put it back
in the trunk. I'll talk to some of my cop buddies and get the

skinny."

"Okay."

"See you in the bar."

"No, I got to sleep."

Zev left the gun in the trunk and walked home. He stripped and took a shower. He crawled into bed and closed his eyes. His last waking thought was that he should call Aaron. He dreamed that he was a young Isaac to Abraham.

Zev was bent back over a rock as his father held a knife to his throat. Tears in his eyes, Abraham, who looked like Chaim, said, "I am sorry, my son. This is God's will."

Zev as Isaac felt around frantically for something with which to hit his father. He found a rock and jammed it into his father's cheek. Abraham staggered back, clutching his face. Zev as Isaac leapt up crying, "Fuck God!" and threw his father's knife into a just-materialized Burning Bush. He looked at the shrub and said, "Okay, if you've got something to say, do so— but it better be good. And don't tell me or my idiot father that he's a virtuous man because he would follow the command of an unseen voice to commit a heinous act! Other people have used that excuse for way too long."

The Bush spoke: "The head of Iran will create a war against Israel that will involve the whole world—three and a half years of peace, three and a half years of war, a thousand years of rule by a Christlike figure. The war will ultimately destroy the world."

Zev woke up in a cold sweat, expecting lightning to strike him down for having such a blasphemous dream. He strained to remember a blessing in Hebrew—something, anything. But all that came was the chorus of his favorite song, "The Unforgiven":

What I've felt,

What I've known

Never shined through in what I've shown.

Never free.

Never me.

So I dub thee unforgiven.

Zev shrugged and said aloud, "Amen." Bathed in sweat, he grabbed his robe and went outside. He'd slept ten hours! In another world, it was Monday, and he would be going back to work. Heather and Tom were eating and watching the news. On-screen, the anchors were discussing Zarafshan's intention to destroy Israel. As Zev brewed tea, he caught Tom's eye. Tom nodded. He gave Heather a hug and came over, leaving her on the sofa.

The two men spoke in low whispers.

"What the fuck, Zev? Who the fuck was your passenger? My cop friend told me that the dude on TV, that Iranian madman, is in town for a couple of weeks. There are probably a hundred nutjobs that might want to off him. Can you remember anything about the fare?"

Zev shook his head. "That's the first thing you taught me: Forget the day at the end of each shift. But I remember the last one, only because I almost fell asleep at the wheel. Fat, pushy. Dropped him at Air Emirates. That's all I recall. He gave me a hundred dollar bill."

Tom nodded. "So much for that. He's long gone."

"But why would he leave an unfired gun in the cab, and why would he leave it in *my jacket*?"

"How do you know it wasn't fired?"

"I smelled it."

Tom was incredulous. "You sniffed it?"

"Yes, I've worked on firearm patent applications. When you fire a gun, there is a distinctive odor."

"So . . . why would someone leave a fully loaded, unused gun wrapped in your jacket—and in *my* cab?"

Zev shrugged. "What does your cop friend say?"

"Leave it in the trunk for now, and play dumb."

"Seriously?"

"Yes. Hey, wait a minute—did you handle the thing?"

Zev thought back. "Yeah, to see if it had been fired, but it was still wrapped in the jacket."

Heather called to them. "Hey, what are you two knuckleheads nattering on about?"

Tom replied, "Knuckleheads?"

Heather said, "Yeah. It's in the script for your newest project, remember? Some creep calls you a knucklehead."

Tom grinned. "Yeah. You're right. Back to work, babe."

Heather groaned. Tom poured her some coffee. "I need you . . ." He clicked off the TV.

Zev walked to the window and looked out. He still couldn't believe that he was living over a bar in Hell's Kitchen in New York City and was rooming with an actor on a TV show, that he had now made up in a few short weeks for all the women he'd never slept with, consulted a psychic, and met a girl—no, wait—met a girl who cared nothing for him. His elation faded. He turned and looked around at the kitchen and living room. The robin's-egg-blue walls and green linoleum floor were chipped and pitted. The furniture was old and patched. Tom and Heather shared a worn leather sofa, but the views through the window of the Hudson River, shining in the morning sunlight, were breathtaking. This was "living" in New York City.

His shift didn't start for another hour.

In his room, Zev clicked on his computer and turned to CNN. No e-mail. He got dressed, went out, and bought a newspaper. As he skimmed the headlines while he sat in a coffee shop munching a giant chocolate croissant with his tea, he realized how insulated from the real world his family was, except for Jewish news. Everything that happened was focused through that cultural lens. His parents leaned Republican—part of his alienation from them. They had liked all of the Bushes because of their relationship to Israel—or not. He tried to read the paper in a nonpartisan way. The girl behind the counter began to flirt with him, and he left the paper untouched. What was he to believe of some *meshugana* psychic three thousand miles away? His phone rang—it was Rachel. She sounded upset.

"You didn't call Aaron yesterday. He moped around the whole day."

"*Oy.* I was under the weather. I spent most of the day sleeping. I almost fell asleep while I was driving the other night."

"Well, okay. In that case, could you call him around three thirty after school today and tell him that? He sent you a gift."

"Really?" Zev felt guilty, but Aaron wasn't his charge—or was he? How much of this Gwydion stuff should he believe, if any? "Okay, why and what is it?"

"It's his science project. The marking period ended on Friday, and it's a big deal. He got an A on it."

"Okay. What is it?"

"I won't tell you. You'll get it in a day or two. Here's a hint—they are studying Rome in his class and all he wants to do is know about the Jews! Can you recommend a book?"

Zev thought about it. "Nothing in particular. Has he read the Old Testament?"

"Not yet—he's six!"

"Oh, right. Well, what about your telling him Bible stories? You read to him before he goes to sleep, right?"

"Actually, no."

"You don't read to him?" Zev was surprised at the anger he felt. "How the heck do you expect him to learn to love reading if you don't do it with him?" He couldn't control the outrage in his voice.

"I know. It's just another one of the ways that I'm a bad mother. I get it."

"So bitter. You're a wonderful mother."

"No. I pick up men in bars; I'm having an affair with my married brother-in-law. I drink. I yelled at my son this morning because he spilled his cereal." Rachel sobbed.

"I'm sorry, Rachel, I'm sorry. I spoke harshly to you."

She said in a strangled voice, "I'm sorry. I'll call you back."

As Zev hung up, he thought, *Why don't I send Aaron a gift?*

He went to a bookstore and bought the boy a beautifully illustrated collection of Bible stories. For Rachel, he got a white leather-bound Bible and a pretty box of folded note stationery with an *R* monogrammed on it, bordered with red roses. He walked to the post office and sent the package Express Mail.

Then it was time for his shift.

He checked the trunk—the gun was still there. He got behind the wheel and entered the void. As he picked up and dropped off fares, each a mini TV melodrama in his rearview mirror, he found himself listening to the news.

Already the euphoric spell of his consultation with Gwydion was wearing off. Zev's rational mind was kicking in with a scathing critique of Gwydion and this mystical nonsense. He imagined what Chaim would say if he knew how Zev was living. *"What? You're going to spend your life driving a cab? Eat treif? Drink treif? Sleep with whores? Worship golden idols? Speak with a blaspheming crackpot who says he talks to the dead? How you have shamed me!"*

Zev felt himself shrinking and turned his mind away from those bitter thoughts. Now he no longer wanted the tape. He wanted to write off that whole experience as a dream and settle into the present. If Heather and Tom stayed together, he would definitely have to move out. Tom would be making more money while his TV show was running. Maybe he would sell Zev the cab.

Zev turned on the radio. "Sometimes I Feel Like a Motherless Child" was playing. The raspy-voiced Richie Havens sang haltingly, *"Sometimes I feel like a motherless child—a long way from my home."* Zev felt himself sinking back into the despair that had prompted him to seek out Gwydion in the first place. Then his cell phone rang. He didn't recognize the phone number. "Hello?"

"Hi. Umm, you don't know me, but my name is Sarah. I think I got your tape . . . from Gwydion, I mean."

CHAPTER 24

THE DINNER PARTY

"YOU *THINK* YOU GOT it?" The lack of certainty put Zev off a little bit.

"It's not marked. I just listened to the tape until Gwydion said your name, 'Zev,' and then I went to the end to get your address and phone. Did you get mine?"

"No, I'm so sorry. When can I pick it up?"

"Do you mind swinging by where I'm working later today? It's down in Chelsea, and I should be there in, say, about two hours. Would that be okay?"

"Sure, I can do that."

She gave him the address and hung up. Zev picked up a few more fares, then turned on the OFF DUTY light and drove to Chelsea, eager to get the cassette. He rang the bell. Sarah opened the door and said, "Great. Come on upstairs." Her red curls were pulled back into a ponytail, but he recognized her right away. It was the woman he'd met in the cab. He was stunned, and all he could think of was what Gwydion had said about there being no accidents, only arrangements. She obviously did not recognize him, and why should she? It had been dark, the middle of the night. Plus, she thought his name was Tom and that he was Irish. But now he was stuck: If he told her he had lied when they met the first time, she might be angry, as Rachel had been. But if he compounded the deceit by not telling her now, she would be even more furious later. *Oy.* What to do? *When in doubt, delay!* was a good saying Ruth had given him.

Zev followed her up the stairs into the opulent parlor. As they climbed, he watched Sarah swaying. She had a tiny brown birthmark in the hollow behind her right ankle that was framed by a gold gladiator-style sandal strap. He wanted to upend her and kiss that spot. He imagined lifting and kissing upward from ankle to pubis.

"Wow." He surveyed the room. Every surface of the kitchen held different foods in various stages of preparation; the eight-burner, stainless steel Viking stovetop was covered with simmering pots. He felt his stomach rumbling.

"It looks like a fancy restaurant."

"Yeah, this is quite a place."

"You live here too?"

"No, I'm a chef. My friend, the regular chef, is away. I'm subbing for him."

"Some big party, huh?"

"It is supposed to be. As my boss put it, 'an intimate dinner for eight,'" she said. "I'll just get your tape—I have to go back to work." She picked up her voluminous, fringed handbag and opened it.

"You seem familiar—it's your voice. Do we know each other somehow? Do you take a lot of cabs?"

Sarah looked up from her search to see if he was being sarcastic, but, if anything, he looked hopeful.

"Of course. Everyone in New York does." Sarah continued to rummage. "Dammit! I must have forgotten it after all that."

He was relieved—as much as he wanted to listen to the tape, this created a definite opportunity to see her again. Should he tell her here that they'd met before? His nerve failed him. Instead, he gestured toward the business end of the kitchen.

"Do you do all this yourself?"

She nodded. "I usually have a helper, but he couldn't make it—down with the flu. Why, are you looking for a job?" He stiffened, then saw she was teasing him. "What do you do, anyway?"

"I drive a cab."

"Okay, cool. I'm so sorry to have brought you all this way for nothing. I'll drop it off tomorrow—I am not booked until evening. Where do you live?" She looked at her watch. "The boss lady wants her *hors d'oeuvres* at six thirty."

"What are you making?"

"A Persian feast! Did you know that the cuisine in Iran has a lot in common with Sephardic food?"

"No, but that makes sense. It smells great in here." He wanted to stay in this warm space.

"Are you hungry?"

"Always! I could eat a horse—if it were kosher."

Sarah smiled. "Great. So your trip shouldn't be a total waste." She opened several covered bowls and took something out of the fridge. "Sit," she said, indicating a large table in the corner near the window. It was set for six. He moved from the corner where he'd been leaning and sat down. She put a plate in front of him filled with hummus, sprouts, fruits and nuts, mini-kebabs, and pita bread. "It's a Persian antipasto." She poured him a glass of water from a crystal pitcher. She surveyed him critically. He hesitated. "Eat," she said. He reached for a fork.

"No, wait, you need pita. And wine." She quickly cut up a pita and placed it on a plate in front of him.

"Don't worry, it's not Persian. It's French." She poured two glasses generously and raised her glass. *"L'chaim."* They drank.

He ate. It was delicious. She went back to her preparations, glancing occasionally in his direction. "So, what do you think?"

"Really good."

She smiled and took a roast out of the oven. The scent of rosemary and garlic stung his nostrils. "Still hungry?" She removed another pan, full of glistening vegetables with slightly blackened skins.

"Always."

She cleared the plate and placed a dish of sliced meat and vegetables before him.

"Eat. I've got to kick you out in fifteen minutes."

He ate while she worked at top speed, humming. For a few minutes, they shared a quiet peace.

The buzzer sounded. Zev got up as Sarah pushed the button. It was the liquor-store deliveryman. Sarah looked at Zev helplessly. "Could you?" She handed him a five dollar bill.

Zev walked down the steps. A muscular Hispanic man with tattoos entered, carrying a case of wine. Zev gave the guy the bill, carried the box up the stairs, and brought it over to the double walk-in fridge.

"Hey, I didn't mean to put you to work"—Sarah smiled—"but thank you. It's my first big dinner for this woman. So wish me luck."

"You won't need it. The food is great." He hesitated.

She nodded. "Thanks. You were my guinea pig."

"Anytime!"

"Okay, I'll call you tomorrow to set up a time. I'm really sorry about that." He nodded and turned to go. She walked him to the door and came out into the hall with a warm smile. "Are we friends now?"

He nodded happily. They hugged, and she pressed her cheek against his. Once again there was that extra something that surprised him so much about these tough New Yorkers—they certainly did a lot of hugging and kissing. He had to bend his six-foot two-inch frame to meet her, and was surprised by a real hug, chest to chest. He smelled her intoxicating perfume, left on a cloud, and decided to take a short walk, drifting down Second Avenue.

After Zev left, Sarah flicked on her iPod to some spirited yoga music, practiced the breath of fire, and got serious. There was so much more to do, and the preparation of the desserts would be so labor intensive that she needed to start them now. She was sweaty and a little lightheaded from all the breathing when Laura peeked in, wearing curlers and a green facial mask, and, with a theatrical flair, circled the kitchen, tasting everything.

"Who was that man I saw on his way out? He's yummy. No

wonder Ed Hirsch left you cold."

Sarah turned off the music. "What? Sorry."

"Tall guy who just left—he your friend? He's hot."

Sarah hadn't registered Zev that way, but as soon as Laura spoke, a mental movie played—of Zev hovering in the doorway, her feeding him, and his sweet goodbye. She felt a tug at her heart. *I am embodying a literary cliché*, she thought, amused at her physical self. Laura interrupted her thought as Sarah opened the oven and peered in at the four chickens cooking away. She had inserted garlic and rosemary into slits she had cut into the meat, and as the oven door was opened, a fresh cloud of fragrant fumes filled the kitchen.

"This looks amazing. You really did your homework. Carlos will have to measure up."

"No, no. I consulted with him. He gets the credit—I am just subbing."

Laura picked up a date that had been soaking in a dish with walnuts, honey, and raisins. She took a bite, closed her eyes, and savored it, then shook her head.

"No. Carlos is good, but you have something special."

"You can tell from one date?"

"How many does it take?"

Sarah laughed. "Yeah. I rarely make it to a second."

Laura smiled. "Uh-huh. Now. Let me catch you up. Ravi will be coming in about five minutes. He will set the table, serve the food, and help you in any way he can. Jimmie arrives at six fifteen, and his guards will be coming right into the kitchen to be fed. One of them will taste all of the food—everything—before it is served. Jimmie has many enemies."

"I can imagine," Sarah said dryly, and Laura chuckled.

"Did you know Jimmie doesn't believe there was a Holocaust?" Laura shook her head incredulously.

Who is this guy? He sounds dangerous. "What does this dignitary do?"

Laura put a finger to her lips. "I can't say."

"Laura, I have to ask. You know I'm Jewish, right?"

Laura winked flirtatiously. "What could be more amusing?"

Sarah turned back to her work. This was indeed getting a little freaky. "Will you tell your guest?"

"At a perfect moment after dinner."

Laura ate another date slowly. Sarah continued slicing and dicing, mentally cursing Santiago. He would have to get the flu now. Laura smacked her lips and said, "Well, think about it and I'll get out of your way. P.S. You're worth a third date." She took one last date from the dish and popped it into her mouth. "Yum, yum," she added, and left. Sarah felt like she'd been groped, at least mentally, but she was definitely turned on.

Sarah ate one of the dates and imitated Laura. "Yum, yum." They were good. The image of Zev came to her mind, and somehow he stood behind her as she leaned back against him and he pressed his hands against the front of her ribs. It was a powerful sensation. She realized that it had been a long time since she had been held.

Ravi, Laura's server, arrived. He reminded Sarah of Hanuman, the monkey god in Hindu mythology. He was a short Bangladeshi with mahogany skin and liquid brown eyes. He was astonishingly handsome but had big feet and walked like a duck, which ruined the illusion.

Ravi surveyed the various dishes and the food. "Smells great," he said. "May I?" And he helped himself to a date. He too closed his eyes in pleasure for a moment. Carlos's cryptic ramblings about how he'd fallen in love with the living embodiment of Curious George hadn't connected with Sarah—until now. This was Carlos's secret squeeze! *All right then*, she thought, *tread softly and carry a big banana.*

"Are you hungry? There's tons of food."

"It's irregular. We usually eat after," Ravi said. "You know who the guest of honor is?"

"No, Laura didn't say. Who is he?"

"Can't say if she didn't. Anyway, he travels with six bodyguards."

"So, it will just be the guest and Laura in the dining room?"

"Yes. The men will be stationed throughout the house. They will be coming in ten minutes or so. Can you feed them?"

"Well, except for the kebabs, everything is cooked, and the salad is ready. I can make them platters, sure. What do they like to drink?"

"They're Muslim, so water, tea, coffee."

Ravi got up and looked into the second fridge. He nodded, took a beer, and offered her one. She shook her head. He said, "Is it religious?" She chuckled. If he only knew that wine was becoming her new religion.

"Then how come you're wearing all white?"

"Not really. I practice a lot of yoga that suggests that white is an ideal color."

Ravi stood up. "Cool. The men will be here. Try to avoid eye contact. These guys are very macho." With that, he left and walked into the dining room, and next she heard the clinking of silverware and dishes as he set up the table.

Sarah now focused in earnest. As she hummed and sang, her mind traveled to that quiet, relaxed place that it did when she cooked, and she added a light breath of fire and the repetitive mantra *Sat Nam, Sat Nam*.

The roasted chickens were ready. Once they'd cooled a little, she stripped the carcasses while she sautéed chopped walnuts and dates, and, on a whim, quickly cut a green apple into cubes and added a few. She was amused—this was like hot *charoses* for Arabs. Used during the Passover Seder, *charoses* was a ritual food created with chopped walnuts, apples, and sweet wine to symbolize the mortar with which the Jews were forced to build the pyramids under the reign of the evil pharaoh. Sylvie had taught her how to crack open a walnut so that it split into perfect sections. Where was Sylvie now? Was she still alive? Why hadn't Sarah asked her folks what had happened to her and where she had gone while they were alive? Stupid, stupid. Sarah checked the basmati rice—it was perfect.

Ravi appeared abruptly with six grim, uniformed Middle Eastern bodyguards. He bustled after them and got them seated.

Shoulder-holstered guns flashed as the men made themselves comfortable.

"Good evening, madam," they said as if with one voice. *Do they know I'm Jewish?* Sarah wondered. *If they knew, would they shoot me right now, or just refuse to eat the food?* She was about to feed men who were probably rabid anti-Semites, men who wanted the Jews wiped out like cockroaches. Who was this man of whom Laura was so fond? For once, Sarah regretted keeping herself so tuned out of current events. The tallest and thinnest of them, who wore a rough beard that partially covered his acne-pitted skin and steel-rimmed glasses, stood and said in heavily accented English, "I am Mohammed. I am the food taster."

Sarah nodded and placed a platter of hummus and olives on the table. It was surreal, as if she had just stepped into some movie thriller. He tasted the hummus and olives, chewed quietly for a moment, then nodded approval. "Very good," he said, flashing a thumbs-up.

I thought he was a food taster, not a food critic, Sarah thought as she laid out other *meze* on the table, including broiled eggplant, fresh herbs, and chickpeas in olive oil and garlic, each of which was greeted with appreciative murmurs. The men waited until Mohammed had vetted the food.

Sarah took a leg of lamb from the warming oven, picked out the garlic that she had embedded into it, and set it on the cutting board for Ravi to carve. Then she pulled out the bed of fragrant rice and gently sautéed veggies, and as Ravi sliced the lamb after she demonstrated, she piled each of six plates with lamb, rice, the *charoses* and dates, and the veggies. Ravi served with an approving grin. He managed to somehow brush her arm or bump against her hip each time he came near her, making her feel cornered near the stove.

The men ate and talked among themselves, and she prepared the presentation plates of *meze* that would be placed on the table for Laura and her guest. She kept her mind focused on her mantra, *Waheguru*.

The men finished eating, and Ravi dutifully served tea. Sarah had made traditional cookies and baklava. With a chorus of a cappella *thank yous* in their distinctive accents, they exited—except for Mohammed.

One thing that intrigued Sarah about Persian food was the delicacy and the unique spicing—so subtle compared with other Middle Eastern cuisines—as well as the extensive use of fruit in meat dishes. She had followed a fantastic recipe for lamb served with a tangy yogurt sauce over a bed of herbed rice, and this was the *pièce de résistance*.

Laura entered wearing a fabulously embroidered caftan of sheer silk over a very low-cut dress with spaghetti straps. Her makeup was subtle yet dramatic, and she wore a perfume so enticing that Sarah longed to ask its name.

Laura ceremoniously inspected everything. She spoke casually to the food taster in his language. "Looks really great, really great."

Sarah beamed and began laying out cake dough in a greased pan.

"Mohammed will taste each food before it comes out, before you put it on the plates."

"That's why you're so chubby, isn't it?" Laura teased Mohammed, whose wry smile revealed a gold tooth that gave a goofy quality to his expression, which Sarah found endearing.

"If Jimmie likes the food, he will want to come in and thank you. Do not bow or show any signs of deference—it embarrasses him." Laura paused and breathed deeply. "How do I look?"

Sarah smiled. "Amazing."

The bell rang and Laura jumped. "Ravi! Please finish getting the table set up pronto." Laura hurried out.

Ravi deftly cleared the kitchen table.

Sarah went into her zone and at top speed created platters of all the appetizer delicacies, which Ravi took to the dining room. Sarah heard the front door open and Laura exclaim excitedly, "Jimmie, Jimmie, so good to see you!" Then a male voice responded, resonant and deep, like that of an opera singer. It was vaguely familiar, but maybe all those Arabs sounded the same. Then it was quiet. Ravi was busy serving, and Sarah could focus on her work.

"It's showtime!" Ravi said.

Sarah put the last touch on the assortment of appetizers. She realized she'd been sweating and now felt clammy and empty. Music began to play—was it Persian? Yoga music? She was not sure, but it was sensuous, plaintive.

Sarah carefully spooned rice onto platters and added the chicken, dates, and figs to complete one dish. On another silver platter, she made a mound of rice, laid slender ribbons of lamb, added the tangy yogurt sauce, and garnished the dish with fresh herbs. Ravi took a plate in each hand and backed through the swinging door to serve them.

For the next forty-five minutes, she prepared dishes as Ravi served. Mohammed carefully watched her every move and dutifully tasted everything before Ravi served it. One of the other bodyguards passed through every ten minutes or so. He and Mohammed would exchange a sentence or two, then the guard would move on. Sarah peeked through the doors; the lights were down and the table was candlelit. She could tell from the clacking of silverware and the tone of the conversation that the dinner was going well. She felt an attack of nerves coming on.

The guest bathroom was down the hall past the dining room. Sarah entered quickly and locked the door. She washed her face and bathed her wrists in icy water to calm herself. The worst was over. She had succeeded. She reached for her phone to text Carlos but had left it in her bag. She hurried out of the bathroom and ran smack into the guest of honor, escorted by a tall, swarthy bodyguard.

The diplomat hesitated, looking at her closely. "Sarah? Can it really be you?"

She looked at him but couldn't quite make the connection. "Do I know you?"

He was a short, slightly chubby man, with a helmet of black hair and pockmarked skin partially hidden by a thin, unkempt beard. Tinted, square wire-rimmed glasses obscured his eyes, and he wore a baggy suit and an open-necked, button-down white shirt. She had seen him somewhere, maybe on the cover of a magazine she'd read when she was getting her hair done. He looked at his bodyguard and said something in Farsi. The bodyguard objected, but the diplomat spoke sharply to him, and he reluctantly moved far enough away that he was out of earshot, though not out of sight.

The diplomat took her hands in his and said in a low voice in English, "It's Mahmoud, from so many years ago. I would recognize your perfume anywhere."

Sarah could only stare. "Jimmie" was Mahmoud Zarafshan, the crazy, Jew-hating Holocaust-denying leader of Iran who was now claiming to somehow know her!

"No, you have mistaken me for someone else."

He leaned closer and said, "No, Sarah. Remember, I gave you my grandmother's necklace."

Yes, he had given her a beautiful antique necklace when they had parted. She suddenly remembered him. *My God, how he's aged*, she thought.

As if reading her mind, he said gently, "I know, I have aged terribly. The burden of responsibility will do that to a man—but you . . . you look the same."

He took off his glasses and brushed his hair back off his forehead. His eyes filled with tears. "Sarah, I can't believe . . . I never thought I would see you again."

His voice broke, and he pressed her palm to his lips. Unbidden tears sprang into her eyes. He kissed her palm again, then her wrist. Electricity shot through her, and she felt weak in the knees.

"This can't be an accident," he said. "What are you doing here?" The bodyguard moved toward them, and again Mahmoud waved him back.

"I cooked the meal you are eating."

"How wonderful." A tear slipped down her cheek, and Mahmoud gently wiped it away. "I want to see you. I am here until the last session of the General Assembly on the twenty-first."

"I can't."

"Please, you must. Why did you never respond to my e-mail? I wasn't married then. I was simply a teacher. I would have come for you."

"That's what I was afraid of. I wasn't ready to be serious."

"And now?"

"You're married."

"So? Are you?"

"No, I'm divorced."

Mahmoud dropped her hand. "Losing you was the greatest regret of my life."

"You'd better go back in."

"Give me your phone number. I want to see you."

She hesitated. She was flattered. "No, I must get back."

She turned and hurried back to the kitchen, but he followed her. Ravi was refilling the coffeepot. "Hey, Sarah, they were raving about your food."

"Thanks."

Mahmoud entered, the bodyguard hovering in the doorway. "I would like a glass of water," he said loudly in English. Ravi scurried out with the coffee.

In a low voice, Mahmoud said, in Farsi, "Mohammed, go and smoke. Nehir, go back inside." The two bodyguards disappeared.

They were alone. Sarah tried to reconcile this ugly man with the beauty she had loved so long ago as she got a bottle of water from the fridge and poured him a glass. Mahmoud walked over to her. "Sarah, I have thought of you every day." He took the glass out of her hand and set it on the nearby table.

Sarah shook her head. "That was ten years ago. This is silly. No good can possibly come of it. Think of your position. What would happen if they ever found out you . . ." —*What is the right word?*— ". . . had been in love with a Jewess?"

"Were you in love?"

Sarah softened. She remembered how she was just starting out, working as a bartender for a large commercial caterer that supplied party services throughout the city. She had cooked for a function that celebrated a conference of international engineers, and Mahmoud had been there among hundreds of other attendees. At the time, he was working as a traffic planner in Tehran.

"I think you read too much into it. It was just one of those crazy things," she said.

He stepped closer and faced her, putting his hands on her shoulders. "How can you say that?" he said fiercely. "You know that wasn't so. It was real." He let go of her and turned away.

"I'm sorry. You're right, that wasn't fair."

"Good." He picked up one of her business cards from the counter, turned it over, and wrote a number on it. "I want to see you." He handed her the card.

Ravi returned with the coffeepot.

Nehir reappeared in the doorway. "You must go back to the table, sir," he said in careful English.

Mahmoud nodded. "Thank you for the water, miss." He spoke loudly, then followed his bodyguard out of the kitchen.

For a moment Sarah was reminded of the scene in *Casablanca* when Ilsa first walks into Rick's café. Bogart later laments to his friend Sam, the piano player, "Of all the gin joints, in all the towns, in all the world, she walks into mine." Then he gets drunk. *That is an excellent idea,* Sarah thought, *as soon as I can get out of here!*

She pocketed the card, sat down abruptly, and poured herself a large glass of wine. She drank it down in a single gulp. Her cell phone rang. It was Zev. Rescued!

"Hi. Can I give you a lift home when you're done?"

"You really want that tape, don't you?"

"No, actually I was hoping for seconds on dinner." A pause. She realized he was joking, and she laughed through quavering nerves. Thank goodness for the call!

For a second, she realized that she was sliding back under Mahmoud's spell. She shook her head to clear it.

"Yes, that would be amazing," Sarah said. "I'll be done in about an hour."

CHAPTER 25

A Lovely Night in Brighton Beach

EV PULLED IN FRONT of Sarah's building. "Let me help you with that stuff."

"Thanks."

He drove into a parking spot and clicked on his blinkers. She got out. Zev opened the trunk, avoiding his jacket, which still concealed the gun, and took out her two canvas carryalls filled with cooking stuff.

"I know exactly where I left the tape," she said. She led the way, and as soon as she opened the door she knew something wasn't right, because it wasn't locked. From the doorway they could see that the place had been ransacked. She started to go inside, but Zev grabbed her by the arm and stopped her. He entered the apartment ahead of her, picking up a broom as an impromptu weapon. He looked fierce as he swept through the apartment quickly.

"Okay."

Sarah walked in and wanted to cry. Everything in her kitchen had been trashed. Spices were opened and strewn all over the floor; pots and pans lay in dented heaps.

"Better see what's missing. I'll call the cops."

"No, wait," she said.

Sarah took a quick inventory. Strange . . . nothing appeared to be missing. The stereo, TV, and her jewelry were all there, though scattered about. Unexpectedly, she burst into tears, great ripping sighs. Zev stood beside her awkwardly, then gently put an arm around her. "There, there, Sarah. I'm here. I'll help you. Don't worry. Don't you want me to call the cops?"

"There's nothing missing." Sarah got the words out between sobs. She realized he had his arm around her and pulled away, trying to regain control.

"Who would do this?" she asked Zev. Her anger helped her focus. "Who would trash my house for no reason?"

"I'm not leaving you here alone. I'm not sure it's safe."

Sarah didn't know what freaked her out more: seeing Mahmoud again or having her apartment destroyed.

"My roommate knows a lot of cops. Let's see what I can find out."

"Why would someone do this to me?"

"Because they were looking for something—something specific. Are you sure everything is here?"

"Seems to be."

"Check your jewelry again." Sarah went back into the bedroom and looked through her stuff as she started straightening up. Her harp-shaped jewelry case, which held her bracelets and necklaces, had been knocked to the floor, but nothing was missing—

Wait! The necklace was gone! The one that Mahmoud had taken off his own neck to give to her—it was gone! *Why that?*

Like Bogart in *Casablanca*, she flashed back—but not to the invasion of Paris by the Nazis, rather, to her last night with Mahmoud ten years earlier. He had taken her home in a cab. They had held hands, unable to speak. Tears had streamed out of her eyes. As they neared her apartment, Mahmoud had taken off his heavy gold necklace with an engraved ruby pendant the size of a quarter and clasped it around her neck. "My grandmother gave me this. I will always be with you, and you with me." She had been crying so hard he had to help her out of the cab and walk her inside.

"I can't come up or I will never leave." These were his last words to her. She had nodded—a last kiss, a hug—then he was gone.

Suddenly she was furious and retrieved the card with his number on it. She looked to see Zev on the phone and figured he must be talking to his roommate. She was grateful he was here. She dialed Mahmoud, and to her surprise he answered.

"Hello, it's Sarah."

"Sarah, how wonderful that you called!"

"Maybe. Look—someone robbed me. But nothing was stolen, so I can't understand . . ." There was silence.

"Broke into your apartment?" Mahmoud said. "I am very concerned now, Sarah. I didn't think anyone knew about us. They might be trying to blackmail me because the speech I will be giving will not be popular."

"Who are 'they'?"

"I can't tell you that right now. Tell me, do you still have souvenirs from our friendship?"

"Friendship?"

"What we had, I mean. Don't believe for an instant that I don't think about you every day, Sarah, and of our brief, sweet time together, even though it was so long ago. You are a beloved thorn in my eternal side."

"Oh, so now it's my fault?"

"No, my dove. What I'm trying to say is that love has a habit of sticking around."

"Tell me about it."

There was silence on the phone.

"I'm coming over."

"No, that would be a bad idea."

She heard him take a breath. "Are you all right? Is someone there with you?"

"Yes, and yes there is."

"Oh, I'm relieved . . . Is it a man?"

"What do you care? It's all water under the bridge."

There was another pause. Then in a quiet tone, he said, "I

think of you constantly."

Sarah felt her heart twist in her chest, and a sharp pain followed. Despite the hour, a Chopin étude was audible nearby, and the melodic piano strains filtered in through the window. She had played Chopin for Mahmoud all those years ago.

"Do you still have the necklace I gave you?"

"Yes, why? Do you want it back now?"

"No, of course not. I gave it to you. It was my grandmother's. I was merely concerned that whoever did this might have taken it from you."

"Why?"

"I will tell you when I see you."

Sarah tried to come to grips with the fact that he was now the president of Iran and one of Israel's archenemies. Maybe being compromised would be a good way to get him out of power.

"That's not going to happen," she said.

"I must see you," he said. Sarah felt herself melting.

She was too upset to speak. She couldn't remember the last time she'd seen the necklace. Was it stolen or in some weird hidey-hole? She had no idea. She decided at that moment to go on the wagon.

Mahmoud pressed her. "Can you meet me at our old place?"

"Now? I have to call the police and make a report."

"No, don't. Please don't do that. I will take care of this. I will send someone to guard you. You must trust me."

Sarah hesitated. "Okay," she said finally.

"Good."

Sarah was silent. *He's married, he's married, he's married,* she told herself repeatedly, but it didn't change anything. She realized now that this was why her marriage could never have worked: Deep down inside, she had been in love with another man. She clicked off her phone and charged back into the bedroom.

"My necklace! Oh, my God—where is it?"

She described it to Zev, and they looked all over. He asked her where she'd gotten it.

"It was a souvenir from the best journey I ever took." He seemed confused, and she recognized the look. "Someone I loved gave it to me."

Zev felt a pang of envy. "Who was it?"

Sarah considered his tone. "Are you jealous?"

"No, of course not. But I think we should call the cops—now."

"No, we can't."

"That's ridiculous. Why not?"

"Mahmoud said it might endanger me."

"Who's Mahmoud?"

"The man at dinner tonight. The president of Iran."

"You call him by his first name?"

"Well, I knew him a long time ago, before he became the president."

"How long ago?" Zev felt a wave of anger at Mahmoud coursing through his veins, as if his blood had turned to acid.

Sarah stiffened, then realized poor Zev was smitten with her. "I dunno . . . ten, eleven years ago."

"You slept with an Arab?"

"Fuck you. That's none of your business."

"Oh. So sorry. And this necklace?"

"He gave it to me. He said it was his grandmother's family heirloom!"

Zev bit his tongue hard to stop his words from coming out in a snarl. He was upset but reined in his rage. He felt like he did when chastised by his mother, and he tried to recover. Meekly, he uttered, "Okay, I understand. Please let me tell my roomie about this. He knows a lot of cops. Someone can check this out under the radar to assess your danger."

He got on the phone. Sarah started to clean up. Zev held up his hand. "No, let's leave this alone 'til we get some answers."

Sarah went out into the hall, where she sat in a chair and covered her eyes. Mahmoud still had the same effect on her. In spite of the fact that he was married now, in spite of the fact that he was the president of a rogue nation, praised in the Muslim world but reviled everywhere else, in spite of the fact that any relationship with him seemed utterly impossible . . . ludicrous, really . . . in spite of all of it, her body still longed for him, and she was obviously a crack junkie for his love.

Zev went into the bathroom and methodically took everything out of the cupboards. Sexy lingerie had been thrown about, and he tried to concentrate on the task at hand but failed. On a shelf stood a faceted crystal bottle with a label that read *La Nuit Exotique*. He opened the flacon and recognized the exotic scent he had smelled on Sarah in the cab. The scent aroused him, and he put the perfume back quickly. Angry at his lust, he kicked a small lined garbage pail, upending it. The contents spilled, and the necklace, wrapped in a pair of tiger-print panties, slid out and lay exposed on the floor amid the garbage.

Zev was confused. All he could surmise was that the jewelry must have been knocked into the garbage by mistake, though he wasn't sure how to factor in the panties. The heavy gold chain threaded into a round pendant almost two inches in diameter, which had a Star of David set across an eye-popping ruby with Hebrew letters—which he couldn't read, and that failing angered him now like it never had before. But he wondered: *Why would a Muslim have a family heirloom that is a Hebrew relic?*

The words of the psychic came to him now, and Zev knew the necklace was the key to the plan to which Gwydion and the guides had alluded, but he had no idea what that scheme might turn out to be. Character assassination, perhaps? Had that been the goal of the thugs who had botched the burglary? In a moment of clarity—tinged with his own sexual fantasy—he wrapped the necklace back in the panties and put everything in his pocket. He knew what he had to do.

Sarah had torn through the house, arriving in the bathroom a moment after Zev had pocketed his find. She was close to tears. Zev was wretchedly conflicted—her sadness and abject grief tempted him to return it to her that instant, but instead he hugged her and she collapsed, crying into his shoulder. "But who would take it?" she cried.

Zev shrugged. "I can't imagine."

Her cell rang again. It was Mahmoud.

Before she could answer it, Zev said, "You can't stay here—there's a sofa at my place you can crash on." Sarah believed he was right. What if whoever broke in came back? She answered the phone.

"I am sending a car for you—let me take you somewhere safe."

Alarmed, Sarah looked over at Zev, and without taking her eyes off him said, "Mahmoud, I'll call you back," and hung up.

Zev was torn. Why had he offered . . .? He couldn't leave her now, and he knew it. It just wasn't an option. This attack on her home was a violation, an outrage, nothing short of a rape of sorts. She broke into his thoughts.

"Do you think your friends can figure out whether this was vandalism, a burglary attempt, or something more?"

"Like what?"

"I don't know, but Mahmoud is here to make some big speech at the UN. Maybe someone knows about our old relationship and wants to stir up dirt. You know: 'President of Iran who wants to blow up Israel once cavorted with Jewish girl.' "

"Were there other things that might link you?"

Sarah shook her head. "Only the necklace."

Zev processed this. If someone was looking to stir up dirt, he had the evidence right in his pocket. "Does anyone else have keys to your place here? There was no break-in, right? I mean, the door was open, wasn't it?"

"Santiago and Carlos." She was already dialing Santiago. "But Santiago would never do anything like this. And Carlos is in Sri Lanka!"

"So, do you have any enemies or rivals that could have gotten in?"

Sarah looked bemused. "I guess everyone has a couple, but no one who would break in—I mean, find a way to get into my apartment to destroy it."

She got Santiago's voicemail. "Hey, call me! Do you still have my keys?"

She texted Carlos in Sri Lanka. "I have his house keys," she said offhandedly.

"Where . . . are . . . my . . . keys?" She said it aloud as she typed. "We're not going to get any info from those guys right away. God! I have to work tomorrow! I better start cleaning up."

"I'll stay and help you."

She was tempted but realized Zev had a crush on her. And Mahmoud was waiting for her call.

Zev waited for an answer. She went to her kitchen junk drawer, dug around until she found Carlos's keys and found Zev's tape in there. Why had she put it in there? It wasn't clear, but perhaps it was a good omen.

"I didn't listen to all of it, as I said. As soon as he called you 'Zev,' I stopped."

Her phone rang again. It was Mahmoud.

"I am coming to your house to get you."

She hung up. "Zev, will you help me?"

He jumped up, alarmed. "Of course."

"Let's go," she said urgently.

"Yes, ma'am. Where to?" Her behavior truly mystified Zev, but he didn't care. He had nowhere to be, no one to see. He had never felt more alive—or more in love. The necklace burned a hole in his pocket, but he could not let it go—not now.

Rachel—the name formed in his mind—Rachel, Aaron . . . then he thought of the rabbi. The rabbi! That's who he needed to see about the necklace. They raced out of the apartment, down the stairs, and got into his cab. And as they pulled away, Zev saw a stretch limo pull up in front of the building.

"Is that him?"

"Yes. Please hurry."

Zev's eyes darted as he ran a red light. "Where do we go?"

"Want to have a midnight picnic?"

"It's three A.M."

"Potato, po-tah-toe! How about a sunrise picnic then? Some-place where we can look out over water."

"Okay. Where do you want to go?"

Tears unwelcome rolled down her cheeks. At a red light, he handed her tissues.

"Poor Sarah," he said.

"Don't insult me."

"No. I meant it. You're in love with a married man. I admire you for not acting on your impulse."

Sarah was quiet, and Zev drove them to Brighton Beach. It was predawn when they arrived—rough-edged, not yet day, the remains of night still clinging to the beach as it slowly surrendered to the eastern horizon. He parked near the boardwalk and opened his window. There was the smell of salt water, the sound of crashing waves.

"Let's get out," she said.

"No. I have no idea if it's safe here."

"Okay."

They sat in the car and ate. Sarah had managed, even in the panic of getting away, to grab some Tupperware tubs of food and a bottle of wine from the fridge as they dashed from her apartment. They drank and ate, and as she chewed she texted Mahmoud furiously: LEAVE ME ALONE!

A rosy dawn filled the sky. A police car pulled up and two cops got out, walking up onto the boardwalk.

"I think it's safe to get out," Zev said.

But Sarah had fallen asleep, phone in hand. Zev felt tenderness, an overwhelming softness—a feeling that somehow seemed to match the pink color of the sky. Her phone fell out of her hand. He couldn't resist looking at the text message: It read: PLEASE, WE NEED TO TALK. I WAS WRONG TO LEAVE YOU FOR ALL THESE YEARS. Zev turned the phone off and watched Sarah sleep.

Then he noticed that, along with the food, she had also grabbed the portable cassette player and shoved it into her bag. The tape recorder had a car-phone power jack, so he plugged it in and listened to his cassette. It was essentially what he remembered—but at the end Gwydion had added something: a question. In his thick British accent, he had asked, presumably rhetorically, "If you knew what Hitler would do, and you could stop him, would you kill him? Even if it meant forfeiting your life?"

Sarah opened her eyes. "Hi," she said shyly. "Thank you. I might have done something stupid."

"There's still time." He smiled.

"We need to find a bathroom," she said.

Reluctantly, Zev drove to Sarah's apartment and dropped her off.

"I don't think you should go back."

"If they went to that much trouble, they got what they were after, and I have to cook tonight. Let's talk later." He couldn't leave the cab double-parked, so he waited while she went upstairs until she waved to him through the window.

Then she turned and walked into her living room, where she was stunned to see that the apartment had been cleaned up!

CHAPTER 26

THE RABBI AND THE NECKLACE

AS ZEV PULLED AWAY from Sarah's building, a Hebrew phrase passed through his mind—the first he had heard since the I-beam incident: *"Shema Yisrael."* He couldn't visualize the words, but the voice sounded like that of the rabbi. The words were from the centerpiece of the morning and evening prayers he'd grown up reciting, and meant loosely, "Hear, O Israel, the Lord is our God, the Lord is one." If he remembered correctly, the verse was from Deuteronomy 6:4.

Rabbi Cohen would know what to do about the necklace. Zev could go down to D.C. to see him, and while there he could stop and see Rachel and Aaron—he'd been neglecting the boy. Zev took a shower and, wrapped in a towel, sat down and checked the Amtrak schedule online. He examined himself in the mirror—he looked pretty much the same, though his hair was fashionably short and his sideburns long. He dressed quickly and came out of the bedroom carrying a small overnight bag.

Tom looked at him. "What's up?"

"Can you cover my shifts? I have to go home for a couple of days."

"Everything okay? Your mom?"

"Yeah."

"Fine. Good timing, actually—we're on hiatus right now. See you in a few."

Zev was about to leave, but Tom gave him a bear hug, and, to Tom's surprise, Zev responded. They stood back, Zev a little embarrassed. "You're a good man," Tom said. "Don't know if you realize it, but you got me and Heather back together again. I owe you, man."

Zev found himself saying, "There is one thing . . ."

"Anything. You name it."

"Can you get a couple of your cop guys to keep an eye on Sarah's place? I still can't understand why she was broken into, but nothing was taken. A little weird, huh?"

"Something more here I should know about?"

"Yeah. She's cooking for the current president of Iran."

"Seriously?"

"Seriously."

"Done. I'll take care of it."

Tom looked like he wanted another hug, so Zev left fast.

☙

Zev wasn't sure what to do about his folks, so he called Rachel and asked if he could sleep on her couch for a night or two.

"Aaron will be thrilled," she responded. "We have an air mattress—you can sleep in his room."

In Penn Station, he picked up gifts for them.

As soon as he got on the train to Washington, Zev called Rabbi Cohen, who answered the phone himself. *Shalom* was the only world Zev recognized. When the rabbi figured out it was Zev, he delightedly launched into a profusion of welcoming greetings—but all in Hebrew.

Zev waited until the rabbi was done, then said quietly, "I can no longer understand the language."

"Oh." The rabbi was silent, thinking. "Come over. It's almost lunchtime. You stop by, and we'll talk. Have you called your folks?"

"No, Rabbi. This is not social. I need your help. I must meet you privately."

"Okay."

"Somewhere we won't be recognized."

"Sounds serious. Okay, where?"

Zev hadn't expected this to go so easily, and he blurted out the first thing that came into his mind.

"The Marriot, near the airport. There's a bar there called Pig and Whistle." To his surprise, the rabbi agreed without further comment.

When Zev entered the bar, he half-expected to see Rachel. He remembered how uncomfortable and self-conscious he had felt the first time he walked into this place. This time he felt no separation because of his Jewishness but casually connected *mano a mano* with the bartender. Zev ordered a club soda. The rabbi appeared in the doorway, looked around, and easily spotted Zev towering over the other lunchtime patrons. Zev waved him over. "Let me get you something. We can sit in the back—it's quiet there. What will you have?"

To Zev's complete surprise, the rabbi ordered a double Scotch. Zev switched to a beer. The barmaid looked with momentary curiosity at the rabbi in his black brimmed hat and heavy beard, but then dismissed it with a shrug.

"So, Zev. This is a mystery! You've lost your ability to understand Hebrew. What about Yiddish?"

"No. Not a word. Actually just two words: *Shema Yisrael.*"

The rabbi frowned. "What happened?"

"You remember. Before I got sick and left, I was almost killed by a falling steel I-beam on my way to work . . . I felt it brush my cheek."

The rabbi nodded. "I remember. Such a blessing."

"Something changed in me at that moment—something radical. Then later, I had this bizarre dream—more like a vision—and I awoke in time to save a little boy from hanging himself. That was the day I drove on *Shabbos.*"

"Wait . . . back up. What boy?"

"I met a woman—actually, right here, in this bar. She took me home. The way life was going for me, I didn't want to meet death without having that pleasure. It turned out she had been widowed and had a son, about six years old. Anyway, I woke up in the middle of the night after having a vivid dream in which *Zayde* appeared and told me to look after this boy. I was delirious with fever—but I drove back and found him in his room, about to hang himself. He said that he missed his father." Zev's voice broke and he swigged his beer. "And that was why."

"So, are we meeting because you need to confess? That's the Catholic Church. We don't believe in heaven, and even if we did, you couldn't buy your way in. It's not His way."

Zev could almost hear Sarah's voice, thickly sarcastic, saying, *Oh, I see—you know God's thoughts now?*

"I have to show you something," Zev said. He looked around to see if anyone was watching, but no one paid them any mind. He reached into his pocket and pulled out the necklace, which earlier he'd had the good sense to put carefully into a Baggie covered in paper towels after unwrapping it from Sarah's panties. The rabbi gasped and drank his Scotch in a gulp. "Where did you get this?"

"From a Jewish woman in New York who had an affair with Zarafshan, years ago, before he became the president of Iran. He had given it to her, saying it was his grandmother's. Someone went to a lot of trouble to get it from her, but it ended up with me."

"This necklace," Rabbi Cohen said in a harsh whisper, "if it is what I think it is, this is the item given to Mary Magdalene by her wealthy Jewish father. Since her last name was the same as the town, it stands to reason that she was a benefactor to Jesus, and may have been his consort—not that I want to publicize my opinion."

Zev stared. This was the rabbi who controlled the Orthodox world in which Zev had grown up.

"You believe in Jesus?"

"No need to *believe* Jesus existed—that's a fact. He may well have been a prophet, but he was not immortal; and besides, from my perspective everyone is the son or daughter of God, so too much has been made of that already."

"What about his rising from the tomb?"

"What about the parting of the Red Sea? What about your saving that boy?"

Zev was silent, then, in a low voice, asked, "Rabbi, does this mean you believe in miracles?"

"Miracles, shmiracles! Do we have to make a *megillah* about something that seems to be a natural part of life? Your own wise grandfather once said to me, 'I think maybe a miracle in life is anything we notice!' "

Zev thought about it. *Zayde* was wise indeed! "So, if the necklace belonged to Mary, how did Zarafshan get ahold of it? He told this woman it had been his grandmother's."

"Yes, you said that already. Go get me another drink—and some nuts or something." Zev obediently walked to the bar, Gwydion's question burning in his mind: *If you knew what Hitler would do . . . . ?*

As he waited at the bar, Rachel came in, this time with a girlfriend. She came up to Zev with a smile. "Hi! What are you doing here?"

"I could ask you the same question."

She dug into her purse. "Oh, just a quick lunch. But since you're here, let me give you the house keys. The air bed is made up in Aaron's room, and he can't wait to see you."

"Is he there alone?"

"Yes, I'll only have one drink. Care to join us? This is my friend Cindy."

"Hi." Cindy was another pretty blonde. She gave him that little smile that let him know she was interested.

"Sorry, I'm already having a drink with someone. Maybe later." Zev saw a flicker of something in Rachel's eyes.

"It's not what you think, Rachel. I'll explain later."

The drinks came. Zev paid and suavely told the bartender that he would cover Rachel's and Cindy's beverages and went back to the rabbi. He was worried. It hadn't occurred to him that Rachel might still be coming to the bar and picking up men. *What about the brother-in-law?* he wondered. *Is that still going on?*

The rabbi sat alone in the back polishing the necklace with his handkerchief. Zev set the drink in front of him, and the rabbi immediately took a sip without taking his eyes off his work. "Listen, the legend behind this necklace is that it was passed down from Tamar, King David's daughter, who is reputed to have written the Book of David. There's no way to scientifically prove any of it, of course, but if that is true, then Zarafshan's paternal grandmother was Jewish—and if his father's mother was Jewish, then Zarafshan is half-Jewish."

Zev thought about this revelatory fact. "Then why would he hate us so much?"

"Identification with the aggressor—Stockholm Syndrome—like the Jews who worked with the Nazis. It is better to be the victimizer than the victim. Who knows?"

"Wow."

"This girl, who is she?"

Zev blushed to the roots of his hair.

"Oh, I see. Your girlfriend. I suppose she's gentile."

"No, and I wish! It's a long story about how we met, but—"

"You want her to love you back."

Zev nodded.

"Okay, so we have a necklace that could prove that Zarafshan is Jewish. There's a girl. What else?"

Zev blurted, "If you knew who was going to be the next Hitler, would you kill him even if you knew your name would live in infamy and he would probably be hailed as a martyred saint?"

Without hesitation, the rabbi said, "Yes, if I could prevent nuclear war."

"Wait. What are you talking about?"

"Zarafshan has been stockpiling weapons. He is a fanatic. He denies the Holocaust because he believes that the Jews used it to justify the taking of Palestinian land—use it to justify the right of the State of Israel to exist at all, which he also denies. There is fear amongst our brethren in Israel that something terrible is about to happen."

The rabbi was thoughtful. "But maybe if we can prove that he gave a Jew this necklace, and if the Iranians found out their beloved leader who claims he is the Twelfth Imam was himself Jewish, even half-Jewish—that might very well topple the whole thing, the whole regime, and prevent a truly horrific tragedy. I must speak to your woman friend. Who is she?"

Zev hesitated, reluctant to get Sarah entangled. "No," he said, "I don't want her involved. I want to protect her. She had an affair with him, true, but that was ten, twelve years ago."

"So he's got another skeleton in his closet."

"Why? Do you really think revealing he's half-Jewish and slept with a Jew would matter enough?"

"Oh, come on, Zev! Think about it. What if Hitler had been revealed to be a Jew during the Final Solution? He would have ended up in one of his own ovens."

Zev was quiet. "I have to think about this. I gotta go."

"Where are you staying?"

Zev shot him a grateful look because the rabbi hadn't brought up Zev's parents. "I am staying with a friend."

"Okay. I will check on this necklace and call you in the morning. Think about whether your obligation is to Israel or to this girl."

"Aren't you exaggerating?"

"I hope so."

Zev accompanied Rabbi Cohen to the hotel lobby, they shook hands, and the rabbi left with the necklace and an admonishment: "You should go see your parents. Your mother has been sick since you left." Zev nodded solemnly but said nothing. So much for premature gratitude.

Zev returned to where Rachel was sitting at the bar. She was chatting with some smarmy middle-management type. Didn't she see that all of this was demeaning? Who was watching Aaron? He sized up the beer-drinking empty suit. *Arrogant cock-*

sucker. When had he begun to use this sort of language?

He felt an overpowering wave of hostility toward this bozo. Rachel was a bit loaded. "I'll take you home now," Zev said loudly enough for every other man at the bar to hear.

Rachel slurred, "I'm not ready."

"Your son is waiting for you." Zev put money on the bar. He glared at the young woman that Rachel had come in with. *What the hell is her name?* Cindy looked back at him vacantly. He took Rachel's arm and said quietly, close to her ear, "Let's go." Rachel struggled slightly, but Zev held her upper arm firmly, making it look like he was simply helping her, and led her out the door.

"Where's your car?"

"Parking lot across the street. Who the hell are you to interfere?"

"I'm sorry, Rachel, I'm sorry. I'll explain later."

"Aaron will be so happy to see you."

"Are you still seeing that idiot? What was his name? Patrick?" Though Zev very well remembered Frank's name.

"No, it's the anniversary of Aaron's dad's death tomorrow. We're going out to visit the gravesite. Will you come?"

It occurred to Zev that his insult ploy had been a blunder, because he didn't know if she meant "No, his name isn't Patrick" or "No, I'm not seeing that idiot anymore." He said nothing further.

They reached the parking lot, and Rachel found her keys—which Zev took away from her, opening the door of the brand-new Volvo. *Where the hell did she get the money for this?* he wondered, and realized that Frank was still very much in the picture.

Rabbi Cohen went home and made some phone calls. In his youth, he had gone to Israel to fight and eventually wound up working in military intelligence. He became a rabbi in his late twenties when an injury destroyed any chance of his continuing an active military career. He locked himself in his study and used the house phone to call an old contact of his who was still highly placed in Israeli intelligence. Ari Ben-Gurim, the man who ran the Mossad, took his call right away. Ari was in his early sixties and had survived the Six-Day War—minus most of his right leg. He enjoyed practicing his English, and the two men always spent time together whenever Rabbi Cohen traveled to Israel for a conference.

"So, Rabbi, what's going on?"

The rabbi told him the situation. Ari was quiet for a while, then said, "This could be the golden opportunity for us. Did you know that the rumor is that Zarafshan is planning to attack Israel with nuclear weapons in the near future? We think they have already decided on a date."

The rabbi was shocked. "He would use them on Israel?"

Ari said grimly, "Not Israel only."

"*Oy vey!*"

"Let me get on this. Find out who this girl is. We need to contact her."

The rabbi's cell phone rang. He looked at the number and recognized it as Zev's. "Hold on, Ari. I may have that information right now."

Zev was now sitting with Aaron at his favorite McDonald's. Much as he had tried to fight it, Zev had realized what he had to do, and had forced himself to make this call to Rabbi Cohen.

"Her name is Sarah," he said, and gave the rabbi her phone number. "Promise me she'll be safe."

"I will try to protect her. Don't tell her about any of this."

Zev texted Sarah, but she did not respond. After three tries, Zev accepted defeat.

CHAPTER 27

Invitation to Betrayal

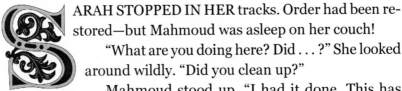ARAH STOPPED IN HER tracks. Order had been restored—but Mahmoud was asleep on her couch!

"What are you doing here? Did . . . ?" She looked around wildly. "Did you clean up?"

Mahmoud stood up. "I had it done. This has nothing to do with me. I have enemies. They may have come here to try to find evidence that they could use against me."

"What kind of enemies?"

"We all have skeletons in our closets. I'm afraid, my darling, that you are mine."

Sarah was shaken. "Thank you for cleaning up," she managed to say. She realized that arriving at her violated apartment had caused her to panic, and she was drawing a blank as she racked her mind trying to remember where she had hidden the necklace *this time*. This unnerved her. She had to call Zev—

Mahmoud interrupted her thoughts. "So, did you find the necklace?"

"After I talked to you, I remembered that I had put it in the vault." Sarah lied.

"Thank goodness!" Mahmoud paused. "I saw your divorce decree. I'm sorry."

"Me too."

"Come. Let me hold you."

"Mahmoud, this is like an addiction—if I embrace you even once, I am doomed."

He looked incredibly sad, and seemed burdened. He sighed heavily. "What if I said to you I do not want to live without you anymore?"

Sarah trembled from head to toe. "You have got to get out of here, Mahmoud. If I am a skeleton in your closet, it may be best to keep me there."

He crossed the room and took her in his arms, but didn't kiss her. They held each other, and both wept unashamedly. After a time, he led her to the sofa.

No need for words. They sat there on the couch, his arm around her shoulders, her head on his chest, and it seemed to Sarah that they shared the same breath, the same rhythm—in and out, in and out.

Finally, he moved gently so he could look into her eyes. "I wish I was still just a traffic planner. Then I would be free to leave my life behind and get a job here."

"I can't picture you as a professor of engineering at City College or Columbia."

He was indignant but tried to cover. "Why? Do you think I am not a good teacher?"

"No, no, not that. It would be wonderful. It's just—"

But Sarah halted and forced herself to focus. "Mahmoud, what if someone saw you come in here?"

"I assure you, no one did. And I want you to leave here and stay somewhere safe until this is all over."

"Until *what* is all over?"

"Sarah, the speech I am giving will be world-changing. There are only a few days before I speak."

He had always been a little full of himself, and she laughed. "Really?"

"Can I kiss you? Please."

He got down on one knee and kissed her hand. "Please, just once?"

"You know what will happen. Would you risk your holy war for a kiss?"

He nodded. "Without hesitation."

Sarah surprised herself by saying, "I will be just fine here. Go back to your hotel or wherever. I will call you later."

To her further surprise, he stood and nodded meekly. "All right. As long as I will see you later."

When did I agree to that? But Sarah said nothing and watched Mahmoud leave and close the door. She took a deep breath and resolved that she absolutely would not get involved in any of this.

As she took a much-needed shower, she found herself asking where God was in all this. One of her friends had told her a funny joke: *How do you know God is male? No female God would have invented the bikini wax.*

Or rape, or marriage, Sarah thought, but the humor in it wore off quickly. She had barely gotten out of the shower when the buzzer sounded. She turned off the water and put on a robe.

"Who is it?"

"Friend of Zev's," a male voice said.

She buzzed him in. She hoped Zev was okay and was surprised how concerned for him she felt. Well, whatever. She opened the door, and a man and a woman dressed in conservative attire stood in her entranceway.

"Are you Sarah?"

"Yes. Is Zev okay?"

"May we come in?" the man said impatiently. He seemed to be in his late forties, with brush-cut gray hair and a neat moustache. The woman had black hair up in a bun, with curly wisps constantly escaping that she kept tucking back in. She was young—maybe in her late thirties.

"Pardon the bathrobe and the wet hair. You caught me in the shower." She led them inside and gestured for them to sit on the couch. She sat opposite on an ottoman.

"Is Zev okay?"

"Yes, Mr. Bronfman is fine."

Sarah was relieved but puzzled. "So, uh, well, who are you?"

"I am Miriam Lev, and this is Ben Halevi. We are from the Mossad."

Sarah blinked. This was ridiculous. She had either been abducted by aliens or teleported into a Hollywood film! She resolved to stop drinking, effective immediately. She asked God to send her the right words—for once. "May I see some identification?" was what came out of her mouth. She repressed a smile at this absurd banality.

The woman sat stone-faced as she took a badge out of her pocket; the man did the same soon thereafter. Sarah examined their credentials. They weren't smiling in their ID photos.

"What do you want with me?" Sarah asked.

"We believe you can help Israel."

"Because I'm Jewish?"

Ben spoke. "Well, partly. But more because of your relationship with the president of Iran."

Sarah got up angrily. "I will not come out and tell the world we had an affair."

Miriam smiled. "No, of course not, and it's always understandable that one wants to put friendship above politics."

"What then?"

"We just want you to renew your relationship with Mr. Zarafshan."

Sarah looked at Miriam askance. "He's married."

Ben nodded. "Yes, we know."

"So, you're pimping me out for Israel."

"I'm afraid it's not that simple."

"Well, I draw the line at 'married'—you know what I mean?"

"At the cost of the destruction of the state of Israel?"

Sarah had a moment of disorientation. Was she dreaming? Was this some practical joke Zev had arranged? He had to be involved, because no one else besides her and Mahmoud knew. "Is this a put-on? Are you actors?" She got up, walked to the door, and opened it. "Is this a sick prank? Please leave."

Miriam opened her briefcase and extracted an eight-by-ten

color photo, handing it to Sarah, whose eyes bugged when she looked at it—it was a picture of her necklace!

"How . . . ?" Sarah was perplexed, then enraged. "So it was you that came in and destroyed my apartment. And stole my necklace! That's a felony. I should call the cops right now and report you!"

"We didn't find it."

"But you did break in."

"Sorry we weren't neater." Ben looked truly repentant.

Sarah closed the door. "If you didn't find it—Mahmoud?"

"No, of course not. Think, Sarah. Mahmoud wouldn't give it to us. It was Zev."

"Zev stole it? Why?"

"We're not comfortable with 'stole.' He took it because he's a patriot and he suspected, quite rightly, the significance of it."

"Other than the fact that the now-president of Iran gave it to his Jewish lover."

"Did Zarafshan tell you nothing about it when you received it?"

"Only that it had been his father's mother's necklace." Sarah thought back. "He did tell me that it had value to him far beyond money—and he swore me to secrecy. He said that I should never tell anyone who had given it to me."

"Did you ever have it appraised?"

"What do you take me for? I did as he asked."

"Where was it last night? Why weren't you wearing it?"

"How do you know I wasn't? How do you even know about me at all?"

Miriam said quietly, "Ms. Bellavita informed us."

"Ms. Bellavita?"

"Laura Bellavita," Ben said. "She called us when she realized you and Mahmoud knew each other."

"*Laura?* Is she some sort of secret agent?" Sarah asked, then thought, *No more drinking—ever!*

Miriam and Ben exchanged a smile. Ben nodded. "Yes, you could say that."

Sarah rubbed her temples. "Where the hell did you find it?"

Ben and Miriam exchanged a look. Miriam said, "We told you, we didn't take it."

"Right, okay, so Zev did."

Miriam nodded. "Apparently he found it in the wastebasket in your bathroom. Perhaps it fell in accidentally?"

The trash can was right next to the sink, and Sarah realized immediately what had happened. In one of her drunken moments, she'd undoubtedly hidden the necklace in the liner—there was more of God's absurdist humor—and it was best not to disclose such.

"Okay. So, Zev took it for some screwed-up patriotic reason. Is he also Mossad?"

"No, he is not."

"Fine. He's just a bastard and a thief then. Just tell me what the hell is going on, and why you want me to be Mata Hari."

"We want you to find out when Mahmoud is planning to launch an attack on Israel."

"I see, the old pillow-talk game. I let him make love to me, and he spills all. That only happens in movies, haven't you heard?"

Miriam looked surprised. "Don't you want to help Israel?"

"Let me be blunt. You don't know for a fact that he plans to blow up Israel. It's just a rumor, and you know it. Besides, Israel hasn't done anything for me lately. Judaism is a sexist religion, in case you haven't heard, Miriam. The big prayer the men say begins with thanking God for not making them women!"

"That's about childbirth," Miriam said, glancing nervously at Ben.

Sarah lost her temper. "Oh, fucking bullshit! You are so brainwashed. It's *not* just about giving birth—it's about all that goes with it! How about just exchanging that morning prayer for one that says, 'Thank you for giving me women, my equals in every way'?"

She saw she had scored a point with Miriam. Ben looked at her with a bitter hostility in that despicable way that all observant Jewish men had used on Sarah throughout her life. "Look at you, Mr. Ben Halevi—you should see the supercilious, superior smirk on your face as these lesser beings complain about the way you treat us. Fuck you, and fuck Israel, and especially fuck Zev. And I want my fucking necklace back right now!" Sarah surprised herself by actually stamping her foot. Her mother had often scolded her for doing so as a young girl. She stood there, arms crossed, determined to have her way and to be free of this lunatic fringe. "And if you don't deliver, I will call Mahmoud right now and tell him what's going on."

Miriam smiled. "Zev said that you were afraid to tell Zarafshan that you lost the necklace."

"I didn't lose it. I misplaced it."

"It was in the trash. If Zev hadn't found it, it would be gone."

"Maybe that was a sign that I was supposed to be kept out of this little drama."

"Perhaps, except that Mr. Bronfman happened to become involved. What sign can you read into that?"

Sarah reflected a bit about this, and it made her uncomfortable. Then she inquired, "Aside from the monetary value, why is it of such interest to you?"

Ben looked at Sarah and said quietly, "We know he has nuclear weapons. We know he plans to use them on Israel. We believe he plans to do it soon—very soon."

Nuclear-bomb Israel? Sarah looked to see if they were kidding. They were grim, deadly serious—and afraid. *How could this have happened? The man I knew was tolerant and could see all perspectives of any problem or issue.* She recalled how she and Mahmoud had talked both sides of the Israel-Palestine question, how he had expressed views that were both tolerant and inclusive. *What happened to him? If what these people are saying is true, he truly must have gone mad.*

To cover her anguish, she said, "Where did you fly in from?"

"Tel Aviv, last night." Miriam looked weary.

"I am being a bad host. Let me make you some coffee. I've got cookies somewhere." Sarah excused herself, went to the kitchen, and tried to think clearly as she brewed java—half Kona, half hazelnut-vanilla—and put some Persian treats on a plate. She picked up her cell phone and speed-dialed Zev. He answered, sounding surprised and pleased.

"Are you okay, Sarah? I called several times but got no answer."

She hated him with every fiber of her being. "I am fine, except that someone I considered a friend stole something very precious from me—and put me in harm's way to boot!"

"But—"

"Fuck you. I never want to speak to you again." She hung up, feeling better, and carried the cookies and coffee in to her new friends, enjoying the relish with which they dug into the Persian goodies. She guessed that they could never get them at home and giggled at the thought.

"Okay. Mahmoud is waiting for my call. Can you prove any of this to me?"

Ben nodded to Miriam, who handed Sarah a file folder filled with photographs of Mahmoud in various secret meetings. Miriam narrated as Sarah flipped through the pictures.

"This is Mr. Zarafshan with the crazy head of Pakistan." Using her pen as a pointer, Miriam continued, "These two men with them are the chief of ISI—Pakistan's intelligence agency—and his top deputy. In this picture, he is with the dictator of Somalia and some of his warlords. In this next one, he is with the leaders of Yemen. These places, you must understand, are where the terrorists have gone since you Americans chased them out of Afghanistan. And here he is with the leaders of Hamas, and in that one there—that's a top-secret picture showing him with the late Chavez at a resort in Venezuela. I particularly like that—"

"Enough." Sarah felt her body go rigid. Did everyone except the U.S. hate Israel? Was the whole world looking for an excuse to get even with America for all of the bullying it had done in the so-called interests of peace? She was overwhelmed.

"Isn't it too late for me to help?"

Ben leaned forward and said, "We also know that he has been

promised absolute power, which he has in the political sense—but he has no sway over you save what he can earn with his love. There's a chance you could influence his choice. The UN summit has been delayed." Ben paused, and there was a twinkle in his eye. With an air of satisfaction, he continued, "It seems there was some sort of problem, but it will give us some time to find out when he plans to attack."

He showed her the CNN feed on his iPhone. The headline read: BREAKING NEWS—UN SUMMIT DELAYED DUE TO BOMB THREAT.

How convenient, Sarah thought. "And if I can 'influence' him?"

"You'll be buying us time to authenticate the necklace."

"And remind me again, what's so important about the necklace?"

"Short-story version: It will prove that Mahmoud is Jewish and utterly discredit him."

"What if I can influence him? Will you still expose him?"

"No, in that case there wouldn't be any need. Perhaps you can persuade him to come to our side—to call off the attack."

"Do you really think his feelings toward me could possibly override the allure of being—"

"Yes, we do!" Miriam interrupted. "Remarkably, he is a humble man at heart. He is kind to his children and has put an end to many of the barbaric police practices within his country—his society. He is open to increasing female rights and to some degree of Westernization, and he continues to teach. In many of these issues, he has differed with the hardline clerics who put him in power, even the Ayatollah. And besides, it's hard to think that a man who drives an old Peugeot is completely power mad." Miriam smiled.

Ben said, "He was put into a position of authority—he did not seek it."

But Sarah was stunned. Her phone buzzed. Mahmoud was waiting for her decision. She looked at the two agents sipping coffee, glanced up, said a final *Fuck you!* to God, and answered the phone.

"What is your answer, my beloved?" Mahmoud asked.

Miriam and Ben held their breath. Sarah couldn't help but enjoy their discomfort.

"Please say it will be yes or my life will be worthless," Mahmoud said in his quiet way.

Surely, this was not the purpose the guides had assigned her. What would Judith have done? She realized in a blinding flash why she had been told about Judith. Judith had successfully outsmarted an Assyrian general and saved her village without any of her kin's blood being spilled. The only casualty—including among her enemies—had been Holofernes. Could Sarah hope to do as well? *This* was her purpose, if she cared to fulfill it.

Like a hologram, an image of Judith seemed to materialize right before her, smiling benignly and nodding. *Yes. Okay, I am way over the edge*, Sarah thought. *I might as well jump.*

"Yes, Mahmoud. Yes. I will see you. I will call you in an hour." She hung up, took a deep breath, and felt her heart pounding.

Her eyes narrowed on Ben and Miriam. "What will I tell him about the necklace?"

Once again, Miriam dug into her briefcase and this time pulled out a jewel box, handing it to Sarah. "Open it."

Sarah did so and there it was: the beautiful necklace, freshly cleaned, gold links rich in the light, the round, ruby pendant with its etched star and strange symbols the color of ripe cherries.

"But how—"

"It's not the real one," Ben said. "That's being authenticated in Jerusalem. This is a perfect copy—it could fool a professional jeweler. It was a miracle that it could be duplicated so quickly."

"A miracle. There seems to be a lot of those going around lately. But how can you *positively* identify something that *may* have belonged to someone who *may* not have even existed?"

Ben smiled for the first time since he came in the door, displaying long sharklike teeth. Sarah wished he hadn't.

"We merely need to trace it back to where his grandmother got it and prove its origin. You see, there is also evidence that his family changed their name—from Sabourjian, which means 'weaver of the Jewish prayer shawl' in Persian—when they emigrated from Aradan. Even then, it wasn't easy to do business as a Jew, long before all this trouble over statehood, Gaza, terrorism, and everything else."

"Really?"

"Yes. If we could discredit him, then his allies would abandon him, and this pending attack would probably fizzle. His whole regime could collapse, and we believe it would take years for his country to regroup."

Sarah laughed. Did this fool drink his own Kool-Aid? "Oh, c'mon. Don't be naïve. I'm sure the president has already paid his supporters off with promises of rich military contracts. He needs another war at this point. And Israel is an albatross."

Miriam laughed. "I appreciate your perspective, but let's wait and see how this plays out before we judge."

Sarah noticed Ben's disapproving look at Miriam. "The point is that this necklace—I'm sorry, *your* necklace—is a relic that links Zarafshan to King David, which is one of the conditions cited to authenticate the Twelfth Imam. Do you know what that means?"

Sarah nodded. "Yeah, that Mahmoud thinks that he is the bringer of the resurrection that will follow a holy war because his grandma gave him a necklace. Give me a fucking break."

"In his very first speech before the UN, he made that very claim." Ben studied her. "You don't keep up with world events very much, do you?"

"I might if we were ever told the truth."

Sarah picked up the fake necklace. It felt so similar. "Is there any way he could tell?"

"No, it's an exact replica."

"Okay, what about my 'job'?" Sarah made air quotes with her fingers.

"Check your phone."

There was a text message from Laura indicating that she had been called out of town unexpectedly and would be away until next week.

"Very convenient."

"Yes, and what's more, we were able to learn his schedule. Interesting—he's keeping it wide open." Ben checked his watch. "Perhaps after you've had your rest, you'll call him and invite him here—to your place?"

Sarah lost her temper again. "Sexist prick!" This was why she didn't date Jewish men! "Oh, I see. Are you running this affair as well? Perhaps you would like to suggest what sexual positions we should use?"

"I'm sorry, Sarah," Ben said. "This is as uncomfortable for us, and me personally, as it must be for you. But, remember, this is a madman who wants to wipe out the Jews."

"No, only Israel," Sarah said before she could stop herself.

"And the difference is?"

"I've been to Israel. They don't think we count."

"You'll probably snap my head off," Ben said, "but what makes you think Zarafshan will stop at Israel?"

Sarah looked at him in amazement. *Is this the Mossad or the Jewish Defense League?*

Miriam said, "Ben, you go too far."

But Ben was unrelenting. "Look, it comes down to this: Will you take responsibility for being a Jew?"

CHAPTER 28

MAHMOUD'S BARGAIN

AHMOUD KNEW THAT HIS mentor, the Ayatollah Hameini, was about to serve him up on a plate. His days as president—very likely as a living human being—were numbered. He felt outrage and betrayal at the situation, but he understood that it was all part of the greater plan. Rather than resist the forces that were at work, he would negotiate his own immortality.

He was staying in a penthouse suite in UN Plaza, a glittering skyscraper that looked out on the monolith of the UN building itself. *What would the Mahdi want me to do? What would the gesture be?* He stared down at the UN and thought about a recent speech he'd given in which he called for the destruction of Israel. Good idea, but too big to be realistic. He walked out onto the terrace and stood by the balcony, the UN still in his view.

He felt his gut contract with the sadness of knowing that he would never live to see his children grow up—and at that moment Nehir, his favorite and most trusted bodyguard, walked out and joined him on the terrace. He offered Mahmoud a cigarette, but Mahmoud refused it.

"May I speak?" Nehir asked.

Mahmoud nodded. Nehir carefully and silently slid the glass

terrace door shut. "I have heard something," he said. His tone was serious and deliberate. "You will never arrive on our native soil again." Mahmoud nodded and smiled almost imperceptibly. Loyalty like this was priceless, something to be rewarded.

"Thank you, Nehir."

Nehir waited expectantly for some sort of instructions, but Mahmoud said nothing more. Nehir was anxious. He had wanted to become a martyr for Islam, but because he was related to the mullahs, he was pressed into this responsibility, and he had served well. He was as patriotic as Mahmoud was, but at this moment he looked terribly sad.

"It is not fair!" he burst out, banging his fist on the balcony railing. "You are the Twelfth Imam! How can they just—"

"Hush, Nehir. Allah hears all."

Nehir collected himself. "What will you do?"

Mahmoud thought for a moment. "What awaits our greatest patriots who give their lives?"

"Seventy-two virgins are promised."

Mahmoud smiled, more broadly this time, but then his expression turned serious. He looked Nehir in the eye. "If I wanted to make the ultimate sacrifice on my terms, would you help me?"

"Anything for you."

"Good! I need to make a phone call on a secure line. I need to speak directly to Hameini—no one else. Do you understand?"

Nehir nodded and left. A few minutes later, he knocked firmly on the glass door and beckoned to Mahmoud. He slid the door open, handed him the cordless phone, and shut the door again.

Mahmoud turned away and gazed once again at the gleaming glass façade of the UN, the phone pressed against his ear. A tear rolled down his cheek as he exchanged salutations with his once beloved former mentor, now his judge and executioner. What had he done?

"Oh, Holy One, I have a plan. I will destroy the UN," Mahmoud said, without emotion. He heard a sharp intake of a breath, then silence. He waited, not breathing at all himself. "Hold on." Now Mahmoud heard the murmur of voices—the mullahs, he realized, were discussing his plan. After a while, Hameini came back on the line.

"Yes. How will you arrange it?"

"Please leave that to me."

"As you wish. How can we ever repay you?"

"There is no need, if it will hasten the end."

"There must be something. Allah would wish that you be rewarded."

"Yes, of course. Support and protection for my family."

"That is a given. What more?"

"I want to be allowed to spend the four days leading up to my speech alone, undisturbed and in prayer. No guards, no surveillance, no contact. In a quiet spot of my choosing, to prepare myself."

Silence. Mahmoud gnawed on a hangnail. Finally, the murmurs subsided and Hameini spoke again.

"Yes. Confide only in Nehir. He will see to it that you leave the hotel undetected, and he will arrange to bring you to the UN at the appointed time. He will help you prepare whatever you need for the deed to be done."

"Thank you, oh Great One, for allowing me this honor."

"It will be impossible to replace you."

You've probably got my successor already lined up, Mahmoud thought. But he said only, "Thank you."

"*Insha'Allah*," Hameini said.

The line went dead.

Mahmoud sat down on the terrace as the faint sound of New York City traffic drifted up from the street. The sky seemed impossibly blue, the clouds like something out of a Surrealist painting he had seen in the Museum of Modern Art many years ago—with Sarah. The image of the vulnerable hollow in the center of her throat where only a single freckle lay caused him to feel weak. He sighed. How great God was! He would accomplish three of his life's goals: to bring about the end of the world, to create immortality for his family, and, before the others, to miraculously have a moment of aliveness he had not experienced since he had left Sarah those many years ago. As he looked up, in praise and thankfulness to God, the sun burst through the billowing clouds and created a sky like the ones he'd only seen in Renaissance paintings. That, too, was when he had toured a museum with Sarah. He remembered the rapture in her eyes as she gazed at the beauty of all of those magnificent renderings.

His heart suddenly clenched, and he admitted to himself that she had never been out of his thoughts. In some private corner of his mind ran an endlessly repeating slideshow of treasured memories, and the truth was, even when he made love to his wife, Sarah was always the one he imagined. He appreciated the irony: that if he was not being cast out, he would never again be with her. He felt humbled that Allah would offer him his reward before his death. Odd that his grief about his family could be so fleeting. Maybe he was a terrible person, but the truth was that he regarded his life back home as listless, his wife as humorless, and his children as dull and dutiful.

He opened the glass door of the terrace and motioned for Nehir, who came with a tray of coffee and sweets.

"Sit, Nehir. We have been charged with a very great mission."

CHAPTER 29

Love Springs Eternal

ARAH FUSSED OVER WHAT to wear. She was numb, but her mind, as if in mockery, nonetheless presented her with a bewildering menu of possible emotions—none of which seemed fully there, none of them being reactions she actually felt. *Nervous?* No. *Pissed off?* Of course, but no. *Apprehensive? Excited? Resigned?* No, no, and no. *What to wear?* Impossible. She selected a pair of jeans, a white button-down shirt, a push-up bra, and thong panties. And, of course, the necklace.

The buzzer sounded. She rushed into the living room and put some music on—soft jazz. Miles Davis playing "My Funny Valentine"—a good start. She opened the door, and in walked Mahmoud, dressed dashingly in a white shirt, jeans, and a base-ball cap shielding movie-star sunglasses.

"I am in disguise," he said gleefully.

You sure are, she thought, but did not speak.

Part of her hoped he would pick her up and carry her to the bedroom right then and there, but instead he stood and looked at her, as if drinking her in. He took off the hat and glasses. He'd brushed his hair back in the old way, and she glimpsed the man she had once loved, thickened by age but still charismatic. Why did he make himself ugly in public, in the presidential persona that he'd created? She couldn't connect the man who now stood before her with the one she'd met the previous night. He looked at her and waited. Without the shield of anger, she felt helpless. She could not believe that Mahmoud—her Mahmoud—was the same man that now called for Israel to be obliterated.

Finally, he held out his hand, and she came forward and took it. He pulled her close to him by pulling her hand down until he held it against the outside of her thigh. There was barely an inch between them. His eyes burned. "I cannot offer you anything beyond this moment." She was perplexed. *How can he look at me this way and yet hate Jews?*

"You are wearing the necklace—the one that belonged to the great-grandmother of my grandmother. Do you remember what it says—in Aramaic?"

"You never told me."

He looked surprised. "Didn't I?" Then he smiled. "It reads: THE ONE WHO WEARS THIS WILL ALWAYS BE LOVED BY THE GIVER OF LIGHT." He put his other hand behind her neck and gently pulled her toward him until their foreheads touched. She trembled and couldn't think, intoxicated by his gravelly voice, the gentle power of his beautiful hands, and his surprisingly delicate fingers, more like a musician's than an engineer's. Sarah feared she would faint from the intensity of the moment, and a part of her disassociated. She imagined that her consciousness was draped against the ceiling like the women in Chagall's painting, looking down on the proceedings with a *Mona Lisa* smile. She sighed loudly. *If he doesn't kiss me, I can walk away.* She took a step backward and moved her head away to free herself, but he moved swiftly and kissed the hollow of her throat—just above where the necklace circled. She was paralyzed like the victim of a cobra—the tender poison rendering her helpless.

"Where is your bedroom?" he asked as he lifted her into his arms.

He's married. He wants to kill the Jews. This is a black comedy. I don't care. I don't care. Judith did not sleep with Holofernes, but she had never been in love with him, and she was still mourning her husband.

Sarah pointed, and Mahmoud carried her up the sweeping spiral staircase and into the bedroom. Afterward, she hoped that she'd be able to recall only the divine moments when he touched her a certain way and spoke her name. Her immersion in the present was so complete that she felt as if their individual beings were fusing—as if they were becoming one physical entity. Their lovemaking went on for five hours.

"How is it you can be here?" she asked much later, as she lay, head on his shoulder, curled around his body. "Where are your bodyguards?"

"That is another person."

"What do you mean?" *Is he schizophrenic as well?*

"The man who is here with you in your bed is Mahmoud, the lover of Sarah, the same man you knew. The other is a persona, a mask if you would like to call it that. I don't. No one but my chief bodyguard knows I am not at the hotel. I am not expected anywhere." Mahmoud stroked her hair. "You never noticed it was me on the television and in the news?"

She looked him over. He held his arms wide, invited her scrutiny.

"No. The man I knew had beautiful black hair, was rail thin and buff, spoke perfect English—and dressed impeccably. That guy on TV is chubby, has disheveled hair and a scraggly beard, only speaks in his native language, and avoids looking directly at anyone."

Mahmoud digested this. "Do you have a razor?"

For some sick, perhaps masochistic reason, in the medicine cabinet Sarah had kept a package of her ex's disposable razors and a leftover can of shaving cream. Over the first few months after their breakup, she would sometimes take a little blob and smell it to remind her of him. *How perverse*, she thought. *But, oh, how fortuitous now! No accidents.*

"Yes, I'll get it for you. And a fresh towel, as I am sure you'll want to shower."

"No, I want your smell on me forever." She looked to see if

he was being facetious, but he was dead serious.

"I'll shower with you," she offered.

"No, let me go alone." She was stung but hid it well, or so she thought.

But he had seen it. "Please. It is not personal. I just need a few moments alone." She nodded.

He went into the bathroom and closed the door behind him. She tiptoed to her study, Googled him on YouTube, and played an interview with Charlie Rose, the sound turned whisper-low. She listened and watched him. His body language, inflection, and demeanor seemed to be those of a different man—frighteningly so. Was he possessed by some *dybbuk*? She had read somewhere that a *dybbuk* had possessed King Saul, which was why he wanted to destroy his protégé, David. Was she even safe with him? Would he suddenly turn into a killer and try to destroy her because she was a Jew?

She frantically e-mailed Gwydion.

Gwydion:

Is Mahmoud schizo? Do I need to fear for my life?

Oh, BTW—the Mossad convinced me to have another affair with him.

Thank you.

What did she expect? She had to talk to someone. Zev's face rose up unbidden. She decided to call now and forgive him later—if she lived.

Gwydion's e-mail came back right away.

You are safe. But don't falter.

She heard a cough and was startled to see Mahmoud standing in the doorway, a towel wrapped around his waist. He was beardless and had cut his hair short. He *did* look like the man she had once loved!

"What do you think?"

"You look very well . . . preserved."

He looked offended, then laughed. "Oh, I remember you with your cute jokes. Come here." She clicked off the screen and walked over to him. He sniffed her. "You smell a little ripe."

For a moment, she was offended, then realized he was teasing her back. She went to tickle him, but he caught her hands and wrestled playfully. Then they both stopped and looked at one another. "You are beautiful, the most gorgeous of all."

"And you do indeed now look like my Mahmoud."

"Come to bed," he said, smiling and advancing. He looked ten years younger.

"Why don't you speak your beautiful English when you appear in public or give interviews?"

Mahmoud smiled. "You should know the answer. Do you recall? I took you to that French restaurant where the waiters didn't seem to be able to understand us."

Sarah nodded, flattered that he remembered. It was their first dinner together. He had wanted to impress her and clearly had done some research about what to order but had no real clue. Still, he had done well enough to order champagne and escargots.

"Are you a teetotaler now?"

"A what? Oh, you mean, do I abstain from liquor? Normally, yes. But let me finish. At the restaurant, I was surprised, but I admit, I actually believed they talked only in French. But you, you savvy New York American, you just sneered and said that all waiters speak perfect English but only when it suits them. So I learned from this, and I found that using my language only and being translated was beneficial. I could understand them, but they thought I didn't comprehend."

"So you did it on purpose?"

"Of course."

They made love many times. Sarah felt herself greatly lost in the sensation. She tried reciting yoga mantras but found herself in a wordless pit of love.

When she awoke, or regained consciousness, or the *spell was broken*—she wasn't sure which—it was dark, and she was alone. She heard something break and leapt up, terrified. A faint glow of dusky light, visible through the open bedroom door, gleamed through the curving staircase just outside. She kept a Louisville

Slugger next to her bed just in case and she grabbed it now, tip-toeing naked down the stairs toward the light, which she could see was coming from the kitchen. Her knees trembled so much she could barely walk, but she forced herself onward.

Mahmoud was sweeping up pieces of something. He had helped himself to the garment that she kept on the back of her bathroom door—a pale-blue chambray men's robe—in the hopes she would have male guests. He looked up, boyish again, without his beard. "I am sorry," he said. "I am . . . how do you say? A *klutz*."

Visibly relieved, she leaned the baseball bat in the corner. She became aware of her body, as Eve must have after biting the apple. She was shaking in fear, which made her look chilled. Mahmoud set down the dustpan, leaned the broom against the counter, then swiftly came over to her and draped his robe so that they were both inside it. Sarah tried to control her body's tremor.

"I love you, Sarah," he said. She felt his hands wrap tightly around her, and responded as she felt him become aroused.

"Are you hungry? I can make us an omelet, or there's great stuff in the freezer."

That was all she remembered of their exchange upon waking up as the dawn seeped into the next morning.

Mahmoud slept on his back, hands crossed over his heart. His face was unlined and calm in repose. He was so handsome, his hands so beautifully formed. She felt the necklace around her throat. How could this man be intending to blow up Israel with nuclear bombs? How had he come to such a state of in-sanity? And how could she have been so unaware that this lu-nacy was developing in the Middle East? She slipped out of bed and went to the kitchen, where she turned on the computer and Googled more information on him. She ascertained that he must have come to New York for the first time right after receiving his Ph.D. in civil engineering and traffic transportation in 1997. What happened to the man who was so proud of his degree and looked forward to serving his country and his people?

How had her lover, the one man who had ever stolen her heart—and was now doing it again—suddenly become capable of annihilating Israel? And ignorant enough to deny the Holocaust? She recalled one afternoon, back when they'd first met. They'd strolled the glistening streets of the city and ended up in a Jewish deli where the owner's mother, who still ran the cash register, had numbers tattooed on the inside of her forearm. Mahmoud had grimaced and made light conversation, asking where her family was from. "Krakow" had been the response. He knew there had been a Holocaust—why would he deny it now?

Her cell phone buzzed—it was a text from Zev: PLEASE FORGIVE ME. THE NECKLACE IS AUTHENTICATED. HE IS JEWISH.

She deleted it.

This was followed immediately by a text from Ben and Miriam: THE NECKLACE HAS BEEN AUTHENTICATED.

She texted back: WHAT DO YOU WANT ME TO DO?

KEEP HIM BUSY, they replied.

WHY ARE WE BEING LEFT ALONE? WHY AREN'T HIS PEOPLE ALL OVER US?

WE'LL EXPLAIN LATER.

She closed her phone and ran a bath. It was now fully light, and she'd caught a chill. She luxuriated in the hot, soapy water. She was sore from the exquisite pain of lovemaking, and her skin felt bruised. She dozed off in the warm suds but jerked awake as she heard the toilet flush and felt Mahmoud climb into the old-fashioned, freestanding tub. She looked into his beautiful dark-brown eyes. They faced each other in the bath. He put one hand on her pubis.

"In two days, I will change the world forever. Until then, I am just a man."

"And after?"

He shrugged and smiled. "I will not have to relive things I have done in my dreams. I will be the Imam."

"The what?"

"A visionary figure."

Yes, she thought, *he is crazy!*

He looked at her seriously, searching her eyes. "I have not

slept so well in so many years until last night. I would like to spend these last two days as I might have if things had been different."

"How do you mean?"

"If I had stayed with you. Gotten a job here. Married. Had children. Celebrated holidays. Read *The New York Times* on Sunday mornings. Taken walks in Central Park. Gone to see a film or a play—your museums . . . do you remember?"

"Yes, I do." Sarah was moved.

"I ask you humbly: Can you give me these two days?"

She nodded and turned to look outside, as she did not want to show him her tears. A flock of birds flew past—it was so gray outside that she had lost all sense of time. Kind of like what happened in the film *Roman Holiday* but in reverse. He was the prince, she the commoner. She thought to herself: *Do I have any regrets? Yes, of course. Who doesn't?* She too would have liked to turn the clock back ten years. *Is there anything I would really want to keep that happened in between the first time we said goodbye and now?* Nothing—not a single thing came to her mind. The pungent irony was there were only things she would prefer to erase.

Her inner voice spoke more. *The line begins now. Over and over. Start here—right where you are—is it where you want to be? If so, enjoy. If not, consider what needs to be done to get you there.*

Mahmoud had just vowed, "In two days, I will change the world forever."

Well, so would she. As Judith said, "Listen to me. I am about to do a thing which will go down through all generations of our descendants." Sarah mentally drew that same line in the sand and stepped over it—and smiled at Mahmoud.

"Yes," she said, "but let's take a nap first." They returned to the bedroom and once again made love 'til they dropped into sleep. What followed was an enjoyable experience that Sarah would term "a Kodak moment"—an all-consuming sense that a romance had reached its most magical, transcendent state.

When these moments happened in films, they were usually de-
picted by a montage of lovers doing romantic things—a horse-
and-buggy ride or a long walk on a deserted beach. But for Sarah
as she slept, it was an endless, blissful, surreal dreamscape.

CHAPTER 30

LOVE IN THE TIME OF ARMAGEDDON

ER VIBRATING PHONE WOKE her. It was a text message from Ben: GO TO THE DOOR NOW. THERE'S A PACKAGE. Mahmoud was asleep, arms wrapped tightly around her. She gently removed herself and went to the door. She opened it and saw Ben standing there.

"I thought I'd drop off the guest list and pick up the menu plans." He said it loudly and handed her an envelope. In a lower voice: "What's in here will make him very ill. It will not kill him—just make him so sick that he won't be able to appear at the summit meeting."

"Isn't this illegal?"

"So is genocide."

"What is it?"

"Do you care?"

"Of course I do!"

"Okay, it's swine flu—seems perfect for a Muslim."

"I do not find that funny—this could kill him."

"I repeat: greater good. One tyrant versus the genocide of a country."

She looked at his smug, sanctimonious face.

"Fuck you and your liberal fucking ideals! No. I won't participate. This would make me as bad as you claim he is."

Ben looked at her coldly. "Okay. Then we'll kill you."

Suddenly she felt something cold against her ribs, and Ben grabbed her shoulder. She looked down and saw the gun pressed against her.

"There are eight bullets in the clip of this gun. I—"

Her head spun. "If you want him dead, why didn't *you* assassinate him? I'm not going to be anyone's patsy. *You* put this crap in his food!" She felt completely indifferent at the idea of her own death.

She glared at him, hating his ever-present five-o'clock shadow and smooth white skin. "Okay," he said at last and lowered the gun. "Go get me what you intend to feed him—I'll put it in. Happy now?"

"No. Is there any other choice?"

"Not unless he has a change of heart."

"And if that happens?"

"It won't."

"Is that a challenge?"

"You think you can fuck him into changing the course of history?"

Sarah had never felt such a desire to hurt somebody.

Mahmoud called out, "Is everything all right?"

"Yes," she called back. "Just a new client picking up a menu plan." Then she turned and hissed at Ben. "History has proven me right—Helen of Troy . . . Yoko Ono . . . Jackie Kennedy . . ."

Ben rolled his eyes. "He denies there was a Holocaust. He thinks he is the Messiah. He thinks Israel should be wiped off the face of the earth."

"He's a patsy . . . a mouthpiece. I don't buy you demonizing him."

Again, she heard Mahmoud call out, "Where are you, my dear one?"

"I've got to go," she cried. "What if he's like Claude Rains in *Mr. Smith Goes to Washington*?"

"In *Mr. Smith Goes to Washington*?" Ben looked at her, stupefied.

"You know, he's the corrupt senator who recruits James Stewart to get a crooked real-estate bill passed. When the crooks go too far, Claude Rains balks and does the right thing."

Ben nodded. "I love that movie."

Sarah crossed her arms. "So, I have got to go to him."

"Okay. Two days, and you put the stuff in his oatmeal."

She nodded and closed the door. She suddenly felt that she was in some movie where the true patriot is being punished for wanting to do the right thing. She shivered. He would really kill her if she didn't poison Mahmoud. Who could she even ask for guidance? There was Laura, but she was on their side. Carlos was away, so that left only Zev.

But first she needed to get on the Internet.

She went to the kitchen computer and Googled "Islam." She discovered that, originally, the prophet of Islam, Mohammed, had gotten along well with Jews—in fact, he married two of them! But as she more deeply researched Mohammed, she was revolted to discover that he had thirteen wives, married a nine-year-old girl, and even had sex with his eldest son's wife. This was the God Mahmoud prayed to five times a day! She read on and dipped into the online Qur'an. Mohammed's prophecies smelled like snake oil to her, and he clearly had taken chunks of the current philosophy of his day and reframed them—corrupted them, as far as she could see. She'd never realized what a repulsive and pathetic fellow this Mohammed was. That one third of the world worshipped a pedophile was beyond her understanding. Suddenly poisoning Mahmoud didn't seem so difficult—nor did it seem undeserved. In fact, she mused that it was a shame that no one had been sensible enough to poison Mohammed. Perhaps a whole lot of misery could have been avoided.

Would she have assassinated Mohammed if she'd been there and somehow known what havoc he would wreak on the world, what atrocities would be committed in his name? The answer, without hesitating, was yes. No one was more surprised by this than she. Such radical ideas. *Who might be "listening in," hacking into my computer and monitoring my searches on the Web, recording my devious thoughts?* she wondered as she sat at the computer. Her guides? God? Mohammed himself? Ugh! Horrible thought. Her beloved worshipped a man who was known to have sex with the wives of generals he had slain on the field of battle the very same day. In fact, he seemed to have fucked everything in sight.

But was the Prophet's behavior justification for her committing what might well be murder? What was really in that vial, anyway? Viruses were not sure shots and probably took time to gestate. She remembered growing molds from bread and water in petri dishes in science class at school.

Her anger at God resurfaced like a giant wave. But then she thought of something Gwydion had told her, which she had completely forgotten until this moment: "God doesn't mind your anger. He would rather you express it and not carry it forward."

This just can't be God's plan, she thought. *No one would design a world where its inhabitants had to kill each other to live.*

Mahmoud called out to her again. She realized she'd come in from seeing Ben, gone straight to the computer, and sat down in a daze. The envelope containing the vial of swine flu—or whatever it was—was safe in the pocket of her robe.

"Love, dearest one, I await you."

What am I, your nine-year-old girl? Her passion for Mahmoud began to dismantle itself—but wait. That could be lies as well. She knew better than to trust Wikipedia or any other online stuff—it could all be propaganda. She had a volume in her study titled *Man's Religions,* which she'd bought when she first started yoga. It covered all the world's religions, and the author, John Noss, was a true scholar, widely respected, and one who could be trusted.

She was scanning her shelves looking for the book when suddenly Mahmoud was there kissing her, wrapping her in his arms. He smelled spicy, and his skin was truly like the suede of an expensive handbag. She wondered: *Has he ever slept with really young girls—underage girls?* She pulled away from him. "Mahmoud, what was the age of the youngest person you have ever slept with?"

Mahmoud took her face in his hands, kissed her nose and her lips, and smiled. "Ah, you are jealous—now I know you truly love me."

"No, seriously."

"Why do you want to know?"

"How do you reconcile the fact that Mohammed had a nine-year-old wife?"

Mahmoud looked confused. "Now that is blasphemy. Where did you hear that? Can that be true?" His tone had become silky and had an edge she had never heard before. She had gone too far. If she kept up this line of questioning, she would never be able to get him to change.

"Well, perhaps I read it incorrectly."

"Yes. My prophet is great and good."

Now she hated God as much as she ever had. How could He have let Mohammed ascend as he did? Free will was bullshit if it allowed men—and mankind—to behave so brutally toward each other. She was sick of the whole business. "Kill me now," she muttered as she untangled herself. Really? Would she really want to die right at this moment? It would solve so many problems: She wouldn't have to hurt him herself, the Mossad could come in and do what she felt was their job anyway, and she would not have to feel anything. She had a sensation of nausea in her throat right where her neck joined her shoulders.

She let him make love to her. She felt oddly detached and unable to abandon herself to the pleasure of him as she had just hours before. He sensed something, stopped in mid-thrust, and said gently, "Where are you?" She was surprised at his sensitivity and found herself suddenly sobbing. He held her gently and whispered, "It's all right, it's all right, it's all right."

⁂

She awoke alone, hearing Mahmoud speaking in Persian in the bathroom on his cell phone. His tone was commanding, urgent, then pleading, then truculent and angry. Finally it was quiet. She dozed again and softly he came to her, touching her in those places she liked the most, telling her he loved her, making love to her with a fierceness she hadn't felt before. She met him halfway, and they were both breathless and covered in sweat by the end.

She looked at the clock—half the day had gone by. "I'm starving," she said, and got up. Her body felt formless and paradoxically like a dry bone that had been sanded by the desert until smooth and white.

"Let's get up. I want to show you something."

"Where are we going?"

They walked out of her building, and he hailed a cab. He helped her climb in and said to the driver, "Ground Zero." He held her hand tightly and put an arm around her shoulders.

"Can we put politics aside?"

"Yes, I'd like that." Somewhat relieved, she looked into his eyes.

"Don't ever doubt my love for you."

"Why are you taking me there?"

"I want to show you where the new mosque will be built."

She looked at him. "Isn't that in rather poor taste?"

He laughed. They pulled up to the huge construction site that the WTC had become. Mahmoud paid the cabbie. Sarah never failed to admire his elegant, square-tipped hands.

"Where were you when the planes hit?" he asked.

"I was at home working on preparations for a dinner party with NY1 on in the background, sound off. I glanced up and saw the first plane hit. I assumed it was a new movie coming out, not thinking for an instant it could be real."

Mahmoud nodded. He looked around. "Do you believe we were responsible?"

Sarah thought about it, and to her surprise she didn't. "No, I think it takes two to tango. Our government at the very least facilitated matters so that it could justify waging yet another war. They used the Arabs to scare the American people into such a state of fear and frenzy that, in effect, tyranny could be secretly introduced in this country."

He looked at her in amazement. "Is this really what you believe?"

"Yes, in my bones I believe the Republicans are far more dangerous than Osama bin Laden ever could have been. After the attacks, bin Laden was marginalized—he was never left alone long enough to coordinate his operations to mount another attack."

"So you do not, how do you say, feel that you are 'sleeping with the enemy'?" He made air quotes with his beautiful fingers.

"Not unless you are Republican." They laughed and laughed. "No, I think I am very democratic in bed." They stood in this tragic spot and kissed. Sarah felt as though a vortex of swirling light much brighter than their surroundings was enveloping them. The warm sunlight, the softness of his mouth, the texture of his fingers against her skin . . . she stumbled suddenly, and he caught her.

"Sorry, you make me dizzy."

"You really believe that?"

"What?"

"That the Americans would bomb their own country?"

"Yes, I do. What other nation would offer no medical care but let crazy people out in the street, elect a movie star to be president, let off a murderer like O. J. Simpson that everyone knew was guilty, allow Wall Street to plunder the middle class, and take money away from education to buy weapons for the Pentagon? Why wouldn't they?"

"Impressive."

"I think greed trumps religion every time. And they make good bedfellows."

Mahmoud said, "I am astonished at your perceptiveness."

"Do you know something?" Sarah asked eagerly.

Mahmoud was quite solemn. "Let's leave it at this: Your instincts are pretty good."

Sarah felt like she'd been slapped. It was one thing to hold a radical view that was unsupported but quite another to have the president of Iran as much as confirm it.

"Don't look at me," he said, staring straight ahead. "I can't bear the accusing gaze I see there. I never asked you—did you lose anyone?"

Sarah was unsure how to answer. She knew he meant a personal connection. *Twenty-nine hundred or so*, she wanted to say, but caught herself. Instead, she asked, "If you knew about it, why didn't you stop it?"

"I did not have power enough. They threatened my family. What would you have expected me to do?"

Sarah thought about it, picturing her mother, father, and siblings dying by way of horrible radical-Muslim torture executions. "Do you really want to nuke Israel?"

He was silent.

"Do you? Goddammit, Mahmoud, what are we doing here?"

He recoiled and began walking away quickly. She ran after him, grabbing his arm. He stopped, looked at her briefly with a tortured gaze, and said, "Those suicide martyrs have it easy. One gesture, one moment of agony, and they are blessed forever. I have to commit suicide a little each day."

"Why? Why are you doing this? Is it for Allah?"

"I thought so, I thought so. Hameini recruited me, made me feel important. I was just a petty official, a teacher, and he promised me glory."

"So . . . what? You're telling me that now you are the victim?"

"I am not a fanatic!" he shouted. She could see that he was actually upset at where this had gone. "I do not see the merit of oppressing women! I do not believe that nuclear weapons should be used on any basis at any time—they will solve nothing. I do not believe in dictatorship. I am aware that much harm has been done in the name of religion. I admit that I have had my own moments of fanatic madness when I wanted to believe these things—but now I am almost fifty, and I see it all differently."

He put his arm through hers, and they walked around the

desolate space. "Look at that. How can there ever be a benefit gained from such destruction? It defies common sense."

"Then . . . why?"

"I am Muslim, Sarah. My faith has been devout—unwavering—and I never understood the concept of free will. That is, until I realized that I actually had a choice—until I met you. That feeling of freedom, which I had for two weeks only, all those years ago with you—that has haunted me ever since, but I had put it away."

"And now?"

"When I knew you were there, when I smelled your scent, it brought back all of my longings for the state of—freedom."

"Okay, so maybe you can make things work out. Why not resign? You could stay with me."

He stopped and his eyes searched hers. "Do you really mean that?"

"You could, umm, I don't know what they call it anymore, but Russian spies used to defect all the time. You could do that."

He laughed and hugged her, but his mirth evaporated when he realized she was serious.

"I am touched by your offer. Let's go back and discuss it."

He gave her that sexy look, and, to Sarah's amazement, she felt like a puddle, melting under his gaze. *I guess this was how Eva Braun felt about Adolf Hitler,* she thought—*though he was probably gay* (she'd heard that from a friend, and oh, *so* wanted to believe it). *Sex always seems to screw* (pun intended) *everyone up.*

He full-on kissed her in a way that seemed to her more filled with love than ever before. She felt him, and in spite of the grave nature of their conversation, and of all that she knew and thought she believed, she succumbed to his request. They went home, making out passionately in the cab, and never made it beyond the living room sofa.

It was night when she awoke.

"It's our last day and night," she whispered to herself. She lay on her side on the floor on a pile of cushions, with Mahmoud wrapped around her. How could he possibly love a Jewish woman? If he was really Hameini's puppet, did it matter what he did? She realized that he was not driving the bus.

It hit like a tsunami: That explained why he had been able to stay with her for so long without being discovered—or sought—by anyone. No one was looking for him! At that moment, she seemed to split into two people: Sarah, the lover of this man whose very breath made her tremble, and Sarah (*or was it Judith?*), the cold-blooded woman who was considering spiking his morning coffee with swine flu—or worse. But what if it didn't matter?

Then another realization hit her: He was going to be the sacrificial lamb and she the deadly killer. He would become a saint. *Wait—this means that the Mossad probably plan to kill me anyway.* She remembered Ben's threat. She excised herself from Mahmoud, covered herself with a faux-fur throw, and grabbed her cell.

She went into the bedroom to get a robe. It was then that she first noticed, in the back of the closet, a heavy, black duffle bag she had never before seen. With trembling hands, she unzipped it. Inside was a metal case. It was too heavy to move. Then she heard Mahmoud calling her. *Shit!* She zipped up the duffle and closed the closet door.

She should call Ben or Miriam—but what if they were in on it as well? She was obviously the sacrificial virgin. What do they say in those war movies? *Collateral damage.* Who was gaining from all of this? Were Ben and Miriam really Mossad, or what? Did the U.S. government want an excuse to sever ties with Israel as well? No doubt that the president would love to get that albatross off his neck—but this rabbit hole was very deep.

Then Mahmoud was there, kissing her, picking her up, carrying her to the bed. "This is our last night. Tomorrow at nine A.M. I stand before the UN—and the world. I only wish I could make love to you seventy-two times."

She had no patience for his caresses or tender words. She felt like Bree, the prostitute/heroine in the film *Klute*, an old movie from the seventies, as if she were replaying the scene in which Bree allows John Klute to make love to her, and appears to respond with uncontrolled passion—which she interrupts to check her watch.

It was six P.M. Six ten P.M. Six fifteen P.M. She could see the oversized alarm clock she kept near her bed. Would he come already?

In spite of the facts, a part of her was really enjoying the sex. He had this way of putting both of her legs between his thighs and gripping her knees just so. She forgot the time. Seven P.M. Finally, he snored, spooning her.

Sarah needed help. The situation was far worse than she had been led to believe. She went downstairs to the den and dialed Zev's number. As she did so, her cell buzzed—a text from Ben. It read: SO? WHAT HAVE YOU DECIDED TO DO? REMEMBER, WE ARE WATCHING.

Had they bugged the house? Planted hidden cameras? Zev would know—he had to!

CHAPTER 31

Mission: Impossible

ZEV RETURNED TO NEW York with a heavy heart and went to pick up the cab, which was sitting idle because Tom's show had resumed filming. The gun was still in the trunk, wrapped in Zev's jacket. He'd bunked at Rachel's place the night before and spent time with Aaron, whom he now thought of as a little brother. Sadly, Frank had left his wife and three kids so that he could marry Rachel, and he had moved in with her. Staying in the house was like having a front-row seat to some biblical tragedy that would not end well, because the sister-in-law was a vindictive and spiteful person. Aaron was devastated, but Zev's promise to visit more often cheered the little fellow up.

Rabbi Cohen had tried to shame Zev into seeing his folks.

"Why should I visit them? So I can make them more miserable? So they can try to persuade me to return to the fold and marry and make babies? That would simply be cruel, because it's never going to happen."

The rabbi shook his head. "What else would you do?"

"Why do I have to do something in particular? I want to travel, see the world."

Rabbi Cohen perked up. "Israel! I have friends you could visit. It would be good. You might gain a better perspective."

Zev actually thought it was a good idea, but he wasn't going to let the rabbi know it. He did at least go to see *Zayde* Hal, who encouraged him to stick to his guns.

Zayde Hal counseled, "Remember what the great teacher Hillel observed, my Zevelah. He said three things: *If you don't stand for yourself, who will? If you only stand for yourself, what are you? If not now, when?*

"When you get to be my age, it becomes very clear where you missed your opportunities."

Zayde Hal had given Zev a sad smile but did not elaborate. "Go—get out of here, back to that Big Apple. Get on with your life!"

Zev's cell phone rang. When he heard Sarah's voice, he imagined that it was how Moses must have felt when the Red Sea parted.

"Yes, Sarah?" Oily sweat drenched him.

"Zev, I need your help."

Zev couldn't stop the sudden pounding of his heart—he felt as if he were standing under a waterfall.

"I'm going to order dinner for us from the Red Pasha on 78th and First. Can you pick it up and pretend to be the delivery person? I will explain later."

"Yes—okay."

"A million thanks."

The line went dead. Zev realized that "us" meant that Mahmoud was with her. How could she? The anguish he felt was unbearable. He pulled the cab over and turned off the engine. He opened the car door and leaned outside, spewing his guts onto the curb. If only he had never found the necklace, he might be there in Mahmoud's place. He turned on the ignition and drove to pick up the food.

☙

Sarah slipped back into bed beside Mahmoud, who stirred and pulled her close. "Hello, beloved," he said. "This is our last night together—how shall we spend it?"

"I have ordered a Persian feast for us. I thought we would eat, and then—"

"I like the 'and then' part." He kissed her, but she wriggled free.

"Let me jump into the tub real quick—the food will be here soon."

"Let's shower together."

"No, there's no time for that. Let me go first and then follow at your leisure." Before he could protest, she got up and rushed into the bathroom. She quickly soaped herself and rinsed. Her cell phone buzzed. There was a new message from Ben and Miriam: LET US KNOW WHEN YOU HAVE DONE THE DEED.

The poison. Somehow, she'd repressed that whole layer. What to tell them? Either way she was totally fucked. She dressed quickly in black leggings and a white lacy T-shirt, keeping her hair long and loose. Her choices were: Poison him and be killed, or not poison him and be killed. If she told Ben and Miriam about the metal case, they would no doubt stage a robbery and she again would probably be murdered, as would Mahmoud.

Judith had gotten Holofernes, the Assyrian general, drunk on her own wine and cheese, then she cut off his head with his own sword. But Judith had no relationship with the general, and she was a widow. She probably had numerous unresolved anger issues, since her husband had essentially dropped dead during harvest season, leaving her to run the whole show. Well, somehow Sarah had to make everything right—see what was in that damn metal case, change Mahmoud's mind, and most of all find a way to survive!

As she put on a touch of makeup and perfume, she reviewed the story of Judith in her mind. Judith had a clear deadline: three days. Sarah had from now—it was seven fifteen P.M.—until roughly the same time tomorrow. But seven fifteen A.M.! What could be accomplished in twelve hours? And what if there was a bomb with a timer in that metal case?

CHAPTER 32

Liquor Is Quicker

ARAH HEARD THE DOORBELL and bolted out of the bathroom. Mahmoud was still in bed.

"Please take your shower," she said, "and allow me to prepare the feast before you join me. I'll come up to get you." She kissed Mahmoud, then rushed downstairs and opened the door—where Zev stood with three bags of food.

"You owe me one hundred fifty dollars, ma'am," he said loudly.

She kissed him—she couldn't help it—then put a finger to his lips and pulled him inside, whispering, "I think the place is bugged. Can you check?"

Zev nodded and transformed before Sarah's eyes into some form of superspy. He nimbly checked the room for bugs, running his fingers along the edges of the furniture, the lamps, and the paintings on the walls as if it were something he did every day of his life. "I think you're safe."

"What the hell was that?" Sarah asked.

"Tricks of the trade. But I am no expert. Better to run the dishwasher as well. What's going on?"

She turned it on. "Get ready for a really bad movie plot . . . that's actually happening right now! The Mossad threatened to kill me if I did not renew my 'friendship' with Mahmoud. They want me to give him poison or they'll kill me, but if I don't they'll probably kill me anyway. They want me to find out when he plans to bomb Israel! Just to put the cherry on top of the whipped cream on the icing of this cake, there's a big metal case in my closet that I doubt very much contains lingerie!"

He couldn't hold back a wry smile. "How ironic!"

When had he gotten this handsome? Sarah wondered. *Absurd thought.*

"Look, he's staying here until he goes to the UN tomorrow. He's going to practice his speech over dinner."

"This metal case, did you open it? What does it look like?"

"It's a big metal trunk, like a suitcase." She made the shape with her hands.

"It could be anything! Why is it in your closet?"

Sarah was getting exasperated. "How the hell should I know?"

"When did you notice it?"

"Today around six—just before I called you. And it wasn't there yesterday."

Zev smiled. "I can open it. And he won't know I did it."

"Really? Why so cocky?"

"I'm a genius."

"Really?"

"Did you know I used to work at the U.S. Patent Office? I tested every kind of gadget or machine you can imagine. I graduated college with honors in engineering. There isn't a mechanical device I can't dismantle or reassemble."

"Really? But what if it's wired to explode? Shouldn't we just call the bomb squad?"

"What if it's not?"

They heard the water pipes clank as the upstairs shower turned off—they were both silent as they heard Mahmoud's feet upstairs. "I need to get into your bedroom."

"This is hardly . . ." Then Sarah got it. "You could disarm a bomb?"

"Yes. I worked on such devices at the Patent Office." Zev crossed his fingers behind his back and looked up at the God he knew wasn't there.

"Okay. After dinner, I'll lure him to the living room. Somehow, you have to get into my room—I'll leave a window open. This building has staircases that lead up to my bedroom, so once Mahmoud is downstairs you can get in pretty easy. Then please text me. Let me know what you find."

Zev produced a gun—a Glock nine-millimeter with a silencer. Sarah's eyes popped. "Where did you get that?'"

"It was left in the trunk of the cab."

"Really?"

"Like Gwydion says: 'No accidents, only arrangements.' "

Mahmoud called out, "Where are you, my dove?"

Zev left, impulsively kissing Sarah on the lips, a kiss that burned through her like boiling honey, stronger than anything Mahmoud elicited in her—ever.

Sarah walked quickly into the kitchen with the three bags, immediately turned on the oven, and slid the lamb kebabs in to heat. Odd that she wasn't cooking. Maybe if she lived through this she'd quit the cooking business—no, it amused her that this was in a way not the Last Supper but a last supper of sorts. Mahmoud entered and walked up behind her as she stood at the counter cutting up pita. He buried his face in the nape of her neck.

"It is unbearable to consider parting."

"Then don't think of it," she said lightly, arranging the pita in a dish and placing it next to the bowls of hummus and olives.

"Please sit."

They faced each other catty-corner. She glanced at the clock—it was seven forty.

"Did I ever tell you about the first speech I gave at the UN?"

She shook her head and passed him the lamb.

"As I was speaking, it was as if a great light surrounded me and those to whom I spoke the words. I saw a celestial light settle upon the room. The whole world's leaders all sat there transfixed as I spoke. It was as if a hand was holding them." He reached across the table and kissed the inside of her wrist. "It was then that I realized that my true mission was to facilitate the arrival of the Mahdi. Do you know what that is?"

Sarah nodded. "It's the Muslim version of the Messiah. There is a similar idea in my religion, and also in Christianity." Then she continued quickly, "Mahmoud, please, just this once— our last night—have a glass of wine." She poured it for him and lifted her glass.

"Let's drink a toast," he declared. "To us!"

They clinked, and he drank again. She refilled his glass with a seductive smile. Judith had been onto something. Mahmoud continued, already slurring his words.

"In all three traditions, the pre-existing condition is a major war. There needs to be such a crisis for the Mahdi to be summoned. I plan to create the right circumstances."

Sarah heard these words as if through a rainstorm. She couldn't quite decipher them. "Sorry, can you say that again?" Mahmoud's eyes glowed with a fervor that Sarah had never seen. "What does that mean?"

"My leader and some other clerics believe that our mission on earth is to facilitate the return of the Mahdi as soon as possible." He took a forkful of basmati rice and lamb. "This is delicious!" She refilled his wine glass.

"Okay. What does 'facilitate' mean, exactly?"

"Terrible upheaval. Crisis and chaos. A war. In Jewish lore, the Imam will be descended through the bloodline of King David, the same as Jesus." Mahmoud smiled. "The necklace that I gave you is proof that I am a descendant of King David."

"But how?"

"My paternal grandmother was Jewish and a descendant of that royal lineage. The necklace has been passed from daughter to daughter for centuries. In order to preserve the bloodline, it has to be handed down only to Jewish women. My mother wasn't Jewish, nor is my"—he hesitated before he continued— "wife."

"But why me?"

"I carried it with me. My grandmother gave it to me, and she prophesied that I would love a Jewish woman, then she said that I should pass the necklace on to her."

"You know what's really weird, Mahmoud? Someone told me that I am a descendant of Judith, a relative of King David." She hoped she hadn't tipped her hand, but Mahmoud's blank look reassured her.

Mahmoud nodded. "Of course. That is perfect. It is a shame I will not be around to see our child."

"Our child?"

"Of course. You will see that you will become pregnant with the Mahdi."

"Wait. Are you the Mahdi or isn't he here yet?"

"That is unclear."

Sarah contemplated this for a moment. "If you believed that I was carrying the Mahdi, would you protect me from death?"

Mahmoud nodded and pulled her into his lap. "Of course."

She was confused. What was he saying here? That he was supposed to create the son who would be the Mahdi—start the Great War so the Messiah would return—or that Mahmoud himself *was* the Messiah, the Mahdi?

"So, are you telling me you're Jewish?"

"Partly. Actually, my father was Jewish. That's why we had to change our name."

"So, what is the objective?"

"I've already explained to you, Sarah. It is to bring about the return of the Mahdi. Let's toast to our child!"

They tapped glasses. Drank again. This was her moment.

"Darling, how will you accomplish this?"

Mahmoud became amorous, and Sarah waited until he was pretty far gone. She felt as if she were in some eighties thriller as he knocked dishes off the table and laid her, and himself, on top of it. At the critical moment of entry, she asked, "When will it start?"

As he rode her, he gasped, "December twenty-fifth."

Luckily, the wine also wore down his self-control, so this was a shorter session. The kitchen looked like there had been a terrible food fight. Somehow, she lay on a spoon and had to pry it out of her back. Mahmoud was staggering drunk, and she helped him to the sofa, where he lay down meekly.

"I'm just going to close my eyes for a moment," he said as he passed out. She covered him with a heavy afghan.

She forced herself to walk calmly up the stairs to the bedroom.

CHAPTER 33

BEWARE OF WHAT YOU WISH FOR

ZEV WAS STRUGGLING WITH the case when Sarah entered.

"Jesus! What's taking you so long?"

Zev flushed, but at that instant the lock released. He gently opened it, laying both halves of the case on the floor.

Sarah stared in confusion. There was no ticking bomb strung with multicolored wires like the one in the movie *Executive Decision*. Instead, there was a pile of stuff packed into foam padding the way camera equipment is prepared for travel.

"What is this?" asked Sarah.

Zev stared at it and blinked. "This is so weird. It's like this weight-loss belt I once worked on in the Patent Office. You strapped it on, then put weights into the pockets and lost weight because you wore it under your clothes . . ."

He stopped. Sarah nodded. They were both quiet. It was a suicide-bomber rig.

Sarah realized that in Mahmoud's mind she would give him the Mahdi and he would instigate the war by blowing up the UN and himself. Bombing Israel was the second phase of the plan. Ben had actually been right, in a way.

"Do you want to call your Mossad people?" Zev asked.

Sarah hesitated. How was Mahmoud planning to put on this rig without her seeing it?

"I can't call them unless I . . . unless I tell them I gave him the poison."

She quickly explained what Ben had told her. Zev rolled his eyes.

"They'll still kill you. You can't stay here."

"I told you that!" Sarah retorted.

"True, you did, but it didn't hit home. You have to come with me now."

"I know, but I can't just leave."

"Why not?"

Sarah realized that, whatever misgivings she had about her religion, deep down it was a heritage that she embraced more often than not. And she further realized that whatever was wrong with God, and there was so much, He had given her what she wanted: a purpose, a place in history. It was no accident. Sylvie had done more than she knew when she gave Sarah that purse with the fortune: *Beware of what you wish for.*

So, should she poison Mahmoud, as Ben wanted? Did the vial actually contain swine flu or was it really some fast-acting deadly toxin? Zev had the gun, but she couldn't imagine shooting Mahmoud. Then again, Judith probably hadn't planned to cut anyone's head off either. But if she did kill Mahmoud, unlike Judith she would surely not be hailed as a heroine—she would probably be reviled as a whore-cum-murderer, whether unfairly or rightly, if she even lived to tell the tale. Just then, Zev interrupted her thoughts.

"I got the gun. Gwydion asked me if I could kill someone I knew would be the next Hitler. I have no problems shooting him while you are sleeping."

There was a pause.

"That would make you a murderer. Your life would be over."

"I consider this war."

She smiled. "Oh, Zev, you were raised religious. You'll never forgive yourself."

"I am worthless," Zev said. "I am a disappointment to every-one who loves me. Maybe—"

Mahmoud called out, "Are you there, my dove?"

"Another minute, beloved." Sarah lit candles and incense. Then the plan came to her with perfect clarity.

"No, Zev, we are not to interfere. I will text Ben that I have given the flu virus. If they intend to kill me, perhaps you can save me. The most important thing is to let Mahmoud make his speech and blow himself up."

"You can't be serious."

"Yes, but with a small twist. You need to either disarm this thing or, maybe better, to replace the explosives—which I as-sume are those square, gray-colored packets. Replace them with something just as heavy, like modeling clay or something, so that this thing can't go off. He goes to the UN, tries to blow him-self up, nothing happens. Total worldwide humiliation!"

Zev said, "Go downstairs. Let me figure this out." Sarah started to leave. "Wait," he said. "I will need a couple of hours. Can you do that?"

She nodded. "Leave the gun in the night table." She opened the top drawer, pushing aside her various creams. "Lock and load. Make sure the safety is off."

"But you don't know how to shoot."

"What makes you think that? I managed a restaurant and de-posited the money. I had a carry permit for years. My instructor told me I was a natural. Look, Zev, I am in this up to my hips, but you fix that belt or vest or whatever we're calling it and go far away. Go back to Washington and kiss whomever you love there."

She turned to leave. "Wait," Zev said.

When she turned, she realized that he was in love with her. "You must forget we ever met," she said. "Destroy any refer-ences, have your phone wiped." She held her hand out for the gun. Reluctantly, he gave it to her. She slid the clip out to make sure it was loaded, with one bullet ready in the chamber and the safety off, and placed the weapon carefully into the drawer. "Put everything back exactly as you found it. I will never see you again." She kissed him and knew then what she was giving up: not just her life but true love. They stared into each other's eyes.

"Don't fuck this up. He needs to get to the UN and be humiliated."

She held up her hand, pinky finger bent. "Pinky swear."

"Are you kidding?"

"I've never been more serious in my life."

Mahmoud called again, "I can't wait for you. I am coming up."

"No!" she called back. "I have something for you." She grabbed perfume off the nightstand and sprayed herself. She left the room without looking back. Zev heard her on the stairs meeting Mahmoud.

"Let's go upstairs."

"No, I have a surprise for you."

Zev felt jealousy overtake him like a wave. All he could think to do was to hurt Mahmoud any way he could. The idea of Mahmoud kissing the same lips as he had was unbearable.

Sarah led Mahmoud downstairs. Oddly, his willingness to martyr himself made her respect him more. This was more like the man with whom she'd fallen in love—passionate with the romance of his religion, and a person of convictions. Death was a perfectly respectable and dignity-restoring conclusion for any love story. God surely had a Jewish sense of humor to make Mahmoud's earthly reward a God-hating Jewish girl.

A strange set of statements came into her mind: "The more you hate God, the more He is with you. He's always with you—you choose the perception of the relationship. His is always loving." *Bullshit to the last part*, she thought. *Probably as true as the other dogma.* She realized suddenly that the father she hated and with whom she was so angry was her earthly one—she had confused "father" with "the Father."

In truth, the person she could imagine shooting point-blank when the Mossad came to kill her was Ben. She smiled. Why didn't she care about living? In fact, she looked forward to the opportunity but hoped Miriam would stay out of harm's way.

CHAPTER 34

Being a Patriot Isn't Fun

ZEV KNEW WHAT TO do. He realized that the C-4 was in one-pound bricks, but there was no way to do what Sarah suggested—not in the amount of time he had. He laid the pieces of the rig on the floor and began to analyze the design. The blocks of C-4 went into pockets around the belt, and electric wiring connected those blocks to a series of blasting caps that were linked to a remote-control master detonator. Zev laughed. The simplicity was marvelous. He would definitely approve a patent application for one of these! With a deft motion, he carefully took out one of the blasting caps and extracted the wire. As he expected, the primary explosive in the caps was diazodinitrophenol powder, usually abbreviated as DDNP. He had seen dozens of these devices from the mining and construction industries. The blasting powder had a yellowish cast to it. If he could find some sort of grainy powder of similar color, maybe he could replace the nasty stuff with something totally inert and harmless. *Sarah must have body powders and such,* he thought.

Zev tiptoed to the bathroom and opened the medicine cabinet. He could not believe his luck. There, right in front, was a roll of yellow antacid tablets—the similarity in color with the DDNP was striking! He got right to work. One by one, he took the blasting caps apart and poured the DDNP down the drain. Then he used a nail file to grind the yellow tablets into a powder that he poured meticulously into each cap, and reinserted the fuse wires. The switch would be undetectable, even if someone went to the trouble of taking apart the caps. He carefully put everything back as he had found it, slid the case into the closet, and smiled with satisfaction. Here was a cache of lethal explosives that he had rendered totally harmless—or almost so.

Then he heard Mahmoud and Sarah going at it and buried his head in his hands. There was nothing he could do about it if he wanted to, which he certainly did.

An hour later, the door opened and Sarah entered, stinking of sex. Her red hair was tousled, her lips bruised and slightly swollen. Zev wanted to slap her and kiss her at the same time. "He's sleeping," she whispered.

"It's done," he said flatly. "Mahmoud will live, dammit."

"How? What did you do?"

"Trust me, you don't need to know."

"Okay."

"You have to leave with me—right now. If the Mossad doesn't kill you, Mahmoud will."

"You're wrong, Zev. Mahmoud expects me to have his child. He's not going to kill me."

"Please, I'm begging you. Please leave with me now, before he wakes up."

She shook her head. "No. It will alert him, and he won't go through with it."

"So the Mossad will kill you—after he leaves for the UN tomorrow morning. What time is he supposed to go?"

"Around seven thirty, eight." Sarah continued, "Look, Zev, I've got the gun. Besides, what does it matter? I'm a God-hating reincarnation of an ancient biblical figure whose only contribution is cooking food. Will you look at the big picture for once?" He felt tears sting his eyes. She saw it and hissed, "I'm a patriot—so are you. Besides, you stole my fricking necklace."

"Back to that, are we—"

"Yeah, you *gonif*! Now get out of here!"

"Please, Sarah. Please."

"Go home, Zev. Your part is over."

"I love you, Sarah." There was a silence. Then a tiny, bitter laugh.

"Yeah, for a minute there I was good with God, but once again I fucking hate Him, with a capital *H*."

Zev looked confused, in a boyish way that charmed her. But she shook her head. "Private joke—between me and Him."

Finally Zev said, "This isn't funny."

"But I'll get what I want. Beware of what you wish for."

"Goddammit, Sarah."

"Sarah, where are you?" Mahmoud called.

"Get out of here," she hissed as the door opened. Zev shot out onto the fire escape. He felt hysterical as he climbed down. Who could he call for advice?

As soon as he hit the street, he crossed to the other side and looked up to her windows. And in the apartment light, he could see Mahmoud in silhouette take Sarah in his arms. At last he understood—and truly believed—that she was sacrificing herself, that he had been wrong if ever he had judged her differently. Zev felt angry and violent enough to climb back up and kill Mahmoud on the spot, but not only had Sarah begged him not to, he realized she was right—the failure of his extremism on the grand stage of the UN was far more important than killing the man. Maybe he could help the cause by holding the Mossad at bay.

He phoned the rabbi. "Call off your dogs," he said bluntly.

"Too late!"

"Did you know they set Sarah up? If she doesn't kill Mahmoud, they will kill her. It's not fair, it's just not fair."

"All right. Look, I can make a call. I'll see what I can do."

"Let them know I'm sitting outside with a gun and I will shoot anyone that comes near her," he bluffed. Now he wished he had kept the Glock with him.

"If you have a gun, go shoot Mahmoud now. You can end this whole thing."

"No, I can't. Trust me, Mahmoud will be stopped in a few hours. I can't tell you how, but we *must* let him go to the UN tomorrow and give his speech. If the Mossad comes after Sarah, I will be waiting."

Zev hung up and began to tremble.

CHAPTER 35

A Shot Rings Out

ARAH TEXTED BEN FROM the bathroom: OK, I DID MY JOB. NOW WHAT? To her immense relief, Ben replied: GOOD WORK. LET US KNOW WHEN HE STARTS TO FAIL. She texted back: OK.

For the remainder of the night, Sarah and Mahmoud abandoned themselves to love. But as dawn broke, he said, "I must leave you soon, my dove. I must make my speech and then fly home. My men will be coming in one hour. I will miss you terribly."

The words came out before she could stop them. "Mahmoud, why did you choose me?"

Mahmoud twirled one of her long red ringlets around his finger.

"Mohammed had Jewish wives. He did not discriminate."

Sarah felt like saying, "Yeah, that's an understatement," but held her tongue. Mahmoud turned on his side, and as Sarah lay on her back, he propped himself on one elbow. He touched her necklace. "What I am going to reveal to you now can never be repeated—"

"Or you'll have to kill me."

There was a silence, then he said, "Don't say such things, even in jest."

"Okay. What do you want to tell me?"

She suddenly felt her eyes fill with tears. She hugged him and found herself sobbing. He held her. "There, there, my darling. Why are you crying?"

"I don't know, Mahmoud." She was so confused.

"I love you, Sarah."

Then there was sad, gentle goodbye sex. Afterward, he stroked her hair.

"I have only fifteen minutes before I must dress. I will ask that you leave the house. I don't want to compromise you or myself."

"Okay. Where do you want me to go?"

He laughed and said, "Your clothes are old, so is your furniture. I would like to take you on, what is it called, a shopping sparkle?"

"A shopping spree?"

"Oh, yes. You are so delicious." He kissed her forehead. "So I am leaving you this." From under the pillow, he took an envelope and opened it. There was a wad of hundred dollar bills.

She sat up, furious. "Do you think I am some whore?"

He looked surprised. "It is only a gift. Please. Be practical. You have lost work because of me. Laura will make sure you are not welcome in those circles, and you may have to deal with . . ."

His tone made her calm down. "Deal with what?"

"My darling Sarah, after today things will never be the same. I have brought attention to you that may not go away for a long time. Perhaps forever. You will need resources. You may find you need to leave the city or even the United States for a while."

He sat up, facing her in the bed. "I have been so selfish in my desire for you. When I am back home, I will not be able to protect you. Please take this, and there is more in your lingerie drawer." She started to get up.

"You're scaring me, Mahmoud."

He looked at the clock. "I must shave and dress. Could I ask a big favor of you?" She nodded. "I want you to leave New York. Is your passport current?"

Sarah looked surprised. "Why?"

"I want you to go to Nepal and visit the Temple of the Living Goddess."

"What? Why there?"

"There is a man you will go see. He will meet you there. He is the son of a very loyal descendant of my great-grandmother's. His name is Ali. He is a Muslim, and he will take care of you. You will be safe there."

Mahmoud reached into his robe and pulled out an Air India packet with a one-way plane ticket to Kathmandu. "Your flight leaves in two hours, so you have only time to dress and get to the airport. Go quickly."

Sarah shook her head vehemently. "I don't want to go."

"You must—if only for our son."

He kissed her—a final act of passion—then gently pushed her away. He looked at Sarah, and right before her eyes, he seemed to harden and become older.

"Enough," he said sharply. "Be on your way. Go now!"

She sobbed at this harsh tone, but the Mahmoud she had come to know was gone. He pulled out a cell phone and barked orders as he walked away from her. She felt invisible and pulled on jeans, a jacket, and boots. She took the cash from her underwear drawer and, when Mahmoud was out of sight, retrieved the gun from the nightstand.

At the door as she was leaving him, for a last fleeting moment, a vestige of the old Mahmoud returned. He wiped tears away and said, "It is like your American movie, the famous *Casablanca*. They always had Paris. We will always have New York. No matter what happens, know that I love you and you hold my secret."

She picked up the change purse Sylvie had given her so long ago and gave it to Mahmoud. Still inside was the fortune cookie, the token, the MetroCard, and the loose coins.

"This is to keep you safe, Mahmoud," she said, then recited the fortune: "Beware of what you wish for." Then she turned and left, wearing a dark hoodie and sunglasses.

Once again, Zev was the answer. She phoned him. "You have to get me out of here—but no one can know it's me. Ben told me to text him when Mahmoud was sick, which I did—so when he leaves for the UN, all hell will break loose!"

"No!" Zev said. "Text him again—tell them Mahmoud is very sick but insists on going. They will let him leave."

"Good." Sarah texted the message to Ben as she raced down the stairs to the street.

She walked briskly out through the tall iron gates of Shively and jumped into the back of the cab. Zev wore a Rasta hat with bright circles and sunglasses, and as they rolled up the street she couldn't help but laugh.

"Where do you want me to take you?" he said.

"Take me to Kennedy."

"Where are you going?"

"To Nepal. To the Temple of the Living Goddess."

"Let's go together then. I can get a job driving anywhere."

"As if that's what you were meant to do."

"Not the point."

"It is the point. You're not coming."

She slipped off her hoodie, wrapped the Glock in it, and leaned forward to hand it to Zev through the partition. "Here," she said. "I won't need this after all." The hoodie caught on the edge of the divider, and as she freed it she noticed the hack license posted next to the window. The name on the document read TOM DOOLEY.

"Tom Dooley?" she exclaimed. "I think I've been in this cab before!"

Zev laughed.

He pulled up in front of the Air India terminal. "Should I park and walk you?"

Sarah wanted to say no, but she realized that she was terribly upset at the idea of leaving Zev behind. "Okay," she said.

Zev jumped out to get the door for Sarah. As soon as he opened it, Sarah emerged—but suddenly, from nowhere, Ben appeared. He was walking toward them really quickly, the gun in his hand at the ready although partially covered by his jacket. Ben looked furious as he came toward Sarah, who was too paralyzed to react. In what might have been the last split second of her life, she thought, *Okay, I did what I was supposed to.* She felt oddly calm and prepared for her end. Out of the corner of her eye she saw Zev fire the Glock. Ben fell to the ground, bleeding from a hole where his tie met his jacket. Time slowed down, then Sarah knew what had to be done.

"Zev!" she hissed. "Drive the cab away, ditch the gun somewhere, and disappear. You'd better go back home. Maybe your family can hide you. Go!"

"I can't leave you."

"You idiot, do you want to go to prison? Go now!"

Sarah knew that she would never see Zev again. So be it. Still, she knew that Zev was in love with her, even if she was unsure about her own feelings for him. He had just killed a man to save her life. Now she wanted to save him.

"Meet me in Nepal when everything calms down!" She prayed that her words would offer enough hope for him to get himself out of there.

And it worked. Zev froze for an instant and stared into her eyes. Then like lightning he jumped behind the wheel, turned on the ignition, burned rubber, and was gone.

CHAPTER 36

THE POVERTY OF 72 VIRGINS

FTER SARAH LEFT, MAHMOUD wept. He would never see his unborn son, he was obviously not the Twelfth Imam as he had believed, and he would never see Sarah again. He stood in the bathroom and touched her cosmetics, opening and closing the perfume bottles. His cell phone buzzed. The text message read: IT IS TIME. WE WILL ARRIVE IN 35 MINUTES.

Mahmoud pulled himself together. He made his peace with God and prayed. He felt very far away from himself, and his eyes kept filling with tears.

As he dressed, he remembered bitterly how the Ayatollah had told him that he, Mahmoud, was the Twelfth Imam—the facilitator of the coming—and that involved creating world chaos. He had been lied to, but he forgave the Ayatollah and focused on his mission. Attacking Israel with nuclear bombs might be sufficient, but blowing up the UN filled with delegates from one hundred and forty nations would be a great appetizer to the main course.

The Americans had been so stupid when they came to look for those "weapons of mass destruction"—a child would have realized they were hidden in other countries, but the UN inspectors were clueless. Had the West really forgotten how the

Nazis stashed money, paintings, and other priceless artifacts in so-called neutral lands? Mahmoud equated "neutral" with "cowardly," and, he thought, even those pretender states would not escape this conflagration. That America and the West had remained so naïve was incomprehensible to him, but it was certainly convenient.

He pulled out his wallet and looked at the photograph of his wife and two boys. He felt a sudden pain in his gut, sharp enough to make his eyes water. In part, it was because he suddenly longed to see them all once again—but it was also the realization that even they would not escape the horror of the destruction that he was to precipitate.

He studied himself in the mirror in Sarah's white, tiled prewar bathroom. He knew that "prewar" referred to World War II, but he did not quite understand how a war defined the arrangement of bathroom tile. But then, there was much he did not understand about this world, and even less about the peoples who had always been his enemies. As he saw it now, as it had always been before, it was mainly these Judeo-Christians who seemed to hate—and to fear—Islam. He could not understand—in a war of attrition, in a life-or-death struggle with one's sworn enemy for one's very survival, where each sought to eradicate the other—how any act that favored your ultimate victory could be excluded as too heinous, as too blasphemous, as too despicable to carry out. In an enterprise that was the very abdication of humanity itself—that of war—what could possibly count or be defined as an "atrocity"? Why had the West always been so sanctimoniously outraged over the things men did in the conduct of war? Why did they make monuments to Auschwitz and Pearl Harbor and Hiroshima and Normandy, as they were so invested in doing now at this Ground Zero?

Suddenly the pain in his gut and in his mind doubled him over, forcing him down on the commode. This was it. The end. He would meet his Lord in just over an hour and a half. He hoped Sarah would be safe on a plane. The buzzer rang, and he knew it was his men. Quickly, he put on his suit pants and a T-shirt.

He left his dress shirt open. He went downstairs and opened the front door. Nehir and Mohammed stood in the doorway, unsmiling and clearly excited about what was to come. He motioned for them to come in. They followed him silently as he led them to Sarah's bedroom and directed them to the case in the closet. Time was racing. "Hurry," he said as they lifted the belt with the C-4 out of the case. Nehir inspected it closely, turned to Mahmoud, and nodded confidently with approval. They fitted the straps over Mahmoud's shoulders and the belt around his waist. Nehir slid the detonator for the belt through his shirt, taping it to his arm, then folded the trigger so that it rested almost at the edge of his shirt cuff. The belt felt oddly comfortable, but a little tight. He had been measured for it, but no one had taken into account the rich food he would enjoy with Sarah.

Sarah. He glanced over at the bed, unmade and retaining the impression they had made the last time they made love. A vision of her long, thin white arms and red hair beneath him appeared. More tears rushed to his eyes. Why was he not praying and thinking of all the glory to come and of the future of the world? Instead, his mind drifted to his two boys hugging him goodbye—would they survive? And his loyal wife, whom he had never loved—would she receive some blessing? She seemed always lost in a veil of sadness, and Mahmoud knew it was his fault. He wished he had said kinder things to her before he left.

Mahmoud buttoned his shirt, leaving his signature top button open, and Nehir helped him on with his black jacket.

He needed a moment for himself. "I will see you in the car. Take the case and dispose of it elsewhere." The men left.

Alone, he looked around the room that had become his living heaven. He spoke aloud in Farsi: "I have had my reward, before my sacrifice, as humbly requested. Thank you."

He walked to the bed and pressed his face into one of the pillows. He inhaled her fragrance, sweet and flowery and mixed with the pungent smell of sex. Mahmoud felt his heart break inside of him. He could not see for the water that was cascading out of his eyes. This was shameful, he thought, not at all the way a man being given such an honor should behave. He looked at his watch—it was time. He sat on the bed and wept uncontrollably. His cell phone buzzed.

⚜

There was traffic on East River Drive as they headed south to the UN. As he sat in the car, Mahmoud realized that this would be the last time he would see the beauty of the sunlight glistening off the East River and illuminating the tall buildings.

There was the speech he needed to recite. He began to rehearse but could not concentrate. Of course, he could push the detonator at any time—there was no specific cue, and the exclamation point of his speech would be apocalyptically obvious no matter where he ended it. He had heard that old saying that your life flashes before you as death nears, but it was only his brief time with Sarah that he wanted to relive. He forced himself to pray, then returned to practicing his speech.

The car arrived at the UN and stopped. Mahmoud got out and entered through the diplomats' entrance. He passed through security without being searched and soon found himself in his chair in the General Assembly Hall.

As the proceedings began, Mahmoud remembered standing with Sarah at Ground Zero when she asked why he hadn't stopped the planes. He had told her only part of the truth, about his family being in danger, and he'd done that shamelessly to get her sympathy—and it had worked. But in fact, it had all been a total lie. He had been a willing volunteer, but now he felt like he was what she would call a heel, though the derivation of that term had always escaped him. The real reason was that he and the Ayatollah were meant to act as a team to facilitate the return of the Imam by plunging the world into chaos. He had naïvely believed that destroying the towers would topple the American regime. Sarah, he well knew, could not have forgiven him for that. *What is her relationship with God?* he thought. *She never told me. I wish that I had asked.*

He realized that the proceedings had started and glanced at his watch. In five minutes, he would begin his brief statement, then pull the trigger. He had better plan on doing that quickly—before the American and Israeli delegates began their insulting march out of the General Assembly, as they always did when he spoke. He wouldn't want them to miss this.

He unbuttoned his cuff and felt the detonator drop into his hand. *Well done, Nehir!* He mentally saluted his ally and confidant. *Sad that he will have to assassinate me if this doesn't work out*, Mahmoud thought.

Mahmoud heard his name announced and stood up. He looked around at the men and women he was about to exterminate. He felt no exaltation or surge of power. His speech was to be brief, and he began, ignoring the traditional greeting and salutations. He realized that this holy war was a farce, that he had no right to kill anyone. Sarah was right—to take such an action was to perpetuate a cycle of murder, and no good could come of it.

And yet, he took hold of the podium with both hands—and squeezed the detonator. But nothing happened.

After what he thought was an eternity, he opened his eyes. He looked to his aides, who were equally shocked to be alive, their expressions like they had all just seen a ghost. He fumbled slightly, but then somehow he regained his composure and finished his speech and left the podium, walking off hurriedly, confused. His mind was utterly blank—he found himself outside on the street as the First Avenue bus rolled up. He ditched the bomber rig in a dumpster near a building that was being renovated and slipped his jacket back on. He remembered that he had Sarah's change purse with the fortune cookie, the subway token, and the MetroCard. Mahmoud had never ridden public transit in New York City—he had no idea what the fare was—but in desperation he climbed aboard, following an old lady wearing a red shawl. He watched as she inserted a yellow-and-blue card into a slot in the farebox mounted next to the driver. That was the odd card he'd seen inside Sarah's change purse! He zipped it open, extracted the card, and, somewhat clumsily, inserted it as the lady had done. Breathless, he waited, hoping it would work. The farebox dinged, and the bus driver nodded as he waved him impatiently to the back. Mahmoud sat down, relieved beyond words, and looked through the window until the magnificent UN Headquarters faded from his view.

CHAPTER 37

THE LIVING GODDESS

 ARAH ARRIVED IN KATHMANDU. During the flight she had slept almost nonstop—a mercy because she could not bear her own thoughts. Zev was most likely dead, or in the custody of the New York City police.

An entire day had passed, which meant that the destruction of Israel was less than three days away. She sent Miriam a text: IRAN PLANNING TO BLOW UP ISRAEL DECEMBER 25TH. She hit send. She was about to toss the phone but decided that it might be wise to make a phone call just in case.

But even before she could dial, Miriam responded with a text: HE WAS A PATRIOT, AND SO ARE YOU. Sarah smiled. She hoped that Judith would have been proud of her.

When she got through customs, Mahmoud's cousin Ali was waiting for her. He wore a chauffeur's cap and black coat and held a discreet sign with one word on it: *Sarah*. She didn't see any police. Suddenly she needed a drink desperately. She walked over.

"Hi, Sarah, I am Ali. Please come."

He took her bag, and she followed him numbly.

"Have you heard from Mahmoud?" she asked as soon as they were in the car.

ACKNOWLEDGMENTS

Janet Appel	My mother,
	Louise S. Horowitz
Danny Baron	
	Anne Kleinman
Jafe Campbell	
	John Koehler
Thomas Chatterton	
	Art Lizza
Joe Coccaro	
	Donna Miller
Aileen Crow	
	Adam Nadler
Donald Hackworth	
	Big Red Ram Das
My brother,	
Adam Horowitz	Cheryl Ross
	Shari Stauch
My father,	
David H. Horowitz	Those Who Watch Over Me

"No." He took a long look at her. "You must rest."

※

Ali lived in a grand house. It was away from the city, secluded and as exotic as she could have imagined, with rattan furniture and wonderful smells wafting from the kitchen. A demure and silent housemaid led her to a pretty room overlooking a garden. "May I take a shower?" The housemaid motioned to the luxurious tiled bath, scented with freshly cut orchids.

She stood in the shower and took stock of her body. There was still the faint trace of a hickey on the inside of her thigh. Hard to imagine Mahmoud at all. He seemed a driving force but from a past life, and Zev—she could imagine his warm brown eyes peering at her. He was her one regret.

She looked upward, in the direction that she imagined God might be. She turned off the shower, fatigue making her feel as though she'd just been hit in the forehead with a mallet. She said aloud, "Okay. This was a pretty good display. Now if I can escape the Mossad, the American government, and Mahmoud's people, I will really know you are my Father."

She began the breath of fire and chanted until she dozed off.

When she awoke, Mahmoud was sitting by her bed.

It took her a minute to get her bearings. She felt incredibly exhausted—like a boned flounder. How had he gotten here in one piece?

She shut her eyes to buy time, but he had seen her and moved to sit on the edge of the bed, taking her hand in his.

"My dove, my dove!"

For the first time, she was afraid of him. While waiting for the connection in Brussels, she had Googled him one more time and realized just how nuts he really was.

"It was the will of al-Mahdi—he was not ready yet. That is why I am here!"

"Is that what you think?"

"It is a miracle. Don't you see?"

Sarah savored the moment. Should she tell him now?

He leaned down to kiss her, but she moved her head away. Mahmoud stopped, looking stunned.

In a serious, perplexed tone, he said, "I am free, Sarah. I have plenty of money—we can disappear and be together. I know where to go where they will never find us."

Sarah couldn't believe her ears—this so-called man of the people, who had until a few days ago been willing to commit any manner of heinous act to throw the world into war so the resurrection and the Twelfth Imam would come, was now talking of money he had embezzled and stashed for his personal worldly pleasure! And what of his wife and children? Was there no feeling for them?

He sensed her fear and took her hand. "I would never hurt you," he said softly. "I have been spared so that I may cherish you and our unborn son."

But if she told him that *she* was the miracle, and that she personally had fucked with the Ayatollah's plans, would he kill her—knowing he would go straight to heaven?

The enormity of what she had done suddenly hit her. With Zev's help, she had prevented the UN from being blown up, as well as maybe saved Israel. The man holding her hand was quite simply a monster.

"Kiss me, my dove," Mahmoud said, and moved toward her.

Sarah's mind left her body. *Kill me now, you fucker!* she inwardly shouted at God, and gasped as she heard shots fired. Finally, an answered prayer. She prepared to die, but it was Mahmoud who crumpled to the floor, blood pouring from his nose and mouth, a red stain forming on his shirt, just above his heart.

Zev stood in the doorway. "We have to go," he said.

Mahmoud was dying. His eyes pleaded with her to stay. Zev held out his hand. Sarah stood up, shaking so much she could barely move.

She looked down at Mahmoud. "It wasn't God's will," she said emphatically. "I had the C-4 in your belt switched with

modeling clay. It's very regrettable, but you are going t[ ] ter all."

Mahmoud nodded and closed his eyes for the la[ ] Sobs rose in her throat, but she pushed them down. Ha[ ] cried? She began the breath of fire.

"He's getting off easy," Zev said. "C'mon, we don't w[ ] here when Ali gets back."

"But how?" she said as she grabbed her bag and[ ] her shoes. She realized that she was crying uncontroll[ ] didn't care.

Zev took her bag and put his arm around her. "God[ ] mysterious ways—He writes straight in crooked lines."

She looked to see if Zev was being funny, but he wa[ ]

I'm leaving one killer to go with another, she though[ ] ever God was or wasn't, she certainly appreciated His[ ] humor. And maybe that was the point.

CPSIA information can be obtained at www.ICGtesting.com
Printed in the USA
BVOW07s1234061114

373976BV00004B/193/P

"No." He took a long look at her. "You must rest."

۞

Ali lived in a grand house. It was away from the city, se-cluded and as exotic as she could have imagined, with rattan furniture and wonderful smells wafting from the kitchen. A de-mure and silent housemaid led her to a pretty room overlooking a garden. "May I take a shower?" The housemaid motioned to the luxurious tiled bath, scented with freshly cut orchids.

She stood in the shower and took stock of her body. There was still the faint trace of a hickey on the inside of her thigh. Hard to imagine Mahmoud at all. He seemed a driving force but from a past life, and Zev—she could imagine his warm brown eyes peering at her. He was her one regret.

She looked upward, in the direction that she imagined God might be. She turned off the shower, fatigue making her feel as though she'd just been hit in the forehead with a mallet. She said aloud, "Okay. This was a pretty good display. Now if I can escape the Mossad, the American government, and Mahmoud's people, I will really know you are my Father."

She began the breath of fire and chanted until she dozed off.

When she awoke, Mahmoud was sitting by her bed.

It took her a minute to get her bearings. She felt incredibly exhausted—like a boned flounder. How had he gotten here in one piece?

She shut her eyes to buy time, but he had seen her and moved to sit on the edge of the bed, taking her hand in his.

"My dove, my dove!"

For the first time, she was afraid of him. While waiting for the connection in Brussels, she had Googled him one more time and realized just how nuts he really was.

"It was the will of al-Mahdi—he was not ready yet. That is why I am here!"

"Is that what you think?"

"It is a miracle. Don't you see?"

Sarah savored the moment. Should she tell him now?

He leaned down to kiss her, but she moved her head away. Mahmoud stopped, looking stunned.

In a serious, perplexed tone, he said, "I am free, Sarah. I have plenty of money—we can disappear and be together. I know where to go where they will never find us."

Sarah couldn't believe her ears—this so-called man of the people, who had until a few days ago been willing to commit any manner of heinous act to throw the world into war so the resurrection and the Twelfth Imam would come, was now talking of money he had embezzled and stashed for his personal worldly pleasure! And what of his wife and children? Was there no feeling for them?

He sensed her fear and took her hand. "I would never hurt you," he said softly. "I have been spared so that I may cherish you and our unborn son."

But if she told him that *she* was the miracle, and that she personally had fucked with the Ayatollah's plans, would he kill her—knowing he would go straight to heaven?

The enormity of what she had done suddenly hit her. With Zev's help, she had prevented the UN from being blown up, as well as maybe saved Israel. The man holding her hand was quite simply a monster.

"Kiss me, my dove," Mahmoud said, and moved toward her.

Sarah's mind left her body. *Kill me now, you fucker!* she inwardly shouted at God, and gasped as she heard shots fired. Finally, an answered prayer. She prepared to die, but it was Mahmoud who crumpled to the floor, blood pouring from his nose and mouth, a red stain forming on his shirt, just above his heart.

Zev stood in the doorway. "We have to go," he said.

Mahmoud was dying. His eyes pleaded with her to stay. Zev held out his hand. Sarah stood up, shaking so much she could barely move.

She looked down at Mahmoud. "It wasn't God's will," she said emphatically. "I had the C-4 in your belt switched with modeling clay. It's very regrettable, but you are going to die after all."

Mahmoud nodded and closed his eyes for the last time. Sobs rose in her throat, but she pushed them down. Had Judith cried? She began the breath of fire.

"He's getting off easy," Zev said. "C'mon, we don't want to be here when Ali gets back."

"But how?" she said as she grabbed her bag and put on her shoes. She realized that she was crying uncontrollably, but didn't care.

Zev took her bag and put his arm around her. "God works in mysterious ways—He writes straight in crooked lines."

She looked to see if Zev was being funny, but he wasn't.

I'm leaving one killer to go with another, she thought. Whatever God was or wasn't, she certainly appreciated His sense of humor. And maybe that was the point.

ACKNOWLEDGMENTS

Janet Appel

Danny Baron

Jafe Campbell

Thomas Chatterton

Joe Coccaro

Aileen Crow

Donald Hackworth

My brother,
Adam Horowitz

My father,
David H. Horowitz

My mother,
Louise S. Horowitz

Anne Kleinman

John Koehler

Art Lizza

Donna Miller

Adam Nadler

Big Red Ram Das

Cheryl Ross

Shari Stauch

Those Who Watch Over Me

CPSIA information can be obtained at www.ICGtesting.com
Printed in the USA
BVOW07s1234061114

373976BV00004B/193/P